T0209220

Other Novels Featuring

Doug Sutherland
by the Author

The Lagarto Stone
Death's Crooked Shadow

WALK
A THIN
WIRE

A NOVEL

GORDON N. MCINTOSH

WALK A THIN WIRE
A NOVEL

iUniverse books may be ordered through booksellers or by contacting:

iUniverse
1663 Liberty Drive
Bloomington, IN 47403
www.iuniverse.com
844-349-9409

ISBN: 978-1-6632-1730-1 (sc)
ISBN: 978-1-6632-1729-5 (e)

Library of Congress Control Number: 2021924545

Print information available on the last page.

iUniverse rev. date: 04/20/2022

For Meridyth, who made all the difference

Luck is a very thin wire between survival and disaster,
and not many people can keep their balance on it.
—Hunter S. Thompson

I think we consider too much the luck of the early bird
and not enough the bad luck of the early worm.
—Franklin D. Roosevelt

Does the flap of a butterfly's wings in Brazil set off a tornado in Texas?
—Edward Lorenz

PROLOGUE

Five nautical miles south of the Dry Tortugas,
Gulf of Mexico, January 1995

The spreading glow to the east heralded the end of the grueling night. Heavy gusts shook the rigging, and the sloop's foredeck lay awash with each cresting wave. Forty-year-old Bernard Sutherland scrambled up the companionway steps into the cockpit and rubbed the sleep from his eyes. He scanned the column of oncoming rollers, assessed the set of the jib and reefed main, and nodded his approval. The fifty-foot Hinckley was built for blue-water passages and had crisscrossed the Atlantic, Gulf, and Caribbean for years. Though the overnight storm had stressed the three-man crew to the limit, the yacht had behaved like the thoroughbred it was designed to be.

"Still blowing stink, I see," Sutherland shouted over the wind to the tall, gangly man at the helm. "What's your heading?"

"One twenty. Need to come about," Sam Baskin yelled back, his face a mask of fatigue and tension as he wrestled the bucking wheel. "Take over, and I'll trim."

As Sutherland seized the wheel, a dark speck on a curling wave caught his attention. "What's that? Two o'clock," he shouted, pointing.

"Can't tell from here," Baskin said, straining to see.

Sutherland bore off toward the dark object, and slowly the features of a raft took form. An eight-foot pole served as its mast, but the sail was in tatters. Waves crashed over two inert bodies sprawled across the makeshift frame as larger rollers threatened to capsize the unstable vessel.

From fifty feet away, Baskin sounded the compressed air horn, but neither body reacted. "Probably dead," he shouted. He held the horn higher and blew it again.

"Take a photo, and we'll send it to the coast guard with the GPS location," Sutherland said. "We'll have to leave them. We'd never get dead weight on board in these seas."

"Wait! One's alive," Baskin cried.

Just then, Sutherland's fourteen-year-old son poked his head out from the companionway. "What's going on?" Doug hollered.

"Get your life jacket and give us a hand, Dougie," Sutherland ordered, starting the inboard engine. "Sam, let off the sails and get ready to throw the man a line."

Baskin released the sheets, letting the sails flail as the engine kicked in. He looked up again and yelled, "What happened? There's only one now."

"I saw it," Doug said. "He pushed him over the side."

They approached the raft from leeward to avoid sinking it, but it was still a precarious maneuver. As the raft slammed against the sloop's hull, the survivor struggled to his knees and crooked one arm around the mast, the other arm hugging a small suitcase he pressed to his chest.

Baskin hurled a looped line, and the man grabbed it.

Hampered by his stubborn hold on the case, the man finally wriggled into the loop, and the three of them hauled him on board. He tumbled into the cockpit with both arms clutching the case in a death grip. While he lay coughing and retching on the deck, the crew trimmed the sails and reset their course to the Florida Keys. The abandoned raft slipped astern and out of sight.

A half hour later, the half-drowned man sat on the cockpit deck with his back to the cabin bulkhead. He stared at the cup of water in his hand as if he wasn't sure what it was. His other hand clutched the handle of the small case. After he finally took a sip of water, he looked up and, realizing that his saviors were staring at him, said in a hoarse voice, "Muchas gracias, amigos. Me salvaron la vida. Me llamo Doctor Jorge Castillo."

"El otro hombre. Qué pasó?" Sutherland asked.

The rescued man barely managed to shake his head. "Muerto." He closed his eyes and seemed to drift off.

"Look at him," Baskin said. "Dumb bastard would've drowned before letting go of that damn case."

"Whatever he's got in there, bet it isn't cigars," Sutherland said.

CHAPTER 1

Twenty-five years later, Chicago, Illinois, January 2020

Doug Sutherland stepped out of the front door of Sam Baskin's Gold Coast town house and shuddered from the assault of frigid air. He was a tall, well-built man closing in on forty years old. As he tucked his scarf under his overcoat's lapels, he gazed across the street at Washington Square Park and reflected on how austere it appeared, dark and deserted, beneath the new blanket of snow. Behind him, Sam Baskin, a seventy-four-year-old investigative reporter, locked his front door, picked up his briefcase, and joined Sutherland, facing the park. He was a lanky man dressed in a tan winter coat, a knit ski hat, and a plaid woolen scarf around his neck.

Baskin pointed across Clark Street. "Beautiful in winter, isn't it? Did you know that park was once known as Bughouse Square?"

"Yeah. But way before my time," Sutherland said.

"Mine too, mostly. Up until the nineteen sixties, communists, anarchists, unionists, nutcases, and all sorts of whackjobs used to voice their views on soapboxes there. A different era then. Today we've got social media and cable news for conspiracy theories and radical opinions. Newspapers like mine that publish factual information are a dying breed. Like me."

"Not you," Sutherland said. "Look at all the awards you earned. The wall in your study is covered with them."

"Well, all things eventually come to an end. I may be working on my swan song. That's why I wanted to get together. You need to know about it before it all comes out."

"Why the mystery?"

"Tell you at dinner," Baskin said and began following Sutherland down the stairs to the sidewalk.

Just as Sutherland reached the bottom step, he saw a flash from the open window of the van parked across the street and heard Baskin cry out behind him. Sutherland spun around in time to see his friend cartwheel off the step and land in the snow behind a row of shrubbery. Sutherland ducked down next him and stared anxiously into Baskin's pain-contorted face. His eyes were squeezed tight, his jaw clenched, and he uttered a deep-throated groan. Sutherland heard an engine rev, and he looked up to see the van racing away, its tires squealing on the wet asphalt as it fishtailed around the corner. As he dug out his phone from his pocket, Sutherland watched a dark stain soak through and spread over Baskin's tan overcoat.

"Slipped on the goddamn ice," Baskin said, grimacing as he tried to sit up. "I think I broke my shoulder when I landed."

"I don't think so," Sutherland said as he punched 911 into his phone. "You've been shot. I saw the gun's muzzle flash. That goddamn ice might have saved your ass—lucky bastard."

The next evening, Sutherland and his long-term partner, Kelly Matthews, were lounging in his high-rise apartment in Chicago's Lincoln Park neighborhood while they watched the local news. Both weary from an active day in their respective offices, he had shed his suit jacket and tie, and she had discarded her cashmere sweater and gathered her long chestnut hair into a ponytail. Outside the floor-to-ceiling windows, snow flurries danced and swirled against the glass, an early sign of the five inches of snow expected to fall overnight.

On the flat-screen television, a carefully coiffed blonde newswoman reported from her desk at CNN. "The Food and Drug Administration announced today that another person has died, the victim of BioVexis, a prescription drug used to treat chronic bronchitis. This brings the total to five deaths, in addition to several dozen in intensive care, over the last month. A spokesperson for Lawrence Laboratories, the maker of the drug, announced today that the company is cooperating with the FDA and has recalled all of the product until an investigation can be completed." The camera shifted to video of a suburban two-story office building with a red Lawrence Laboratories sign over its portal.

The news anchor continued, "This is an astonishing setback for the company's founder, Dr. Jorge Castillo, considered a genius in the pharmaceutical community, with his string of successful products. The company was to go public in a few months, but under the shadow of this recall, analysts say the initial public offering is doubtful."

"See what you got me into?" Kelly said as she muted the telecast. "Three months in the job, and now this pile of crap lands on me."

"For the record, I tried to discourage you," Sutherland said. "I thought you could do better. Any number of law firms would have scooped up one of the City of Chicago's top attorneys."

"But it's still your fault," Kelly said. "I only knew Doc Castillo through you. He would never have recruited me otherwise. To cap it all off, my predecessor quit today. Too old, too much pressure."

"So you're the chief corporate counsel now? Congratulations," Sutherland said and held up his martini glass in salute.

"That's not funny," she snapped.

"I wasn't being snarky. I meant it. As long as you're in the kitchen, you might as well be the master chef."

"It's an apt metaphor. Defending the company and Doc Castillo's reputation is going to get hot. These deaths, the media attention, recall, canceled IPO … what'd I get myself into?"

"Ah, the lure of money," he sighed. "A lucrative salary and generous stock options. You do have green eyes after all."

"Again, not funny," Kelly said bitterly. "*Worthless* stock options now." Suddenly she sat upright and pointed at the screen. "Look. A photo of Sam. It's about the shooting."

Sutherland grabbed the remote and unmuted the television. A reporter dressed in a ski jacket and knit hat stood holding a microphone as he faced the camera. A brick town house loomed in the background, its stairway rising to the front door. The reporter said, "Last evening, *Chicago Tribune* journalist Sam Baskin was attacked by an unknown gunman as he was leaving this his town house in Chicago's Gold Coast. Mr. Baskin was taken to Northwestern Hospital to be treated for a gunshot wound. So far, the police have no leads."

"No leads. Do you believe it?" Sutherland said, muting the television. "I gave the police a description of the van and its license number. A white Ford with one rear window removed, where the shot came from."

"Never mind the van. I'm just thankful that neither of you were killed. You both could have been targets. How's he doing?"

"I couldn't talk to him today. His daughters were with him when I called the hospital. Said he was out of the operating room and it supposedly went well. He was sleeping off the anesthetics."

"Poor Sam," Kelly said. "To think that just yesterday I was cursing him. Did you read his *Tribune* columns the last couple of days? He says he's got evidence from a whistleblower of criminal negligence and a cover-up at Lawrence."

"That's what Sam does. Digs up crap like that. But unless this was just a random shooting, I'll bet this attack had something to do with the casino corruption he's been writing about. Those guys don't like to be in the news."

"I hate to see Sam hurt, but he's not making life any easier on me either."

"Is the cover-up claim true?"

"I'm still trying to get to the bottom of it. I'd like to know what I'm defending."

"You'll do fine. The Chicago police force gave you tons of defense practice."

"One frying pan into another," she said before polishing off her wine.

Sutherland yawned and said he was going to take a shower before going to bed. Kelly told him to go ahead, and she carried the wineglasses into the kitchen. In the bedroom, Sutherland stripped down, hung up his clothes, and stepped into the shower stall.

He was toweling off after the shower when his cell phone buzzed. "Sutherland here," he answered as he walked into his bedroom, where Kelly was slipping into her side of the bed.

"Doug, it's Sam. Alive and still kicking, my friend. Can't keep these old bones down."

"You at home?" Sutherland asked, pleased to hear Baskin in good spirits.

"I'm out of the hospital, but I'm not at home. Can you meet me tomorrow night for dinner? We never got to discuss the reason I wanted to see you."

"I've got dinner with Kelly, but I'm free for a drink. You said this was about my deal?" Sutherland's real estate company had been chosen to build a forty-story office building for Lawrence Laboratories. The deal had been finalized two months before Kelly joined the company, and they had been shooting for a summer groundbreaking. Because of the negative ramifications of the BioVexis fiasco, Lawrence's board was considering canceling and had defaulted on several commitments.

"That's not the half of it. But I don't want to get into it on the phone. Let's meet in the lobby bar of the Royal Suites Hotel. Say six o'clock? You and Kelly have no idea what crap is going on there," he said before disconnecting.

"What did he say?" Kelly asked, placing her book on the bedside table. "He sound OK?"

"He was even chipper. But you and I may not have a reason to be. Says neither one of us knows how bad things are at Lawrence."

"Great," she said. "Just what I needed. I'm already having nightmares."

A solid giant of a man, Matt Kirkland, in a leather sports jacket and with his dark brown hair in a ponytail, was sitting at the blackjack table peeking at his faced-down ace when his cell phone vibrated. He was having a decent night—more than could be said for the other three at the table. Two out-of-town conventioneers were reckless players, taking risks and missing opportunities. The fourth player was a middle-aged woman handicapped by too many scotches. Slipping his cell phone from his jacket, he glanced at the caller's number and swore under his breath.

The dealer pointed to the woman's cards a second time, seeking an answer. She glanced at her down card, bit her lip, and scrunched her eyes in a boozy show of uncertainty.

Matt's phone buzzed again. It was a caller he couldn't put off, so he chucked his twin aces, spun off his chair, and strode away from the table. "Yeah?" he said, growling into his smartphone.

"*Buenas tardes*, Matt. I found you at the casino again, *verdad*?" Paolo Aguilar had the deep, throaty voice of a man who had smoked all his life. In his case, it had been the hand-rolled cigars made by fellow Cuban expatriates. He was short and stocky, in his late seventies, with dark hair and eyes. His coarse skin showed the pockmarks of infantile chickenpox.

"How'd you guess?" Matt retorted. Slots pinging and music pounding, the background sound was unmistakable, especially to a longtime casino owner.

"The reason I interrupt your *diversión* … you know of this reporter Sam Baskin?"

"From the *Tribune*? I just heard someone tried to kill him and missed. That your deal?"

"He's been writing some dangerous columns," Aguilar said.

"That's what he does," Matt said. "Must have you worried." Baskin had written several articles about the casino gambling industry, and Matt suspected this was the subject of Aguilar's concern.

"It is sufficient that he interests me," Aguilar said in his typical close-to-the-vest fashion. One never knew the why—only what he required of you.

"And so …?" Matt held his breath and waited. He was about to get his marching orders.

"Baskin is planning to meet with a state prosecutor and FBI agents in several days. I don't want that to happen or for any of his research material to change hands."

The fact that Aguilar knew about a meeting with the FBI didn't surprise Matt; he had witnessed numerous examples of the conglomerate magnate's connections over the years. And he didn't need to guess what was next. "Kind of obvious, isn't it?" Matt said. "He writes about corruption in your casinos, then he's whacked?"

"Not necessarily. If you read his articles, you will know he investigates others as well. Two weeks ago, this *cabrón* writes about Senator Roth's questionable election finances and marital infidelities. Last week, it was the Midway Airport contract fix. On his blog, he exposes the waste hauler's outfit connections. Finally, this morning, he attacks Lawrence Laboratories and this BioVexis drug causing those deaths. Samuel Baskin has many, many enemies. A long line to see him gone."

"Why not use the ace shooter who missed him the first time? He knows the target's movements," Matt said. His resistance wasn't for what the assignment might entail—nothing had ever strained his scruples, and their having worked together for so long, Aguilar knew it. Matt had another reason to sidestep this job: for months, he'd been preparing to escape Aguilar's servitude, and he sensed that his plans may have been discovered. Even if this wasn't a trap, the hit could easily entangle him. Now the reporter would be wary and on the defensive, making the assignment riskier.

"I never reveal my reasons, only my decisions. This is your assignment. It should be personal for you."

"How so?"

"The national media are saying a certain Clark Kirkland should be crucified for selling pills that killed those people. This Clark person is your *gemelo*, no? Your twin brother? Big man in Lawrence Laboratories?"

"It's just twenty-four-hour news hype. Something to rant about."

"This Baskin writes that a whistleblower from your brother's company has given him new information. What if it put your brother in jail?"

"My brother's innocent. Not a corrupt bone in his body," Matt said.

"But there are those around him who have such bones. They'll cast the blame on him," Aguilar said. "My daughter Renata is sending you a link to incriminating internal emails and wire transfers. Sam Baskin has the same emails and will use them if he's not stopped."

"These links … hacked by your spook friends?"

"If helping your brother isn't enough," Aguilar said, ignoring the question, "I'll consider your debt paid, and I'll wire another hundred thousand into your Panama account. After this, you can do what you like."

"This reporter's findings must be pretty incriminating if you're willing to do that," Matt said. "I thought your casinos were covering their tracks pretty well. I guess not."

"Never mind that," Aguilar growled. "I just want it done."

The promise of relief from his debt and another hundred thousand should have been the tipping point for Matt, but he knew that a man as careful as Aguilar would never let him walk away knowing what he did. Yet saying no to Aguilar was a certain death sentence. If he was going to disappear, Matt wanted it on his terms, not as fish food. His only remedy was to agree and accelerate his arrangements to leave the country.

"Carlos, head of casino security, has the details," Aguilar said. "Baskin is moving into a hotel, and Carlos will see you get Baskin's room key. There are no guards, and my grandson will be with you for backup."

"Your grandson?"

"Rodolfo. We can't afford another fuckup."

Matt was already wary, but the mere idea that Matt needed backup set off blaring alarms. In all the dirty assignments he'd handled for Aguilar, Matt had never needed help or backup. "Won't Baskin's paper pursue the story anyway? He's sure to have everything backed up."

"Just concern yourself with Baskin," Aguilar said. "And stop fighting this. I know that after gambling and sex, murder is your favorite indulgence. Make the routine cash collections with Rodolfo during the day, and finish this matter that evening. You'll pick up Rodolfo at the airport that morning and have a weapon ready for him. As a felon, he won't be able to carry or check one on the plane."

After Aguilar disconnected, Matt cashed in his chips and went to the casino lounge, where he downloaded the material from the link Renata had sent. The files contained evidence that Lawrence executives around Matt's brother were protecting themselves and setting up Clark as a scapegoat. Renata had also included Baskin's newspaper column claiming Clark could be criminally responsible for the BioVexis fiasco. If the allegation was true, Aguilar's argument was ostensibly persuasive: Matt could finally escape Aguilar's yoke and at the same time make one last payment on an old debt to his brother. But there was another incentive that convinced Matt to go ahead with the Baskin hit. Not the hundred thousand that Aguilar never expected to pay but the millions collected from Aguilar's casinos and betting parlors earlier in the day—millions that Uncle Sam would never tax and Aguilar would never see.

Matt realized that Aguilar would pursue him relentlessly for robbing and humiliating him in the eyes of his minions and associates. Not only did he have connections in every country that allowed casino gambling; he had a secret connection to some government spooks, an arrangement that Matt wasn't privy to. There would be no civilized place in the world for Matt to hide. So after killing Baskin, Matt would have no choice but to eliminate Aguilar as well, and he planned for Aguilar's last moments to be particularly agonizing.

Finally, Matt could think of no valid reason for the grandson to be there other than to kill him. The question was when he was planning to do it—before or after taking out Baskin. Matt intended to make sure it didn't matter.

CHAPTER 2

Kelly sat at the conference table with Dr. Jim Ridgeway, the company's chief microbiologist; Clark Kirkland, president of the Pharmodyne Division, which sold BioVexis; and Hugh Trent, Clark's executive assistant. She looked at her watch and frowned. "Twenty after, and Doc's still not here. Is he always this hard to corral? I called his assistant, and she said the meeting was on his agenda."

"Don't take it personally," Clark said. He was a tall, handsome man, with a full head of dark brown hair, who carried his surplus sixty pounds with authority. "We barely get a minute even when he's in the office, which is rare."

"This is critical," Kelly said, jabbing her finger at the *Chicago Tribune* lying open on the table. "You've read it. How much of what Sam Baskin wrote is true?"

Ridgeway and Trent looked at each other uneasily. Ridgeway, a balding man with glasses and a haughty air, picked up the newspaper, scanned the article, and pushed it away with a scowl.

"None of it, as far as I'm concerned," Clark said. "Payoffs, cover-up, no way. Still, the media's making me the poster boy. CNN, Fox, *Times*—all ready to feed me to the wolves."

"That's not Baskin's doing," Kelly countered. "The deaths and hospitalizations speak for themselves, and you're the face of BioVexis's division. I know Sam Baskin, and he doesn't fabricate stories. Says he has a source inside the company. If that's true, what could he have? And don't tell me nothing." She cold-stared Ridgeway, Trent, and Clark in turn. All three men shrugged, shaking their heads.

"Let me ask another way," she said, glaring at Ridgeway. "Did we know about the side effects before the media got a hold of it?"

"At first, we didn't know about them, and when we did begin to hear, we thought they might just be anomalies. You know how these things are," Ridgeway said, smoothing his hand over his balding head.

"Actually, I don't," Kelly replied. "So you tell me. Someone dies using our product, and you don't wonder—you don't check? How long had it been going on?"

"There were reports from the field starting a couple months ago," Ridgeway said, shrugging indifferently.

Clark bolted upright and scowled at Ridgeway. "I never got any reports until last week."

"I read your email replies to the concerns the field offices were writing in about," Ridgeway said assertively. "Everything under control, you said."

"My replies?" Clark said and looked at Trent. "Mine? Hugh, was that you?"

Trent recoiled from Kirkland's gaze. "You were traveling. Busy. I went to Doc, and he told me we had to settle the field force down. I just thought …"

Appraising Trent's startling blue eyes and dimpled chin, Kelly ventured that some women would consider him boyishly handsome. But she found his smile insincere, like so many of the city's aldermen she'd had to deal with in her former job.

"Jesus Christ," Kelly said. "Just great! Doc goes into denial mode; Hugh replies for his boss; and Jim, the one who understands the goddamn science best, just sits on his ass?"

"Idiots," Clark said, his face turning red. "If I'd seen reports of those problems, I'd have pulled the product in a second. This is criminal."

"I'll say it is," Kelly said. "I'm afraid to ask about Baskin's claims of falsifying reports and the bribe of an FDA inspector." She turned to Trent. "Well?"

Trent shook his head. "They won't be able to trace it. Wire transfer from a secret fund."

"We are so fucked," Kelly said, shaking her head. Then she gave Trent a steely-eyed stare and said, "I think you both better get out of my office before I start throwing things."

Like scolded puppies, Ridgeway and Trent jumped out of their chairs and left Kelly's office, leaving Clark behind, slumped in his chair.

"What?" Kelly said, sensing Clark wanted to talk.

"Now I know what's going on," he said. "It's making sense now."

"This makes sense?" Kelly said. "People died, and we're trying to cover it up? As if we could get away with it? Sense?"

"I'm talking about the board. Two board members called me and offered me a settlement if I resigned. Make the media happy, they said. A scapegoat. I didn't realize …"

"But it's not your fault. None of it."

"The pressure, the publicity … now my wife's threatening to leave—not that I give a shit anymore."

"Sounds like you're going to do it."

"I'm hanging in for now. I'll let you know," he said and then stood and left the room.

No sooner had Clark left than Kelly sprang from her chair and stormed down the corridor to Doc Castillo's corner suite, bypassing Cheryl, his assistant, who tried to head her off. Kelly rapped once on Castillo's door and entered without waiting for a response. The office measured twenty by thirty feet, with a modern glass desk with two facing guest chairs, a wet bar in one corner, and a conversation grouping of a table and four chairs in another. Upon spotting Sutherland Associates' rolled-up building plans lying on the table, Kelly winced. It was a disappointing reminder of their plan to move into a new downtown headquarters, a project that now seemed doomed because of the BioVexis problems.

Castillo was a burly man in his sixties with thick black hair, an unsmiling face, and dark wary eyes. He sat at his desk with his back to the door. When he glanced at Kelly from the corner of his eye, he quickly minimized the document on his screen, as if the contents were confidential.

"Oh, Kelly," he said, turning toward her. He was chewing on an unlit cigar, a habit so common it seemed like part of his face. "Sorry about the meeting … phone call."

"You missed a doozy, Doc," Kelly said as she plopped into one of the two armchairs in front of his desk.

"This is more about BioVexis, I suppose," Castillo said, frowning and waving the cigar. With only a trace of an accent, his English was excellent and imbued with an extensive vocabulary, assets he'd acquired with practice and voracious reading. Behind Castillo, the wall was covered with framed magazine and newspaper articles about him and Lawrence

Laboratories, letters of appreciation, awards, and photographs of him with various politicians and doctors, as well as his deceased wife.

"The company knew about the problems and didn't stop it," Kelly began breathlessly. "Even told the field force that all was well and went about trying to cover it up by falsifying reports. It's all in internal emails. It was Hugh acting and writing for Clark on your orders. Clark was as surprised as I was. And you want him to resign. He's innocent."

"He is our face to the world for this matter, after all. Head of the division," Castillo said.

"There seems to be enough blame to go around. Ignoring adverse field reports, denying them, covering up afterward. Someone inside Lawrence may have leaked those emails to Sam Baskin. Your messages may be included. If so, between the feds and the class-action factions, we're really screwed."

"Do we know Sam has them?"

"You know Sam as well as I do. He's not the type to lie about that. What's more, we actually tried to pay off an FDA inspector."

"That can't be proven, can it?"

"Did you know about all this?" Kelly asked, shocked by his question.

"Let's just say I spoke to Jim Ridgeway about it, but what's done is done. Now you'll have to hold off the class-action leeches until those emails can be redacted," Castillo said nonchalantly.

"I have to advise against that. It will look suspicious, guilty, and probably illegal. Besides, Sam may already have them from the leaks."

"He'll never publish any of that—believe me," Castillo said. "We have friends who'll keep it under wraps … buried."

"What kind of friends are going keep the feds and a pack of hungry lawyers at bay?"

"Just do your job, Kelly. We'll be fine. We may even move into a new headquarters once this gets sorted out. That should make Doug's day," Castillo said and pointed to the roll of blueprints on the corner table. "Anything else?" he said and jammed the cigar back in his mouth.

"Just that I think you have your head in the sand, Doc," she said, shaking her head. As she closed the door behind her on her way out, she said to herself, "Or someplace just as dark."

☙

Mother O'Brien's Pub was an Irish saloon decked out with green crepe paper, shamrocks, and leprechauns as if it were permanently Saint Patrick's Day. The bar stank of stale beer, whiskey, and sauerkraut, and the floor looked like it hadn't been swept in a week. Matt Kirkland had chosen the pub because it was far enough away from Lawrence Laboratories' campus headquarters to ensure secrecy. Matt, clad in sweater and sports jacket, waited in a corner booth, his muscular frame wedged uncomfortably into a space designed for an average-sized man. He checked the time, expecting Jim Ridgeway, Lawrence Laboratories' top microbiologist, to arrive any minute.

The large barroom was almost empty, only a few diehards hanging at the bar after happy hour. Ridgeway, wearing a knit cap and overcoat, walked in the front door, spotted Matt in the booth, and walked over. His thick glasses were misted from the temperature change. "Sorry I'm late. Damned snow."

"You sure Clark doesn't know about this meeting?" Matt asked.

"Why the mystery … keeping this from him?" Ridgeway took off his coat, revealing a sports coat and turtleneck.

"My brother doesn't approve of my methods. My life, for that matter."

"I gathered that," Ridgeway said. "I asked Hugh Trent to join us. He's your brother's right-hand man."

"I know who he is."

As if on cue, Hugh Trent came to the table, brushing snow off his shoulders with his gloved hands. "Nasty out there," he said to Ridgeway as he took off his gloves and overcoat. He wore a navy-blue suit, white shirt, and silk tie.

"Easy to see you're Clark's brother," Trent said, sliding into the booth across from Matt. "In better shape, though. He's put on a few."

Matt beckoned to the blonde waitress and ordered a Guinness draft. Ridgeway asked for a scotch on the rocks, and Trent ordered a Maker's Mark neat.

When the waitress left, Ridgeway said, "So what's this about?"

"This drug, BioVexis," Matt said. "A big problem, right? Killed some people."

"Allegedly," Trent said, shrugging. "What about it?"

"The national media have suggested criminal negligence, a cover-up, and attempted bribery and claim my brother is responsible. But they don't have proof. Sam Baskin, on the other hand, writes that he has two sources and can prove those charges and a lot more. The problem is that Baskin doesn't know that you two are the real guilty parties."

"Guilty parties?" Trent demanded. "That's some accusation coming from the guy who barely avoided jail time years back."

"That was me all right. But Clark? He would never do anything unscrupulous," Matt said. "But he's naive. He delegated all kinds of shit to his treacherous assistant while assuming his chief biologist would put science ahead of a fucking IPO. Sam Baskin's material could implicate Clark for the crimes related to BioVexis even though he was out of the loop and innocent. He'd be your scapegoat."

"You don't know that," Ridgeway said.

"You'd be surprised what I know," Matt said, glowering. "Here's the thing: Sam Baskin is on a crusade and plans to make that leaked material public. But his story goes far beyond the BioVexis matter, delving into unethical product development and who they are clandestinely collaborating with. If he publishes, it's going to put you out of business—not that I give a damn. But it will damage Clark's reputation or, worse, his freedom, and I don't intend to let that happen. So here's what you're going to do." Matt handed Ridgeway a note with numbered bank routings on it. "Two hundred thousand in that Panamanian account by tomorrow, and Baskin, his research, and your problems go away. No story."

"That's outrageous," Ridgeway bellowed, loud enough to turn heads at the bar. He lowered his voice to an angry whisper, saying, "We can't be party to anything like that."

"You can't mean …" Trent began. "That's … you couldn't."

"With Baskin out of the way," Matt said, "this matter will die down and be forgotten. But if my brother becomes the fall guy, gets blamed, arrested, or indicted for any of this, you'll have me to deal with."

"What's that supposed to mean?" Trent asked.

The waitress arrived with their drinks and, sensing the hostile mood at the table, abruptly set her tray down, turned on her heels, and scurried away without a word.

Matt hissed, "I fix this for you, or your problems will get a lot worse … personal and very unpleasant. Two hundred grand, twenty-four hours."

Neither man dared to return Matt's glare. Trent looked at his hands, his jaw muscles twitching. Ridgeway stared at a shamrock on the wall, his lips a tightened thin line.

Matt picked up his Guinness and drank it down in deep swallows, then replaced the empty glass on the tray. "Thanks for the drink," he said before he stood and strode out of the pub, leaving the other two with the bar bill and a dilemma to gnaw on. It didn't matter much what they decided, but as a betting man, Matt would give odds that they'd pay up.

Matt sloshed down the gloomy alley through the melting snow to a rusty steel door with a burned-out light overhead. He pounded on the door, and a shadow swept across the eyehole, followed by the clatter of a bolt and chain. The door opened, and Luther, a tall, bony man, grinned widely from a wrinkled black face. He wore an oversize T-shirt covered by a well-worn leather apron.

"Ho there. If it ain't old Matt the Knife," Luther said. "Every time he show up, a darkness come down on some poor soul. What the big man up to this time?"

"Money, you old coon, you. What else?"

"Music to an old nigga's ears. Come on in."

Matt was led into a metal machine shop filled with cluttered workbenches and well-used lathes, drill presses, routers, saws, grinders, and planers. The shop smelled of oil and turpentine, and the floor was covered with metal filings and odd bits of iron and steel. Luther sat on a rickety desk chair and cleared off a stool for Matt.

"So? What kinda skulduggery we up to today?"

Matt reached into his pocket and pulled out an unopened box of nine-millimeter cartridges and handed it to Luther.

"What's that about?" Luther said, confused. "Where's the hardware? No silencers, no reworking a semi? What am I supposed to do with these?"

"I got hardware. I need you to take the powder out and make them look and weigh the same as the real thing. Then you can put them back in the box like you found them. Got it?"

Luther grinned at Matt with a knowing gleam in his eye. "I guess old Matt never believe a gunfight got to be fair."

CHAPTER 3

Sutherland stood at the entrance of the Royal Suites Hotel lobby and spotted Baskin waving at him from a table near the bar. Besides losing his hair, Baskin hadn't changed much over the decades that Sutherland had known him. Tall and thin, with a beak nose and long corded neck, he had affectionately earned the nickname Professor Crane among some of his law students during his teaching years. He wore a navy-blue sports jacket, faded jeans, and worn tennis shoes, unusually casual for a man who normally wore a suit and tie. His left arm hung loosely in a sling, and with his right hand, he lifted a half-empty martini glass in a welcoming gesture. The two friends had shared many conversations over gin or aged rum.

Baskin's phone rang, and he gestured for Sutherland to sit down across from him, mouthing, "One minute," while he answered the call.

Sutherland took off his camel-hair topcoat and tossed it over one of the empty chairs. As he waited for Baskin to finish his call, Sutherland reflected on the years he'd known him. Baskin and Sutherland's father, Bernard, had gone to law school together. They had continued their friendship during their respective careers, often sailing, playing poker, or arguing politics and world affairs. On one sailing trip, they had taken fourteen-year-old Sutherland along, and it was on that voyage that they had rescued Dr. Jorge Castillo from a drifting raft in the Florida Straits. It was Baskin who had convinced Sutherland to go to law school, and Sutherland ended up taking classes from him at Northwestern University in Evanston.

After Bernard died, Baskin did his best to fill in the paternal gap with dinners, advice, and help, even trying to interest Sutherland in one of his daughters. During his tenure teaching at Northwestern University's law school, Baskin began working with law and journalism students, investigating and sometimes overturning questionable criminal convictions involving police-forced confessions. He then decided to dedicate more of his skills and curiosity delving into matters of suspected corruption that no one else had the courage to pursue. After publishing the results of a few notable cases, he earned a contributing spot with the *Chicago Tribune*, and over time, his columns gained national attention, won awards, and led many to believe he should have received a Pulitzer. He minced no words and didn't care who he offended in his columns if blunt coverage was deserved. But the private Sam Baskin was a different man. Sharp-witted, humorous, kind, and warm, he was who people thought of when they used the term *mensch*. Approaching seventy-five, he'd been married and widowed twice and had two daughters and five grandkids, who Sutherland had met at various birthday parties.

"Tomorrow, then. Nine o'clock. And then I'm gone," he said into his phone and then slipped it into his jacket pocket. "Quite a stroke of luck the other night, huh? Saved by a patch of ice."

"Any idea why you were targeted?" Sutherland asked.

"Probably a story I was working on. Anyway, I owe you for taking care of the ambulance and everything after it happened. So I'm buying the drinks." Baskin finished off his glass and waved to the bartender, holding up two fingers. "So how's Kelly doing? I really wanted to talk to her too."

"You're a reporter, Sam. Maybe a friend, but still a reporter, and she's in the middle of a media frenzy. She can't talk to you without opening it up to everyone."

Baskin nodded. "It's not going to get any easier for her. She should bail out before it's too late."

"She's only been there three months."

"Better to be gone while she can keep her reputation. After CNN and the rest began covering the side effects and deaths, I started looking into the BioVexis matter. It gets personal; don't forget that we both were there when we pulled Doc Castillo out of the drink. Your father and I even helped Doc find his first pharmaceutical position here."

"A few home runs there, and soon the venture capital boys came looking for him."

"That's right," Baskin said. "So anyway, after I started following this BioVexis thing in my column, I began receiving correspondence from someone inside Lawrence Labs, a fact that I eventually wrote about. The whistleblower sent communications proving a cover-up and payoffs related to BioVexis. Soon after that, another source sent a sample of files with an international angle and promised more. But it was what happened next that made me even more suspicious. I'm used to disturbing people with my columns, but one particular piece I wrote got some unexpected people worried."

Baskin explained that after he'd written that Lawrence's research center was the source of the BioVexis problem and should be investigated, a federal agent showed up at his door advising him to back off and let the agency handle it. Then the editor at the paper ordered him to forget those anonymous tips and anything else involving Lawrence. He'd been cooperating with the FBI and the state's attorney on the gambling-casinos story, and suddenly they started treating him like a criminal for snooping around Lawrence Labs. When he called Doc Castillo as a courtesy, Castillo said he was wasting his time, that there was nothing to it. He had actually told Baskin to stop for his own good. "Is that how you talk to a friend?" Baskin asked.

"My father advised me not to put too much stock in Doc's friendship," Sutherland said. "Fact is, I cautioned Kelly about taking the job, but she was dissatisfied with city politics, and the lure of stock options and a public offering won out."

The bartender arrived with the martinis, placed them on napkins, and whisked away Baskin's empty glass without saying a word. The drinks sat like trophies, ice crystals sparkling, condensation sweating down the stems. Both men lifted their glasses and said, "L'chaim," their customary toast.

"I'm glad we could meet tonight because I'm leaving Chicago tomorrow for Florida," Baskin said. "I'm supposedly retiring to write my memoirs after turning my files over to the feds in the morning. They'll get all the gambling dirt, but I'm holding back most of what I have on Lawrence Laboratories. That's what I wanted to see you and Kelly about. Join me upstairs in my suite, and I'll explain."

"Upstairs?" Sutherland asked. "Your house is ten blocks away."

"After being shot there, I'm not taking chances. I'm checked in under an assumed name, and only a few people know I'm here. A nurse from the hospital is coming to change the dressing on my shoulder. It's a messy wound. I'll meet you in my suite, rooms 635 and 637. I'm ordering room service for a sandwich. Join me?"

"I'm meeting Kelly for a bite later," Sutherland said and finished his drink. "I'll see you upstairs in ten minutes. Got to call the office."

On his way out of the bar, Sutherland glanced in the direction of a table at the far end of the bar and saw two men who seemed to be looking his way. The larger man had a baseball hat on and looked vaguely familiar, but the light was too dim for Sutherland to place the face before the man abruptly turned away. The smaller man didn't take his eyes off him, and as Sutherland went through the double doors into the lobby, he wondered where he'd seen that big man before.

Baskin paid off his bar bill, leaving the cash next to the empty glasses. Handicapped by the arm in the sling, he fumbled his laptop into his briefcase, draped his trench coat over his shoulder, and walked across the bar to the exit, then stopped. For a moment, he thought he saw someone he knew, but he couldn't place him. He continued across the hotel lobby while carefully scanning the faces of the patrons waiting in the lounge chairs. Seeing no one familiar or anyone showing interest in him, he entered an open elevator cab and pushed the sixth-floor button. Before the doors closed, he checked to see that no one had followed him, a habit that he had acquired years before and that seemed even more important now.

After someone had shot him, he dug out the Smith & Wesson .38 that he'd bought for his now deceased wife when she worked for the district attorney. He disliked firearms, but it was either that or a bodyguard. In this hotel under an anonymous name, neither should be necessary.

As he inserted his key card in the door to his sixth-floor suite, the face he'd seen in the bar finally registered. Clark Kirkland's photo was all over the media, and the man he saw in the bar with the baseball hat on looked a lot like him. He had been sitting next to a smaller man dressed in flashy clothes and enough bling around his neck, wrist, and fingers to start a pawnshop. He asked himself whether it could have been Clark Kirkland watching him but dismissed the idea as ludicrous. Clark was a division president of a multimillion-dollar corporation. He didn't spend his time in bars shadowing professors or journalists.

Matt and his unwelcome associate Rodolfo Aguilar sat in the Royal Suites Hotel bar nursing their lattes. They watched Sam Baskin and another man, with his back to them, sitting at a table near the unoccupied bandstand. The bartender walked over and delivered two martinis, and the two men raised their glasses in a toast. After a few minutes of conversation, the other man finished his drink, stood, and walked away. But on his way to the exit, the man glanced across the room, stopped, and stared straight in Matt's direction before leaving.

"Shit," Matt said under his breath, pulling down the visor of his baseball hat and turning away. A witness misidentifying Matt as Clark in Baskin's hotel might complicate matters for his brother.

"What?" Rodolfo asked, startled by Matt's expletive.

"Nothing. Just keep watching."

Baskin paid his bill in cash, grabbed his coat and briefcase in his good hand, and headed for the elevators. He was over six feet tall, but his stoop and shambling gait made him look every year of his age. Satisfied that their intelligence had been correct about his whereabouts, they would only have to wait until after room service delivered Baskin's dinner. Then, instead of the nurse's assistance Baskin expected, Matt and Rodolfo would be employing their own skills.

After Baskin disappeared down the corridor to the elevators, Matt turned to Rodolfo. "Any idea why your grandfather sent you here? To make your mark? Prove something?"

"I don't have to prove dick," Rodolfo snapped. He was a dark-complexioned twenty-nine-year-old with slicked-back black hair. To Matt, at six feet five, most men seemed small, but Rodolfo was shorter than the average man. "He thought you wanted backup is all."

"Thoughtful of him," Matt said sarcastically. He was supposed to believe that this cocky pip-squeak was intended as backup. Matt mentally mocked Rodolfo's jewel-encrusted Rolex, the heavy gold necklace, the gilded wedding band, and the diamond pinkie ring. Rodolfo's aqua-blue shirt, silk handkerchief, and sky-blue sports coat cried out to be noticed. Matt couldn't help his own size, but given his line of work, he walked through life as inconspicuously as possible. Under his trench coat, he wore a faded blue blazer large enough to conceal his gun, a pair of khakis, and an oxford-blue button-down shirt.

"You never finished the story about the money you took from the hedge fund," Rodolfo said. "How much?"

"I lost count. Millions, anyway," Matt said.

"And my family bailed you out," Rodolfo said. "So, besides the cash collections, what else do you do for the old man?"

They had spent the morning making a few of Matt's regular stops at Paolo Aguilar and his partners' offices and casinos. In the parking lot of a suburban tavern, they pulled next to a new Porsche and were given a heavy suitcase filled with cash by a well-dressed man in sunglasses.

"What else do I do? Shit like tonight," Matt said. "Why do you think we're carrying? We're not trying to scare him."

"Yeah, I got it," Rodolfo said, patting the bulge in his sports coat. Matt had handed over the nine-millimeter and the box of altered cartridges after their last cash pickup, and he had watched for any signs of suspicion as Rodolfo loaded his magazine. But Luther had done a perfect job. Now Matt was curious about when Rodolfo would try to take him out—before or after Baskin was murdered?

"Just give me a second or two with the shears first," Rodolfo said. That afternoon, they'd stopped at an Ace Hardware store in Oak Brook. In addition to the duct tape, Rodolfo showed up at the cash register with a pair of pruning shears. Matt didn't ask what they were for. Working for Aguilar as long as he had, he knew. The family had acquired many bloody habits from the Mafia back in Cuba. Aguilar once advised Matt to always send a message. That way, others will fear you.

"After we pop him," Rodolfo said, "I deliver today's cash to our airport baggage guy and fly outta here."

Except that Rodolfo wouldn't be taking any money. Matt considered the $2 million in bundled bills in the trunk of his car an exit bonus.

CHAPTER 4

Sutherland knocked on the door of room 637 and waited. As he stood there, a bellman pushing a meal cart arrived. The door opened, and Baskin let them both into what was obviously the living room of the two-room suite. The furniture consisted of a grouping of a couch, two armchairs, and a coffee table in the room's middle, and a heavy round table with two chairs in the far right-hand corner, next to a wet bar. On the left, an interior door led to what must have been the suite's bedroom. The floor was covered with a thick green-and-black-patterned carpet, and the windows were framed in lighter green drapes. It reminded Sutherland of other residential suites he had stayed in over the years—clean and functional but hardly luxurious.

After covering the granite tabletop with a white cloth, the bellman set out a napkin, cutlery, a water glass, and a wineglass and then uncovered a plate laden with a corned beef sandwich, coleslaw, and french fries. After he opened a half bottle of red wine, he handed Baskin the check to sign and left with the cart.

Baskin winced as he took his arm out of the sling and wriggled out of his sports jacket. He draped it over the chair back, slipped off the leather holster and revolver from under his left armpit, and hung the strap over the other chair.

"That loaded?" Sutherland asked, pointing at the gun.

"If someone's out to kill you, would you carry around an empty one?" he said and cracked a smile. He pointed to the laptop. "Start with the computer directory. I'll fill you in while I eat." Baskin poured a glass of wine and with his free hand gathered up his sandwich for a bite. Between mouthfuls, he said, "We've only got a few minutes before the hospital nurse arrives. They didn't want me to leave the hotel."

Sutherland opened the directory. "Holy shit, Sam. How many stories you got in here?" he said and scrolled. "Let me see … river casino, Midway Airport contract, Senator Weiss, waste products, Lawrence Labs, code enforcement … You've been busy."

"The really damaging stuff on Lawrence is in here," Baskin said, handing Sutherland a flash drive he'd dug out of his briefcase. "Kelly and you need to understand the depth of corruption you're dealing with. You both have a decision to make. She should walk out now, and you should cut your losses, cancel the lease for cause, and sue them while they still have any money."

"A little severe, don't you think? Not easy decisions."

"Read what's in there, and tell me that," Baskin said.

A flat-screen TV hung on the wall between the windows, and two news anchors were talking about BioVexis. They showed a video of Clark Kirkland, president of BioVexis's division, ducking his head as he lowered his large frame through a limousine's door. A blonde female talking head remarked, "There's suggestions of a cover-up now, a case of a criminal negligence followed by closing ranks and denials. Mr. Kirkland is the center figure in the story."

"That guy looks like the guy I saw in the lobby twenty minutes ago," Sutherland said, pointing at Clark's image on the screen. "Must have a doppelgänger. He was with a small guy dressed like a pimp," he added with a chuckle.

"Kirkland's not the big story. Neither are BioVexis and a few deaths. It begins decades ago with a doctor in the tradition of Nazi Josef Mengele, and I think there's a direct link between that diabolical doctor's practices and what's going on with Lawrence's research labs today. Come to Florida, and I'll show you what my new source sent me. I left it in my lockbox on the boat a couple weeks ago."

Baskin took a last bite of sandwich and washed it down with a swallow of red wine. Then he glanced at his phone lying next to his wineglass and said, "Whoa. I need to clean up for the nurse. I won't be long. Make yourself a drink while I'm gone. There's gin and scotch on the bar."

"I really shouldn't. Supposed to meet Kelly for dinner later," Sutherland said, consulting his watch with an uncertain expression on his face.

"If you're indecisive, let's make it easy," Baskin said as he reached into his pocket and produced a quarter. "Heads, you stay; tails, you go, leaving this poor old man to drink alone." He tossed the coin in the air and let it fall on the table. It came up heads.

"OK, one drink, and then I really have to go," Sutherland said.

"That's my boy," Baskin said before picking up his laptop, walking into the bedroom, and closing the connecting door behind him.

Sutherland poured a gin on the rocks and sat staring uneasily at Sam's flash drive before pocketing it again. *Let Kelly deal with it*, he thought. After all, Lawrence was her company.

After a few minutes, he heard masculine voices coming from the bedroom. He hadn't pictured a male nurse, but why not?

Matt inserted the key card to room 635, waited for the click, and launched his large frame through the door, gun in gloved hand and ready for anything. Seeing the bedroom vacant, Matt pushed open the bathroom door to find Sam Baskin bent over the sink, washing his face with his free hand. Baskin looked up into the mirror, saw Matt behind him, and shouted, "What the hell?"

Before Baskin could defend himself, Matt had his arm crooked around his neck and his hand over his mouth. He dragged him out of the bathroom and threw him onto the bed, burying his face in the slipcover to silence another shout. Rodolfo was ready with the duct tape, slapping a strip across Baskin's mouth. Baskin struggled and kicked, but Matt's weight and grip were too much for the older man, and soon his thrashing subsided and his muffled bawling ended in a moan.

"That's better, Sam," Matt said, motioning to Rodolfo to tape Baskin's wrists and ankles. The binding complete, Matt lifted the reporter and carried him to the corner chair, kicking the ottoman aside as he went. Rodolfo taped his torso to the back of the chair and his bound ankles to a chair leg. When he was finished, Baskin was totally immobilized, looking defiantly into the two faces confronting him.

Matt stood over him and said calmly, "If you're still expecting your nurse, forget it. We'll be treating you tonight. We have a few questions, and then we'll be out of here. I'm going to take the tape off, and if I hear a peep, pain—and lots of it. Got it?"

Baskin, eyes wide and angry, nodded.

"Good. First question: Your laptop and your notes on Lawrence Labs—where are they?" Matt asked and ripped off the duct tape.

"Ouch," Baskin yelped. "Take it easy. This is about Lawrence?"

Over his shoulder, Matt said to Rodolfo, "Is there a security box in the closet?"

"The safe's open," Rodolfo said, standing in front of the closet. "Laptop's here, and there's a stack of folders stuffed with papers, and a wallet."

"Hand me the laptop, and grab everything else and load it into those cases," Matt ordered. He opened the laptop and turned to Baskin. "You're going to tell me your password, right, Sam? And don't make me resort to force."

Baskin shrugged and recited a series of numbers, letters, and characters. Matt tried it. "Excellent."

"If you intend to destroy the files, you're wasting your time," Baskin said. "They're all backed up."

"Not my problem. Someone else is cleaning up after me. Your office, the cloud, whatever," Matt said, remembering Aguilar's directions. On another occasion, Matt might have ended this matter with a warning. But Baskin might remember incriminating details that Aguilar's cleanup team, whoever they were, couldn't destroy. "So … laptop and papers collected from the safe, I guess that's all she wrote."

"Not quite," Rodolfo said. He had finished packing Baskin's possessions and was standing at the foot of the bed opening and closing the pruning shears, his eyes a sheen of malice.

Baskin, his gaze fixed on the shears, strained against his bindings. "What's that for? You got what you wanted. Why hurt an old man?"

"You pissed off the wrong people, old man," Rodolfo said.

As Rodolfo stepped forward brandishing the shears in his gloved hand, Baskin twisted and pulled against the duct tape and hollered at the top of his lungs, "Get out! Get out now—"

Before Baskin could shout out another word, Matt pulled his Glock from under his coat and drilled a hole in the center of Baskin's forehead. "That's done. Now let's finish up here and get out."

"I wanted to do it with him alive," Rodolfo grumbled as he watched blood dribble from the hole in Baskin's skull.

"What's the fucking difference? Finish your sicko entertainment, and search the other room for his phone. It isn't in here."

His grisly handiwork completed, Rodolfo toweled off his bloodied gloved hands, tossed the washcloth and shears on the carpet, and opened the connecting door to the living room. The first thing he saw was a very surprised man standing behind a table that was cluttered with the remnants of a room-service meal.

In the living room of Baskin's hotel suite, Sutherland was sipping his gin when he heard Baskin shout from the bedroom, "Get out! Get out now!" followed by a muffled pop. *What the hell's the nurse doing?* Sutherland thought. He put down his glass and stood, ready to check on what was happening in the other room. But before he could take a step, the bedroom door opened, and a small man appeared.

"Who the fuck are you?" the man hissed as he fumbled a semiautomatic fitted with a silencer from under his jacket.

"I was just leaving," Sutherland said, sensing his dire situation. If the gun wasn't enough, the silencer made it clear: this was an assassin.

The man's cruel smile oozed malevolence as he sidestepped to his right, closing the path to the door. "You're leaving all right," he said, edging forward, his gloved finger firmly on the trigger.

Sutherland was standing by the card table where Baskin had left his holstered gun hanging on the chair back. Could he grab it and fire in time? The answer was no—unless the other guy was blind and slower than drying paint, which didn't seem to be the case.

"You the fed that the reporter's ratting to?" The gunman stepped closer, smirking.

"You don't want to shoot a federal official, do you?" Sutherland said, grasping the first straw that came to mind.

"Do I look like I care? Only good fed is a dead one," the man said as he aimed and pulled the trigger.

Click.

It was the sound of the firing pin against metal. Flustered, the gunman racked the Glock's slide, ejecting a round and chambering another. Meanwhile, in a desperate attempt to shield himself, Sutherland heaved the heavy table toward him, cascading the soiled plates and glasses over him as he tumbled to the floor. Then, with his back against the wall, he grabbed Baskin's holster from the chair back and yanked out the revolver. But when he looked up, the gunman was glaring down at him, aiming and pulling the trigger again.

Click.

"What the fuck?" the man howled and frantically pulled at the trigger two more times in a futile frenzy.

Sitting pressed against the wall, Sutherland fired up at the gunman hovering over him. The shot struck the attacker in the chest, and he stood for a moment with a disbelieving expression on his face before his legs buckled and he collapsed onto the carpet in a heap of bling and garish clothes.

The dead intruder had barely hit the carpet before another man appeared at the connecting door. His bulk nearly filled the frame, and he was pointing his gun in Sutherland's direction. Reacting out of instinct, Sutherland crouched behind the overturned table, hoping that a bullet wouldn't penetrate the heavy granite top. He heard two muffled pops, followed by a spattering of dust and a sharp sting in his left temple from a flying granite chip. From behind the overturned table, he aimed and fired, but the shooter had sprung back behind the doorframe. How many rounds did Baskin's gun hold? He knew some .38 revolvers held five, others six, and he was afraid to take his eyes off the door to count. To be safe, he had to figure on only three remaining shots.

A pistol and an arm appeared around the margin of the doorframe, and another round hit the tabletop with a loud crack. More stone fragments scattered, but the round didn't penetrate the granite. But the next shot tore through Sutherland's flesh just above his left clavicle. The searing pain coursed down his arm and across his neck, but he had to bear it and concentrate on staying alive. He aimed again, this time at the drywall hiding the man. The shot tore into the wall, and Sutherland heard a grunt and a muffled "Fuck." He'd hit the bastard and still had two rounds left—or, with any luck, three. He aimed the gun again in case the man mounted a desperate attack.

"OK, OK!" the shooter shouted. "Let's stay cool, buddy. You did me a favor shooting that little prick. I've got no fight with you."

"Then why are you trying to kill me?"

"No more. Is Aguilar dead? The guy you shot?"

"Yeah. What about Sam Baskin?" Sutherland asked, thinking how odd it was having a conversation with a man he had just exchanged shots and injuries with. He maintained a steady eye on the doorway, the revolver in his sweating hand, his finger testing the trigger.

"He's in a chair right behind me," the shooter said.

"Let me talk to him."

"He's tied up right now. So let's call it a draw. I'm going to leave by the bedroom door, and if I see you in the corridor, I'll shoot. Got it?"

"Got it," Sutherland said, happy to avoid another exchange. He might not get away so easily if it got any more heated.

"If you're smart, you'll wait five minutes and split yourself. Once that prick's people find out you killed him, you're a dead man."

Split? How is that going to work? Sutherland asked himself. His prints were everywhere, Baskin had emailed him a couple of times, they'd talked on the phone, and he'd had a drink with him in the bar a half hour before.

The connecting door swung closed, and Sutherland let out a long, relieved breath. He found a napkin on the floor and put pressure to the side of his face that was sticky with blood. Nothing he could do with his shoulder except hope his shirt and suit jacket would stanch the bleeding until help came. He was worried about Baskin's condition but didn't want to risk bumping into his adversary in the other room. Instead, he crept on hands and knees to the cell phone lying on the carpet, crept back behind the table, and dialed 911.

After the call, Sutherland waited for a minute to allow sufficient time for the shooter to leave before he emerged from behind the table and scrambled to the side of the closed door. Gun at the ready, he turned the knob, pushed open the door, and peered into the dark and silent room.

"Sam?" he shouted into the shadows. By the light from the living room, he spotted spent brass casings and a stained towel and shears on the carpet. Peeking around the doorjamb, he saw the silhouette of a man in a chair. "Sam?" He groped along the wall and clicked on the light switch, momentarily blinding himself. When his vision returned, all he needed was a glance to grasp the horror. Baskin's head was slung back, the eyes were wide and lifeless, and the middle of that face that Sutherland had loved and admired was a gruesome mass where his nose had once been. Sutherland dropped the gun to the floor and pressed his fist to his mouth to repress the primal bellow of outrage that smoldered inside. He bit into his fist so hard he tasted blood. But he forced himself to gaze intently at the gory scene, wanting to etch it forever in his memory, until he had finished what he was determined to do—put a bullet into everyone who had a part in Sam's murder.

CHAPTER 5

Matt winced at the fire in his abdomen as he carried the suitcases with Baskin's belongings along the hotel corridor toward the elevators. He cursed his own stupidity, having thought that flimsy drywall would protect him from a .38 round. If the slug's force hadn't been blunted as it passed through the wall and his clothing, he might've been totally incapacitated. As it was, the wound seemed serious and meant he would have to endure a lot of pain until he had the lead removed.

Matt had one suitcase jammed under his right arm, the other in his right hand. His left hand pressed the wound through his coat in an attempt to stanch the bleeding. Thirty yards down the corridor, the door to room 631 opened, and a small man in a suit and tie rushed out and crashed into Matt, bouncing off and nearly falling over in the process. When he regained his balance, he looked up at Matt and said, "Sorry. My fault. I'm late."

"No worries, mate," Matt said and kept walking. He continued down the hall past the elevators, not wanting to share one with the other man for fear he'd notice the blood. After waiting for the elevator doors to close behind the man, Matt returned, descended to the lobby, and walked out into the cold. It couldn't be helped that he'd left a direct witness at the scene. Continuing the noisy gunfight was bound to attract attention. The only thing that mattered was that Matt had another $2 million of Aguilar's money and would soon be in another country. Why would he care about witnesses?

Two uniformed police officers responded to Sutherland's 911 call within minutes. They double-parked on Rush Street in front of the Royal Suites Hotel and strode across the lobby to the reception desk, where they were met by a frenzied night manager who informed them that a guest had heard shots coming from one of the suites on the sixth floor. Minutes later, two plainclothes detectives arrived. One of them, Detective Arlo Demming, took the officers aside, where they conferred for a few seconds before asking the night manager for a key to the suite where the 911 call had originated.

After knocking and hearing no response from Baskin's bedroom, the two detectives entered, leaving the two uniformed cops in the corridor to watch the other door. As a career policeman, Detective Demming had seen dozens of dead bodies. But when he focused on the bound man in the chair, he struggled to understand what he was looking at. It was only after he noticed the pruning shears on the floor near the slumped-back body that reality set in. The other detective crossed himself and muttered, "Jesus! Why?"

"Never mind the Jesus crap—check the other room," Demming said as he looked into the bathroom. "This one's clear. Bullet hole in the wall by the door. Blood. Take it slow."

Entering the living room, they found a man slouched against the back of the sofa with his head in his hands. He looked up with a blistering glare, his forehead bloody, his shirt and suit coat stained with wine, ketchup, and blood. When they approached him, he said in an intense, resolute tone, "You can write this down: I'm going to put a bullet in that bastard's brain if it's the last thing I do."

Two EMT specialists arrived a few minutes after Sutherland finished summarizing to the detectives what had happened. They quickly verified that Baskin and Aguilar were dead and then turned their attention to Sutherland's injuries while he sat on the couch in the suite's living area. A bandage was all that was needed for the cut on his face, and after removing Sutherland's suit and shirt, the lead tech examined the gunshot and said, "Not bad. Right through, clean. We still need to get you to the ER."

"No friggin' way," Sutherland said. "It barely grazed me. Just put a bandage on it. I'm not spending the night in a hospital."

"We're not allowed to do that," the tech said. "We have to take you—"

"Look," Sutherland said. "Either put a bandage on it or get out. After what happened here, the last thing I'm doing is going to a hospital."

"OK," the tech said, intimidated. "Against our protocol, but given everything, OK."

The tech and his assistant cleaned the wound while Sutherland watched, clenching his teeth. After applying antibiotics and bandaging it, they left without another word.

"I don't blame you," Detective Demming said as he eased himself onto the chair across from Sutherland. "Come out sicker than when you went in. I've seen lots of gunshot wounds, and that was a lucky one."

"It hardly broke the skin. Hurts like hell, though."

"As long as we're here," Demming said, tapping his notebook with his pen, "we got the main picture of what happened here. While it's fresh in your mind, you remember anything else?" The detective was in his forties, tall, and blue eyed, with blond hair cut short on top but swept back on the sides. He looked like he'd boxed some, because his nose was crooked and one eyebrow was crowned with scar tissue.

"Yeah. Downstairs in the bar," Sutherland said. "I saw the two gunmen when I left there. They must have been watching us. I don't know whether they were waiting in the other room or came in later. I heard voices but thought it was the nurse. No one else was supposed to know he was here."

"Someone did," Demming said. "After the second shooter closed the door, why'd you go in there?"

"I wasn't sure Sam was alive, dead, or dying."

"Shame you had to see that. Awful."

Awful didn't cover it, Sutherland thought, reliving the scene—the spent brass on the floor, the bloody towel and the shears, his friend who'd been alive only minutes earlier.

"OK," Demming said as he consulted his notes. "The dead man, the one you shot, is Rodolfo Aguilar, from Fort Lauderdale. Mean anything to you?"

"Sam mentioned the name Aguilar pertaining to a gambling investigation he was working on and planning to hand over to the state's attorney and FBI."

The other plainclothes detective came in and said something in Demming's ear, causing him to furrow his brow. He turned back to Sutherland and said, "One mystery's solved, Mr. Sutherland. After they got the prints from the dead man's Glock, they found out why you're still alive."

"Did it jam?"

"Nope. Magazine was filled with dummy rounds. Took the techs a while to figure it out they appeared so genuine. Even the weight with lead replacing the gunpowder. There's a story there, for sure."

It wasn't the first time Matt had taken a bullet in the course of working for Aguilar. This time, it was royally fucking up his plans for the evening. He should have been on the way to the airport, where a private plane was waiting to take him to Florida, where he intended to kill Aguilar. But his pain was so intense he could barely concentrate on driving his car. He knew that unless he received medical attention soon, he could pass out or bleed to death. Remembering a retired doctor he'd used when he was wounded before, he stopped off at the man's Logan Square home. Matt wasn't worried about secrecy. He knew that since the doctor had lost his license, he'd drained what little money he had remaining after fighting various lawsuits. The cash Matt would offer him was enough to keep him quiet and in booze for many months.

"How bad is it?" Matt groaned after he stripped to the waist and watched as Dr. Wilbur Whitehead examined the injury and took his blood pressure.

"Let's hope it didn't hit the liver," Whitehead said. "Won't know until I dig it out to see. You've lost a lot of blood, and I can't help you with that. But at least I've got something to put you out."

"You can't. I'm supposed to be on a flight out of town," Matt said and grimaced.

"Son, you're not going anywhere tonight. Your blood pressure's falling, and you're white as a sheet. I don't care how brave you are—I don't have any help with this, and I need you immobile. Just lie down on the table, and I'll wake you in the morning." His breath smelled of scotch, but he seemed sober and steady when he filled the syringe, flicked it with his finger, and slipped the hypodermic needle into Matt's vein.

After Rodolfo's bagged body was shuttled out of Baskin's suite on a gurney, Sutherland turned on his phone and saw a text from Kelly: "Where are you?"

"Oh shit," Sutherland groaned to Demming. "That's my girlfriend. Supposed to meet her for dinner."

"Got a pretty good excuse, y'ask me," the detective replied.

Sutherland clicked her number.

"This better be good," Kelly answered tersely. "I've been sitting at the bar for over a half hour and already have several decent offers. Should I accept one, or are you coming?"

"Sorry. The police had me turn off my phone," Sutherland said.

Seconds passed before she responded. "This isn't funny. What's going on?"

"I'm serious. Sam Baskin is dead."

"Stop it, Doug. Tasteless, crude—sick, even."

"True, I'm afraid. Sorry about dinner. Been a terrible night, and I'm going home for a large scotch and crash."

"And leave me hanging?" she cried. "Oh no you're not, buster. You think you can drop that bomb on me and hang up? Where are you?"

"Leaving the Royal Suites Hotel to find a cab."

"Then you better take it right to my place, where I'm heading right now. I won't sleep until I know what's going on."

"Better meet at my place," he said. "I need to change out of these wet and stained clothes. Be there in twenty minutes."

"Wet and stained? Now you've really got me worried."

Better not to be alone tonight, he thought. He needed the company of someone besides the jaded detectives who probably viewed the evening's events as routine. He had lost an old and dear friend and shot and killed a man. It didn't matter that the stranger had intended to kill him; he'd pulled the trigger, and an instant later, a life was snuffed. How did one forget the sound of the deafening shot, the shocked eyes draining of light, and the stink of bowels and bladder evacuating in the man's final humiliation? So now he had one more gruesome sensory loop imprinted forever in memory and psyche.

Driving to Sutherland's place, Kelly agonized over what he had told her. Sam Baskin dead, wet and stained clothes … what the hell! Just like him to drop a bomb like that and leave her hanging, wondering, and worrying. He'd never been one for openness, but she'd be damned if he was going to drink his scotch and crash before telling her every damn thing.

As she drove east on Chicago Avenue, she reflected on their relationship and how learning consequential details about him was like pulling teeth. After they'd been dating for months, he finally told her about his failed marriage to Margo, who he described as a self-centered and needy woman. Kelly tried to imagine Doug with a needy person and gave up the effort, just as he had given up on Margo. From Kelly's experience, he wanted neither to need nor to be needed.

He'd been secretive about his father as well. She finally learned that he was deceased after they'd been seeing each other for six months. Much later, it came out that his mother—his Mexican mother—was still living in San Miguel de Allende. His Mexican heritage would never have occurred to Kelly. When they first met at an archaeology dig in Chiapas a couple of decades earlier, the first thing she noticed were those startling blue eyes shining from that deeply tanned face. She'd been attracted to his assured manner, good looks, and the special feeling she got when they were together, digging side by side or practicing Spanish over *cerveza fría* with Arturo, the head of the excavation. Their relationship at the dig had never had time to develop beyond friendship. They both had too many plans, which sent them in different directions.

Since they reconnected, each after a divorce, they'd enjoyed years of quasi-domestic tranquility, contentedly living in separate homes and working at their respective professions. Unfortunately, this tranquility had been twice interrupted by enough life-and-death drama to last a lifetime.

And now it seemed that the black cloud was hovering again. What was it with Doug's karma? Was this another instance of fate throwing him a curveball?

After the twenty-minute drive from her condominium in West Town, Kelly arrived at Sutherland's apartment building and dropped her car off with the parking valet. She rushed to the back door, used her keys to enter, and took the elevator to the twentieth floor. When she entered Sutherland's apartment and saw him in his stained clothes, all she could utter was, "Jesus, Doug. What ...?"

"Make us both a stiff drink while I change," he said. "I'll give you the whole fucking story."

"Is that blood? Are you hurt?"

"It's blood. Some of it's even mine," he said. "Settle down. Give me a minute."

"Then hurry up. Suspense is killing me."

"A poor choice of words given everything," he said as he walked to his bedroom, tearing off his shirt.

Kelly insisted that they stay up until he recounted every detail of the evening's events. When he finished his narrative with the discovery of Baskin's body, Sutherland felt his eyes well up and noticed that Kelly was looking at him, speechless.

"My god, Doug," she finally said, shaking her head. "You're talking *Pulp Fiction* or *Kill Bill*. Sam tortured and killed, you nearly the same ..."

"All I can think of now is seeing the responsible people punished. The shooter and whoever sent him. I'll do it myself if I have the chance."

"You don't know who they are."

"It starts with a name: Aguilar. The man I shot."

Paolo Aguilar sipped his fifteen-year-old Havana Club rum and tried to quell his growing sense of foreboding. He leaned against the railing of his penthouse balcony and gazed out at the dark waters of Key Biscayne. A brightly lit cruise ship passed to the south, headed for points unknown, a silver reflection of the moon in its wake. The night was chilly but not as cold as Chicago, the city that had occupied his mind for the last few hours. His grandson was supposed to call as soon as he left the hotel. Worse, the airport carrier hadn't seen or heard from him.

Aguilar's daughter Renata joined him on the balcony. She was in her late forties, with her hair pulled tight back against her scalp, her features sharp and severe. "It's after midnight and still no news."

He turned to face her and nodded. Then, noting her irritated expression, he sighed. "What?"

"If this is fucked up, it's your own fault for using Matt. You could have had our friends take care of it. It's too delicate to trust to a loose cannon like Matt."

"Our friends already took a shot and missed—remember? They can take care of Baskin's backup files and his Lawrence whistleblower," Aguilar replied.

"But what were you thinking promising to forgive Matt's debt? What does he still owe?"

"About a half million," Aguilar said. "We wouldn't see the money anyway. He was already making secret plans to disappear, and he's a serious liability if we didn't stop him from leaving. Next time he's in trouble with the law, who knows what deal he'd cut for what he knows."

Renata thought for a moment, and then her face lit up in a shrewd grin. "That's why you sent Rodolfo to be with him. You're diabolical, Papi. Two birds … I just hope your plan worked."

Aguilar finished off his rum and shouted to the woman waiting inside the balcony door. "Margarita. Any calls on my other lines?"

Margarita was a pretty twenty-five-year-old undocumented refugee from Guatemala who Aguilar had illegally taken in at a very early age. For years, she had functioned as personal assistant, nurse, waitress, and, as far as he was concerned, slave.

"No, señor," Margarita said nervously.

"Don't just stand there like a kicked dog. Get me another rum, *puta*," he demanded.

After Margarita went inside to pour Aguilar's drink at the wet bar, Renata said, "Someday she's going to poison your rum, Papi. Treat her like a dog, she might bite."

Before Aguilar could respond, his phone buzzed. He listened for a few moments and disconnected without saying a word to the caller. He turned to Renata. "They found two dead men. No names yet, but it should be Baskin and Kirkland. So why hasn't Rodolfo called?"

Aguilar had lain in bed most of the night wondering what had occurred in Chicago the night before and why he hadn't heard from Rodolfo. The lack of specifics, other than that there had been two dead bodies, made for seemingly endless dread. It was hard to imagine much good news behind the silence.

At ten o'clock the next morning, Aguilar, Renata, and Margarita left his penthouse apartment in his limousine, destined for his Palm Beach mansion. They were silent, all deep in their own thoughts and fears. In the bay, there were a number of sailboats and motor cruisers scattered over the calm waters. Aguilar imagined the people on the boats laughing and enjoying themselves as if life never ended.

But life did end. Renata's phone buzzed, and she picked it up and listened while Aguilar continued staring through the window brooding. After a minute, Renata disconnected and sighed.

"Well?" Aguilar grunted. "Who was that?"

"It's official, Papi. Two bodies were found. One was Sam Baskin, and the other was Rodolfo, shot with the reporter's gun."

"How could that be?"

"Someone else was there. A person we didn't plan on."

Scrunched in a corner of the limo's back seat, Margarita crossed herself. "Aiii, Dios," she whimpered.

"Cállate, puta," Aguilar growled at Margarita. Then, addressing Renata, he said, "How would Rodolfo let himself be shot with the reporter's gun? You're saying he was that careless? Something's fishy here."

"Rodolfo's gun had fake rounds in it," Renata said. "Remember? Matt was to supply the gun so that Rodolfo wouldn't have any hassle on the flight. As a felon, he couldn't carry one."

"Ese carajo Matt!" Aguilar shouted as the limo's phone rang.

Margarita reached to answer it. "Dígame."

"Hola, Querida. Cómo estás, dulcita?" Rafael, Aguilar's son, said from his office in Boulder, Colorado. "Is my father, Satan's servant, there?"

"Who is it, *bruja*?" Aguilar snapped.

"Your son, Rafael," she replied, cowering.

"The traitor," Aguilar said. "You speak to him, Renata. I can't bear the sound of his voice."

Renata took the phone and cleared her throat. "He won't talk to you, Rafael," she said. "You know that."

"Of course he won't—the coward," Rafael said. "His corruption killed my son, your nephew, and you do nothing but enable him."

"We will have revenge; you can be sure," she said.

"He had two children. What good will revenge do them?"

"They will be taken care of," she said. "Rodolfo was his favorite."

"And he corrupted him like everything else he touches. Like you. You're as perverted as he is. You tell the child-molesting fuck I hope someone cuts off his balls and your fake tits and makes you eat them." He hung up.

Renata, taken aback, slammed the handset into its hook.

"Let me guess," Aguilar said. "More insults. First, he goes to the feds, tries to destroy me; now he pecks away from a distance. I've got a mind to silence him for good."

"Bad idea, Papi," Renata said. "We've already been over that. When you sent Matt to Boulder to take Rafael out, I had to call him off. Despite what Rafael did, many in the family would be very upset."

"Fuck them," he said. "Who's the boss of the family? Who made them all fat and lazy?"

"Still. There is a limit to what measures the newer generation will accept."

"Weaklings. If it wasn't for my father, they'd all be starving in Cuba," Aguilar said. He puffed angrily at his cigar. "This was Matt's doing. What do you hear about him?"

"They checked his apartment. Gone," Renata said.

"Kills my grandson and runs away with my money."

"You won't miss it, Papi," Renata said.

"Can't let him make a fool of me."

"Besides, it was someone else who killed Rodolfo."

"Because Matt gave Rodolfo fake rounds," Aguilar replied. "Research that *hijo de puta* who shot him, whoever he is."

"His name is Sutherland."

"And Matt's brother. He must have known what Matt had planned. He is equally guilty of Rodolfo's murder."

"You don't know that," Renata said.

"Sutherland and Clark Kirkland! Both of them, you hear?"

"Calm down, old man," she said. "Rushing into this would look too suspicious. We have to be smart about it, choose the right time and method. While we're hunting down Matt, I'll do the research on his brother and Rodolfo's killer."

"Not too long," Aguilar growled. "I'm not getting any younger."

CHAPTER 6

The morning after Baskin's murder, Sutherland awoke late to find that Kelly had already left for her Lawrence Laboratories office in Lake County. Sitting up in his bed, he could look out his windows at a panoramic view of the city. It stretched east past the tapered Hancock Building to the long tongue of Navy Pier, the conspicuous Ferris wheel, and the lighthouse and lake beyond. South, the ragged profile of Loop office and apartment towers was crowned with the skyscraper originally named Sears Tower: tall, distant, and as imperious as Everest. Forget Willis Tower. To Sutherland, the building would always be the Sears Tower, a symbol of the company's pioneering role in American merchandizing and Chicago's history.

Planning to call his office, he discovered that he couldn't open his iPhone. He tried his pass code several times, and it wouldn't open. Puzzled, he examined the device closer and realized it was slightly larger than his. It meant that this wasn't his phone. He was often in meetings with others who had iPhones, and he figured he must have pocketed one of them by mistake. He set the unfamiliar phone aside and dug out his own from his briefcase to tell his assistant he had an appointment with the police. A shower, a shave, and a cup of coffee, and he was ready to meet Detective Demming in the Central Area on Larrabee Street.

The detective looked as tired as Sutherland felt as he led Sutherland into an elevator to the second floor. It wasn't the first time Sutherland had been in a police interview room, but that didn't make the experience any less stressful. He hadn't merely witnessed a crime; the previous night, he had killed a man. It had clearly been self-defense, but his past experiences taught him that "clearly" was subjective and didn't always coincide with the way the police or prosecutors viewed events. Sutherland had awakened several times envisioning what other interpretations or conspiracies a detective could play out in his mind. It had happened before.

When they entered the interview room, it was stuffy and overheated. Sutherland guessed eighty degrees.

"Dammit. Janitors can't get it right," Demming said, hanging his sports coat on the back of a steel chair.

Sutherland did the same with his suit jacket, thinking with a hint of paranoia that the heat was intentional, an attempt to make him sweat.

As if to ease Sutherland's mind, Demming chuckled softly to himself and smiled. "You see the end of the game last night?"

"Not really," Sutherland answered.

"Overtime. Last-second three-pointer, Bulls win. From half-court, for Christ's sake. Should've seen the face of my partner. He's a Lakers fan."

"Have a bet on it?" Sutherland asked.

"Just enough to make it interesting. I love to give him crap," he said, opening a folder and his notebook and spreading them out on the table. "But on to business. I told you last night about the gun—that it wasn't meant to fire. Blanks. Any ideas why?"

"Not a clue."

"His partner had a Glock too, which obviously worked fine. Don't make sense showing up with a worthless piece."

"He tried four or five times. He was more surprised than me."

"The man you killed was Rodolfo Aguilar, the grandson of Paolo Aguilar," Demming said, reading from a folder on the table. "Aguilar and his partner were probably there to kill Baskin for his investigations into the casinos his grandfather controlled. Aguilar and the other assassin arrived together, had coffee in the lobby lounge where you and Baskin met, and then entered Baskin's suite while you were in the living room. We got it on the closed-circuit video, so we have the times nailed down."

"Video of the killers?" Sutherland asked. "The big one looked familiar."

"He wore a Sox hat and must have known where the cameras were."

"If I saw him again, I'd recognize him for sure."

"Speaking of recognizing," Demming said, "when I was a rookie, maybe twenty years ago, there was a guy named Sutherland. He looked something like you."

"What about him?"

"Former prosecutor. Sent to jail for bribing the mayor, something like that. Any relation?"

"He was part of an FBI ploy that was eventually divulged, and he was totally exonerated. My father."

"See that?" Demming said proudly. "I never forget a name or a face. And you were the one that found the murdered alderman's tapes that brought down the governor candidate. Damn, I'm good."

After his statement was ready, Sutherland signed it, handed it to the detective, and stood to leave.

"Take a look at the Lotto today," Demming said. "Over a hundred million and counting. Getting out of that clusterfuck last night with only a flesh wound ... you may be on a roll."

On the television screen, a reporter in an overcoat and knit cap stood in front of a downtown Chicago hotel while snowflakes drifted around her. Eyes into the camera, microphone in gloved hand, she was delivering the latest news on the murders that had taken place in the building behind her. "Two men fatally shot, another injured, while the police try to piece together what happened and who the unknown assailant was. But sadly, this much is known for certain: Samuel Baskin, the prizewinning columnist and investigative reporter, has been brutally murdered. Back to you, Dale."

Dr. Jorge Castillo nodded, relieved. He sipped his morning *café con leche* his houseman had brought while he sat in the dining room of his Lake Forest home. His betrayal of a supposed old friend couldn't have been avoided. Baskin had been delving too close to the truth and wasn't going to be dissuaded. Even cautions from government agents and orders from the newspaper's management wouldn't deter the man. Fortunately, nothing about Baskin's death could be directly traced to Castillo or, as far as he knew, to Lawrence Laboratories, the company he'd founded. Though Aguilar's ploy to eliminate Matt Kirkland had failed, in Castillo's mind, the outcome was roundly successful. Baskin may have saved Castillo's life decades earlier, but for the doctor, loyalty and gratitude had their limits.

Castillo, a widower and childless, was nevertheless well cared for by his live-in houseman, cook, and groundskeeper. Satisfied with his hot breakfast and the morning news about Baskin, he finished his coffee and lit a cigar while he gazed out at the morning scene that never failed to cheer him, even in the depths of winter. The home was perched on a bluff overlooking Lake Michigan, with a wide lawn sloping down to the water. The lawn was newly white with a covering of snow, and the shoreline had partially iced over, a gray sheet extending several hundred yards to meet the open water. In the summer, the lawn would shimmer with dew, and the water would glimmer in the reflection of the dawn light. He had bought the property from a prominent Chicago family in the process of liquidating assets to maintain harmony among the grandchildren. That had been a decade before, the tenth anniversary of the year Castillo had started Lawrence Laboratories with seed money from Morrow Partners. The home purchase was his way of showing his former countrymen in Florida that he had made it. Unlike many of the wealthy *exiliados* in Miami, he hadn't fled Cuba in the exodus of 1959 and 1960, when Castro came to power. It was much later before he took off from a remote beach east of Havana on his makeshift raft bound for the United States and a new existence.

His breakfast over and the cigar drawing smoothly, he went into his library and picked up the leather-bound copy of Dostoevsky's *Crime and Punishment* and continued reading where he had left off. His bookcase was filled with hundreds of volumes he'd consumed over the years, beginning with the Greek philosophers and progressing through all the important themes throughout the ages. It was ten o'clock, but he saw no need to hurry into the office. With Jim Ridgeway and his team, the company functioned just as well without him, and he much preferred staying at home reading the classics in English to dealing with the complexities of running a company and plumbing the arcane depths of microbiology and immunology.

Kelly let herself into Sutherland's apartment, tore off her winter coat, threw it over the back of an armchair, and collapsed onto the couch with a groan. Recognizing the taut jaw, hard-edged eyes, and knitted forehead, Sutherland knew she was either very pissed off or overly stressed, or possibly both. The symptoms were enough to send Sutherland straight to the kitchen, where he poured a glass of sauvignon blanc.

Sutherland handed her the glass and asked, "Is something stronger in order?"

She took a thirsty gulp. "Thanks. After my commute, the whole scotch bottle wouldn't help. I can't tell you how pissed off I am that we're not moving downtown. It was promised when I took this job. I used to commute to city hall with a fifteen-minute walk from my place."

"Can't you work from your condo?"

"I intend to, as much as I can. But I'm also thinking about getting a small apartment near the labs during the week."

"I'm not in favor of that idea," Sutherland said. "Hardly see you as it is."

"I know. But see how you would enjoy that commute," she said. "An hour on a good day."

"You might as well face it. I don't see your HQ move ever happening," he said. "Not after hearing what Sam had to say."

"How much money will you be out?" she asked, slipping off her shoes and putting her feet on the coffee table.

"I shouldn't be telling you. You're their lawyer."

"Yeah, yeah," she said. "I already know enough. The company's lab specs required major design, stringent codes, sophisticated labs—all unnecessary for any other tenant."

"The only way to win the deal." His competitors had accused him of securing the headquarters deal through his acquaintance with Castillo, but it was only sour grapes. He responded to the request for proposal just as every other developer had. As far as Sutherland knew, Castillo had never been involved. And Kelly certainly wasn't. The lease had been signed months before she took the job. "Anyway, there's the cost of the option on the site and the architecture and engineering fees, but that won't break me even if I have to wait years until winning the damage suit against Lawrence. I still have the other properties bringing in revenues. I could even close up the development side of the company and retire if it came to that. I've been giving that idea some thought lately, with all this going on with your company and now with what happened to Sam. Life's too short."

"You'd retire while I'm saddled with this BioVexis curse?" Kelly said. "You wouldn't do that to me, would you?"

"According to Sam, it's not just BioVexis, Kelly. Otherwise, why would the government suits and his editor want to gag him? He was onto something bigger."

"And that something's on that flash drive he gave you?"

"Part of it. He said he was expecting more," Sutherland said. "There may be clues in those files to who wanted Sam dead."

"Won't the police or the FBI need it?"

"My guess is they already know what's in those files. That's why they wanted the story killed. I've got no faith in their enthusiasm for finding the killer."

"You're saying they'll do nothing?"

"We'll see. Meanwhile, we've got Sam's files, evidence that may lead to the people who wanted him dead."

"And then what? What can you do?"

"Let's not get ahead of ourselves. But know this—Sam was a friend, like a second father to me, and I will see that his story is published and his death avenged, even if I have to sink to their level."

Kelly shook her head. "You say that now because you're emotional. You know damn well you're not a killer."

"And you know this wouldn't be my first rodeo," he said. In the last ten years, there had been several circumstances in which Sutherland had had to eliminate a dangerous enemy in self-defense. "But let's not dwell on that. We need to begin digging into what Sam left. He said it was important for both of us. My project and business and your reputation."

He plugged Baskin's flash drive into the USB of his laptop, and they sat together at the dining-room table, scanning a folder labeled "Centro." After Sutherland paged through a dozen emails, Kelly stopped him and said, "There's a lot of scientific material in Spanish here. This one's subject reads, 'Vacuna AC508,' and it's addressed to Doc at jcastillo@lawrencel. com. It says, 'Aquí tiene el protocolo para la vacuna AC508. Fíjese en la sección 6 que contiene un cambio significante.'"

"A vaccine protocol with some changes," he said. "Is this info coming from Puerto Rico?"

"Because of the Spanish? Probably. We have a lab there and are talking about building more there when things improve," she said. "Speaking of improving, how's your shoulder? Still hurt?"

Sutherland rotated his wounded shoulder and winced. "Some. Didn't hit anything important, so it won't bother my squash game."

"Thank goodness for that," she said. "That would have been earth-shattering."

৵

At ten o'clock, Sutherland and Kelly decided they'd slogged through enough of Baskin's research for one night. Between the Spanish texts and the medical jargon, it wasn't easygoing. The internal Lawrence emails in English were welcome respites from the confounding texts, but the implications of what was known about BioVexis early on were increasingly troubling to Kelly.

"Nightcap?" Sutherland said as he walked to the kitchen. "Something to counteract all the coffee?"

"Scotch, if you please," Kelly replied, stretching her arms out and up while she walked to the east window. The half-moon was peeking through the clouds, its silver reflection sketching a wavy line on the dark lake. "What do you hear from Jenny?"

"I called and left a message this morning, but I didn't tell her about Sam. I worry about how she's going to take it," he said, dropping ice cubes into crystal glasses. "It's because of him she's decided to become a journalist. He was encouraging her to go to Northwestern, but she's undecided. She wants to get away from home, away from her mom. Can't say I blame her."

"I remember that time of life. You're sure your whole future depends on that decision," she said. "It's scary."

He poured two scotches and brought them to the living room and sat on the couch.

Kelly turned from the window and joined him. "You call her back?"

"I'm not looking forward to it."

"Why not FaceTime her now? I can help you deal with it." Kelly and Sutherland's daughter always got along like sisters. Their friendship had continued during the span of time that Sutherland's ex-wife moved to California, got remarried, divorced, and moved back to the Chicago suburbs. "You think Margo will mind?"

"She'll be passed out by now," he said. "But it is late for a school night."

"You don't understand seventeen-year-olds. Let's do it."

Ten minutes later, the image of a blonde with Scandinavian features was staring through teary eyes at them from Sutherland's screen. Jenny had her mother Margo's exceptional beauty, enhanced by the Sutherland dimple nestled in her cheek and the same subtle twist of the mouth, which on her looked impish when she grinned. But this time, she was far from smiling.

"I just heard," Jenny said, wiping her eyes with her fists. "Sam was killed."

"I'm sorry, honey. I should have told you earlier," Sutherland said, feeling like a rotten father. Baskin had always doted on Jenny, and she treasured him, sometimes calling him Uncle. "A terrible thing."

"But you were there," she said, sobbing. "Couldn't you do anything to stop it?"

"No, honey. There were two very dangerous men with guns."

"You killed one, though," she said. "Didn't you? Are you OK?"

"Yes, I'm OK," Sutherland said. "Just shaken up. He was my oldest and probably my best friend."

Kelly said, "Your father was very brave, Jenny, but he couldn't have done anything more. He even wounded the other killer."

"Are you going to catch him—the one you shot?" Jenny asked.

"That's not up to me," he said. "That's the FBI and the police's job right now."

"You've done it before," she insisted.

"Where did you get that idea?" he asked, baffled.

"I asked questions. That's what reporters do. Last term, there was a journalism assignment in school, and I chose a crime story. I got an A. It was about a Mexican drug and artifacts trafficker and a bad federal agent. I didn't use your name, though."

Sutherland and Kelly looked wide-eyed at each other.

"You're joking," Sutherland said.

"No. I always knew there was something going on."

"Well," he said, trying to gauge where to go from there. "That had to do with your grandmother Gabriela. She was in danger."

"You saved her," she said. "She told me all about it."

"And I was almost killed in the process," he said, remembering how close he'd come to dying in the last moments before the explosion killed

Enrique Arias and his gorillas in Mexico. And it easily could have been him rather than Agent Christopher who drowned under the icy waters of Chicago's Montrose Harbor. Sutherland didn't like being reminded of how many times he'd narrowly escaped death. He sometimes wondered whether those who believed that providence governed events also assumed it could impose an upper limit on good luck. If so, the episode with Rodolfo Aguilar brought Sutherland one step closer to his quota. Not a comforting thought.

"Don't think of me as some kind of superhero, Jenny," Sutherland said. "I can't do miracles. But I would like to read your story."

"Only if you promise," she said, sniffling, her eyes still wet.

"I can only promise to do everything I can," he said. "I know it's hard. Kelly and I are going through the same thing about Sam. Try to get some sleep remembering the great times we had with him."

They disconnected, and for a few moments, Sutherland and Kelly sat silently, sipping their drinks.

"It might have been me," Kelly said.

"What?"

"When the lagarto-stone thing was going on, she sensed something even though she was living with her mother in California. After all, you warned Margo to leave the house and take Jenny to stay with a friend. Jenny called and asked me about it, why you were going to Mexico, things like that. I told her Gabriela was in trouble. She must have taken it from there, because I never mentioned any more than that."

"If she squeezed that story out of my tight-lipped mother, she'll make a hell of a journalist."

Aguilar finished reading the report he'd received from his Chicago sources. It had taken only twenty-four hours for their connections to assemble a more complete picture of the events of the night Sam Baskin and Rodolfo were killed. Matt Kirkland had guessed that Rodolfo had been sent to kill him and gave Rodolfo ammunition that had been tampered with. Defenseless, Rodolfo was shot with Baskin's gun, in the hand of a third person. Shots were traded between Matt and this wild card, and Matt may have been wounded—one of the few positive notes in the report. Aguilar's people in Chicago were still researching Douglas Sutherland and would forward the material in another day. The only information they could provide at the time was that he was a commercial real estate developer. The last detail of the report was that there was no sign of Matt.

Matt Kirkland had been vetted and recruited ten years before, when Aguilar bought him out of his legal problems with the hedge fund Matt managed. He was a high-stakes gambler, and he'd begun dipping into client funds to finance his losses. Before his fraud was discovered, he had siphoned off several million from his clients' accounts and hadn't changed his luck.

Matt was broke and unable to replace what he'd embezzled from the hedge fund clients or pay off his debts to Aguilar's private card games. Killing him would be a message to other deadbeats, but Aguilar had a better plan. Matt was extremely intelligent and had other attributes Aguilar could use.

Matt was a CPA and had passed all the SEC certifications for security trading. He would delve into company financials and find the dirty secrets, the organization's hidden flaws or the unexploited potential, and during his early tenure at the hedge fund, his real returns beat most of the street averages by an impressive margin. In addition, Matt wasn't afraid to get his hands dirty or step over legal or moral lines. He had not only demonstrated his amorality by defrauding the hedge fund, but he had frequently used his formidable size to satisfy his psychopathic, sadistic impulses. As linebacker for the Northwestern Wildcats, he'd crippled a rival quarterback and several running backs before he was suspended, and a college roommate related how Matt had broken the arms of two card players who tried to cheat him. But the most convincing evidence of Matt's potential usefulness surfaced during Aguilar's investigators' deep background research. Their findings uncovered Matt's suspicious proximity to a number of fatal incidents that began in his teen years. They included the gruesome death of an adult camp counselor, the drowning of a young woman, and the tragic demise of his and his twin brother's parents. Surviving unscathed after flying so close to the flames would be an invaluable asset in Aguilar's nefarious world.

So rather than writing off the loss and letting Matt be indicted for fraud, Aguilar flew Matt to Miami. The proposition was simple: The hedge fund would forgo prosecuting Matt in exchange for Aguilar's substantial investment in the fund. As for Matt's debts to Aguilar, he would work them off, however long it took. The interview took place on Aguilar's yacht, and he remembered the discussion well. "What would I do?" Matt had asked after hearing the proposal.

"For now, I want you to immerse yourself in the accounting practices of my Midwest casinos. I want you to know more about them than the managers. I'll give you all the proven industry percentages and statistics, and you'll see how well the casinos' results conform. I want you in the trenches looking for anomalies. Later, I'll have other assignments that shouldn't stretch your scruples too much."

"And if I don't take the job?" Matt had asked.

"The best thing? You go to jail."

"I don't suppose I have to ask what the worst would be."

"Oh, one more positive note," Aguilar had added. "You can gamble all you want, but only at my casinos. No more private games, no horses, no pro games, no bookies. If you lose in my casinos, no problem—it won't go on your account. If you win, you return the winnings to the house."

The next day, Matt returned to Chicago and began his new career as another set of eyes inspecting the intricate workings of Aguilar's expansive empire. Over ten years, his duties evolved into more confidential and underhanded matters. Like his brother, he was a good salesman, and combined with his imposing size, it made him an effective unofficial lobbyist. When reason wasn't successful, he leaned on politicians and other public officials, sometimes bribing, blackmailing, or threatening them when necessary. Cash pickups and drop-offs were as regular as the mail, and once in a while, he had to clean up after a mess another of Aguilar's minions had left. More than once, his warnings weren't taken seriously, and he had to make good on his threats. Matt had been a great asset for years until he felt the urge to retire.

Grant Reynolds, an agent for Allstate insurance, returned to the lobby of the Royal Suites Hotel and sank into a cocktail lounge chair. It was to be his last night in Chicago after a three-day seminar with his counterparts from other sales branches across the Midwest. He ordered a beer from a passing waitress and began to page through the *Chicago Tribune*. The front page had the headline "Sam Baskin Murdered," along with a photo of a thin older man. Reynolds scanned the article and stopped when he saw that the murder had taken place in the Royal Suites Hotel on the same floor as his and at about the time Reynolds had been leaving for dinner. He'd been running late, and he tore out of his room and crashed into a big man. When he returned later in the evening, he saw a policeman standing a few doors down from his room on the sixth floor, but he'd been too tired and drunk to think of anything but sleep.

In the newspaper's business section, he was surprised to see a face he recognized. A photo showed a man in an overcoat getting out of the back seat of a limousine. He was caught looking directly into the camera with an angry expression, as if he considered the photographer's presence an intrusion. The caption underneath said, "Clark Kirkland, President of Lawrence Laboratories' Pharmodyne Division, Manufacturer of BioVexis."

The man Reynolds had collided with in the corridor looked exactly like Clark Kirkland. A man of that size wasn't easily forgotten, and Reynolds had bounced off him like he was a brick wall. Even considering his surprise at the time, Reynolds knew his glimpse of the man's face was enough. It had to be the same person. His first impulse was to call 911, but he didn't want to be involved as a witness. So after polishing off his beer, he called a friend who worked for CNN.

Sergeant Daryl Durant, a freckled redhead in civilian clothes, sat in a secure basement room in a rural Virginia office building in front of a half dozen color screens. The sergeant headed a twenty-four-hour center that monitored a number of organizations around the United States. Shifts were spent reviewing closed-circuit surveillance video, watching for anomalies in voice and data traffic, and reporting any security breaches to his superior. All this was for a unit that had recruited him from the US Army after his second Afghanistan tour. He didn't know, and he didn't ask, what their overall mission was. He knew only that the outfit was very secret and it didn't pay to ask questions.

He crushed out his cigarette into the overflowing ashtray and studied the screen that had just refreshed itself. He keyed a few strokes on his computer, and a phone number popped up and was automatically dialed.

He never had met the woman who would answer, just as he had never laid eyes on any of the others in the organization.

"Lansing here. What is it, soldier?" the woman answered in clipped military fashion.

"Ma'am, I tracked down the information you requested. On three separate occasions in the last thirty days, location number fourteen transmitted a high volume of data. Compressed and encrypted, as if someone was dumping files. And just as you suspected, the recipient was a private account owned by a Samuel Baskin. Is this serious?"

"We wouldn't be monitoring that company otherwise. There's no legitimate reason why Lawrence Laboratories should have been exporting mass data to a reporter. Have you identified the sender?"

"He's a microbiologist. Must know a lot about computers and systems because he ducked the IT department's internal protocols. Even used other employees' computers to hack, download, and send the material."

"If he's so smart, how do you know it's him?" Lansing asked.

"The transmissions occurred at night or early morning. I got into their security system and checked entry and exit times in the various sections of the building. He was the only one who matched."

"Good detective work, Sergeant," Lansing said.

"Do you want me to send you the transmissions?"

"Our team already downloaded and expunged them from Baskin's backup and cloud files. What information do you have on the reporter's source?"

"Got an address."

CHAPTER 7

Jim Ridgeway sat in his home office sipping his coffee and reflecting on Sam Baskin's murder. He speculated that Baskin had come upon the BioVexis story after the *New York Times* and national television networks began to look into the drug's side effects. But Baskin only became dangerous after the whistleblower sent him correspondence from doctors, clinics, and hospitals across the country reporting BioVexis side effects to Lawrence management. The reports should have set off alarms, but concerns about profits and the imminent initial public offering had taken precedence. If the reporter possessed memos to that effect, any defense against the company's culpability would be impossible.

Days earlier, when Baskin's column stated that he had evidence of unethical methods being employed in Lawrence's research centers, Ridgeway had gasped. If Sam Baskin had been able to follow that circuitous trail to its beginning, Lawrence's problems with BioVexis would seem trivial. Everything considered, Ridgeway felt relieved and somewhat vindicated for his part in the reporter's demise. It was only the guilty who knew of his involvement, and why would they go public?

Ridgeway joined his wife in the kitchen. She was filling the coffee machine and watching the local morning news on channel 2. She turned as he entered and said, "Jim, you must know Kenneth Wright, don't you? They're saying he worked at Lawrence Labs. Had something to do with BioVexis."

"Kenny? Sure," Ridgeway said, surprised. "He's a senior microbiologist. Why?"

"The news. They just showed his house on TV. He was killed last night. Went out to meet someone, and they found him in a ditch this morning," she said. "You want eggs?"

Ridgeway sank into a kitchen-table chair and exhaled loudly.

"Are you all right, dear? Would you rather have cereal?"

First Baskin, then Ken Wright. It made sense—the whistleblower.

Clark Kirkland squeezed into the driver's seat of his wife's BMW and adjusted the seat to make room for his 290-pound body. He couldn't begin to count the number of lunches, dinners, manhattans, and cognacs responsible for the damage he'd done to his once-athletic frame. Came with the territory, he liked to tell himself. With his work, travel, and entertainment schedule as division president, he had no time for exercise. He rarely drove his wife's cars, but his Porsche didn't behave on slippery roads, and besides, Melanie had left Chicago on an early-morning flight, escaping all the publicity surrounding his name and BioVexis. Based on their last exchange and the yearslong deterioration of their relationship, she might have left for good. It was the least of his problems.

"Have you seen the evening news?" Melanie had screeched when he'd entered his den the night before. She stood with the TV remote in her hand, still dressed in her tennis warm-up clothes, long pants and sequined Dior jacket. A sweatband held her shoulder-length blonde hair in place, but her makeup hadn't been disturbed by her evening at the club. She never seemed to sweat.

"I've been in meetings," he said, falling into his favorite leather chair. "What's it this time?"

"A witness saw you leaving the suite where that reporter was killed. It's all over the local channels and CNN."

"That's fucking ridiculous," he said. "Who put them up to this? Some smut rag?"

"I don't know, Clark, but this is too much. First, it's that damned drug—now you're involved in a murder? What am I supposed to think?"

"You're supposed to think it's bullshit. That's what. Do you actually believe it?"

"It's on TV. All my friends have seen it. Our phone's been ringing off the hook tonight, and I'm getting all kinds of texts. What am I supposed to tell them? How can I even show my face?"

"Since it's clearly bullshit, it won't stand up. It'll be easy to refute. Fucking sue the bastards while we're at it. I'll call Victor Grossman now."

"What's your lawyer going to do? Can he undo the embarrassment you've caused? Maybe he'll resolve this claim, but what about all this other notoriety? People died from that drug, and I feel like everyone's talking behind my back."

That was the last of the conversation. He had called his attorney, and by the time he went to bed, his wife was feigning sleep. When he woke up, she had already left the house. He found her note: "Early flight west. Staying with Sandy Dennison in Palm Springs."

The temperature was in the twenties again, with a few snowflakes kissing the windshield and melting. He turned on the radio and found it tuned to an oldies station. Searching around, he skipped past public radio during a pledge drive, then some bluegrass music, and stopped when he heard the name Lawrence Laboratories being criticized by a ranting talk show host. There was no getting away from it. CNN, MSNBC, FOX, the *Tribune*, the *Sun-Times*—everyone was sensationalizing the BioVexis deaths. And the worst of it was that if he had been paying attention, he would have stopped it before anyone died. Now the media had another angle to weigh in on and hype: the murders of Sam Baskin, Rodolfo Aguilar, and Kenneth Wright.

The news was only days old, and Clark Kirkland's name, already notorious for his connection to BioVexis, was being linked to the reporter's murder by an anonymous tipster. But Clark knew it wouldn't take his attorney long to debunk the allegation. Clark had been having dinner at Gene & Georgetti steakhouse in Chicago with a well-known judge and had the credit card receipt and the witnesses to prove it.

It was nearly nine o'clock when he arrived at the gated driveway to Lawrence Laboratories' Lincolnshire campus. He wondered how much longer he could withstand the pressure before passing through the gate for the last time.

❧

Matt Kirkland had needed a full day's rest after Dr. Whitehead removed the bullet from his abdomen and stitched up the opening. The following morning, the pain was tolerable enough that Matt could go to work altering the arrangements for his private flight to Florida.

The two-day delay caused him to miss the critical window his preparations called for in Miami. During visits to Aguilar's mansion, Matt had struck up a friendship with a gardener who shared a mutual fondness for coke. The day before killing Baskin, Matt had called the gardener under the pretext of arranging a drug buy and learned that Aguilar would be away from the mansion until the day after Baskin was to be assassinated.

When Aguilar wasn't in residence at the mansion, the remaining staff consisted of a security guard, a gardener, several maids, and a cook, all of whom would have been easy for Matt to deal with. After the private flight to a remote airport in southern Florida, Matt expected to enter the mansion and wait until Aguilar and his bodyguards arrived. It was to be a surprise party, and Matt would have been well prepared to take them all out as they walked in the door. But with the opportunity squandered because of the injury, he was forced to wait until Aguilar was vulnerable again. It wouldn't be long.

Three inches of snow had settled overnight, and the temperature had already plummeted to below zero. Cold and snow were nothing new to Sutherland. He had been born and raised in Chicago; briefly attended college in Ithaca, New York; and graduated from Northwestern University in Evanston, a Chicago suburb. During those years, whenever someone would complain about the cold, he would brusquely tell them to put another layer of clothes on and remember how loudly they'd bitched about the suffocating Chicago summers.

But with passing time and age, his dogged capacity to endure ice, snow, sleet, slush, wind, and arctic temperatures had gradually deteriorated. Sutherland now looked on the shorter days and longer nights of autumn with the dread of a man facing oral surgery the next morning. He felt that if he hadn't been anchored in the North by his business, he might be living among swaying palm trees at that very moment. He owned three office buildings and a residential apartment complex, so he had sufficient net worth and cash flow to retire if he really wanted to. Adding an exclamation point to Sutherland's aversion for the cold, two days after Baskin's death, he stepped from a taxi into a freezing ankle-deep puddle of slush.

In the coffee room of the Eighteenth District office on Larrabee Street, Detectives Arlo Demming and Willie Grant sat scowling at the coffee in their paper cups as if the bitter contents were responsible for their visitor's presence. They were waiting for out-of-town agent Donald Radoff to finish his phone call and rejoin them at the table. The Chicago detectives had no choice in the matter. Their lieutenant had told them that Sam Baskin had already been in negotiations with the FBI, as well as the state and federal prosecutors, and had promised to hand over the evidence he'd accumulated relating to several cases of federal interest. One was the Illinois gambling casinos, and other was the BioVexis deaths occurring in three states—making the case federal. The protocol was clear: the Chicago detectives were to cooperate.

"Pisses me off," Grant grumbled under his breath. He was a tall, thin black man with a shaved head, glasses, and a mustache and whose favorite sports jacket was a muddy-brown shade that rarely went with the blue or green tie he wore on alternate days.

"It's not as if we had everything locked up," Demming whispered back, making sure the agent didn't hear. "We thought we did until Clark Kirkland came up with the alibi. Now we got a bucket of nothing. Besides, how were we supposed to deal with the Aguilar family in Miami?"

"I've been thinking," Grant said, fingering his mustache.

"That's something new," Demming jibed as Radoff hung up and sat down at their table.

"Just got some interesting intel," Radoff said. "Puts another spin on things. We keep thinking it's all about gambling, which it partly is. Why else would the head of the casino empire's grandson be involved? What did you find out about his gun?"

"He flew into Chicago and didn't check any luggage. So it had to be supplied. Sutherland said Aguilar was totally surprised, tried to fire a bunch of times," Demming said.

"Dummy rounds," Radoff said. "Either the other shooter or whoever hired them sent Rodolfo Aguilar in there with a useless weapon with the expectation that he wouldn't leave alive."

"High noon with nothin' but your pecker in your hand," Grant said and chortled.

"We just learned a couple other things," Radoff said. "Clark Kirkland, the guy who was fingered by the anonymous tip, has a twin brother. His name is Matt Kirkland and looks a lot like him. He works around the casinos as a fixer, a Jack of dirty deeds." Radoff looked at the detectives, waiting for their reactions. "Well?"

"It fits," Grant said. "Is someone picking up this Matt Kirkland?"

"Too late," Radoff said. "No sign of him. We just put a watch on the airports and immigration."

"It explains how Clark Kirkland got fingered," Demming said. "So maybe this brother arranged for Aguilar to be holding a useless piece. Then you gotta ask, What kind of disappearing did Matt Kirkland do? Skip-the-country disappear or bottom-of-the-lake disappear?"

"Something more," Radoff continued. "Everyone knew Baskin was also writing about Lawrence Laboratories and that BioVexis mess, claiming he had new information. Does that sound like too much of a coincidence? Clark Kirkland is head of the division that made the drug."

"You're saying maybe the hit man was doing it for his brother? Not for the casino bosses? Damn," Grant said, his face screwed up as he considered the idea.

"Or the hit man had two clients," Demming said. "Someone in the casino organization, maybe the boss himself, and Clark Kirkland, protecting his ass for what happened with that fucking drug."

"And this Sutherland?" Radoff said. "He a wild card? He said it was a last-minute thing that he was there, but we don't know that. Sounds too pat. Let's see if there's any connections before we forget about him. He did kill a man, after all, and he might have a motive."

Agent Radoff was waiting in Sutherland's office reception area when Sutherland arrived the next morning. Shaking the man's hand, Sutherland had the feeling he was looking into the eyes of someone who wouldn't trust his own mother. His held his head at an angle, and he squinted, as if trying to bore through the lies and evasions of everyone he encountered. He was tall, close to Sutherland's height, with a sinewy physique and a sharp nose that added to the overall impression of a raptor assessing its prey. Judging by the agent's graying hair at his temples and the creases near his deep-set eyes, Sutherland guessed he was well over fifty and wondered whether that was unusually old for a field agent.

"This shouldn't take long," the agent said as he showed Sutherland his ID. "Just a couple questions."

"I told everything I know to the police."

"This is more complicated than that," Radoff said.

"I got a few minutes, so follow me," Sutherland said, leading the way past a conference room, several empty cubicles, an office where his accountant was peering into his computer screen, a coffee station, a copy room, and his secretary's desk, which guarded his corner office. When he waved to a few of his project team, Sutherland felt a twinge of guilt. He knew that he might have to let them go if Lawrence Laboratories canceled and he couldn't find a replacement anchor immediately, an unlikely possibility. Sutherland hung his topcoat behind the door and plopped into the leather chair behind his desk. Radoff sat opposite in one of the guest chairs and unbuttoned what looked like an expensive suit jacket.

"So … the complications," Sutherland said.

Radoff pulled a folder from his briefcase and opened it. "How well do you know Clark Kirkland?"

"Not at all. Why?"

"How about his brother? Matt?"

"He played football at Northwestern when I was in law school there. A linebacker, I think, but I never met him."

"Ah," the agent said before turning over a page in his lap. "OK. The night Sam Baskin was killed. Why were you in his room?"

"If you watch television, you'd know that Sam Baskin was shot a couple nights ago. I was with him. We were going to dinner but never made it. He called me after he was out of the hospital and arranged for us to meet in the hotel bar and afterward invited me up to his suite. He had information that he wanted to pass on that could affect my development business," Sutherland said, pointing to the office-building photos hanging on the wall. "It was about Lawrence Laboratories, the company that I was going to build a new headquarters for. You must have read about it in his columns and seen it on the news. The problem drug."

"Right. And now they're making suggestions that they won't go ahead with the deal because of the bad publicity and its effect on their profits, which is understandable. What information about Lawrence did he have for you?" Radoff asked.

"What difference does that make? His murder wasn't about Lawrence," Sutherland said. "Those two murderers were part of that casino business Sam was writing about. That guy I killed was part of the casinos family."

Radoff took a deep breath and turned a page in his folder. "Mr. Sutherland, we're talking about Lawrence because there are important connections here that need explaining. Like your Lawrence HQ office development, your timely presence at the murders, your girlfriend's position at the company, and the murderer's possible relationship to the Lawrence executive responsible for the problems. You'll tell me it is all coincidence, and maybe it is. But we have to be sure."

"Jesus fucking Christ," Sutherland moaned. "How do you guys come up with shit like this? What's your theory? That I'm part of a conspiracy to kill my friend Sam so his story won't hurt my development? And Kelly's in on it. And that executive too? Jesus, you read too many crime books."

"As I said, we have to be sure. Do you want to finish this here, or would you like an invitation to come to our offices?"

"I'd love to visit your offices, but I've got another conspiracy meeting to attend. So ask your fucking questions, and let's get it over with."

"This isn't a joking matter, Mr. Sutherland," Radoff said, consulting his notes. "So I'll ask again. What did Mr. Baskin have for you?"

"Sam told me that my development deal would never work out and I would be better off cutting my losses. The company's drug problem was only the beginning of the corruption and crimes he'd uncovered. That it would all come out despite the warnings he'd been given. He said he'd taken precautions."

Radoff cocked his head and paused. "Warnings?"

"He said some government men visited him and told him to back off."

"These men … did he give you any names?"

"No. But it wouldn't be like Sam not to ask for credentials. Could have been you. You tell me."

Radoff ignored the comment and made a note in his folder. "But he didn't back off, though, did he?"

"I only know he was told to give what he had to you guys or the state. According to them, there were bigger issues involved, but he didn't buy it. Thought it was bullshit. Then his editor told him the same thing, so someone got to her as well. Between that and being shot during an attempt on his life a few days ago, he decided to call it quits and write a memoir. Since he was handing over his findings, you guys should have protected him."

Radoff shrugged. "You said he told you he had taken precautions. That his story would get out despite the warnings. What did he mean?"

"I have no idea," Sutherland said.

"We believe Mr. Baskin had a couple sources, one inside Lawrence and another from somewhere else. Did Mr. Baskin mention who they were?"

"Just that he had them. I think he mentioned that in one of his articles."

Radoff sighed and shook his head. "Mr. Sutherland, it's hard to believe you spoke to Mr. Baskin in the bar and then in his suite and you didn't learn anything. What were you talking about all that time?"

"He was my father's best friend, and when my father died, Sam became a mentor and a good friend as well. What do friends talk about?"

"Lawrence Laboratories, you said. But no details? Did he mention el Centro?"

"I saw the comment about research centers in one of his articles," Sutherland said. "No details, just that he intended to write about it in his next column. He liked to end each article with a teaser. He never did write about it, though, because he was warned off and then killed."

"And you didn't talk about it that night?" Radoff asked. "Or maybe the initials CIGB?"

"No. What do they stand for?"

"No matter," Radoff said and flipped a page in his folder.

Sutherland shook his head. "I don't understand. Why isn't this about the casinos? Rodolfo Aguilar's presence there wasn't a coincidence. His family owns the casinos Sam was investigating and writing about. It strikes me that you're more worried about how much I know rather than acquiring information—making sure there are no loose ends. Because if he didn't tell me anything, you could be confident that his investigation died with him."

"That's a curious thing to say," Radoff said, glaring down his sharp nose. "Why would I do that?"

"You tell me. You want the story dead, don't you? Like the agent who visited Sam. Or was that you?"

"Now who's been reading too many conspiracy stories?" Radoff said. "We want to know if he uncovered a crime, and if so, what it was. That's our job."

"Don't you have his files? His computer? Or his backup?"

"The killer took his laptop, his backup servers were destroyed by arson, and the cloud data vanished. His source inside Lawrence was killed soon afterward. As far as we know, all the information Sam Baskin had is gone."

Sutherland was stunned, alarmed by the efforts taken to eliminate Sam's research. "All of it? Backup, arson, cloud? Surely that couldn't be accomplished by one wounded gunman. That would take a whole fucking team, don't you think? A coordinated attack by arsonists and technical geeks. Spooks. Now that's a conspiracy I could believe."

Agent Radoff shook his head and frowned sadly. Then he looked up, pursing his lips as if trying to recall something. "You've got quite a history, Mr. Sutherland. Quite a record."

"Innocently dragged into situations like this. A clean sheet," Sutherland said. "What's your point?"

"A trail of unexplained deaths and mishaps. Even in some place in Mexico. Skeletons in the closet, you might say. Am I right?"

"I'm still waiting for your point," Sutherland said.

"My advice is to put this behind you and forget those theories of yours. It occurs to me that with Mr. Baskin's death and his findings lost, things at Lawrence can go back to normal, and your real estate deal could be revived. If that fortunate turn of events should transpire, your presence in that hotel room could very well be construed as more than a coincidence. And it wouldn't be a matter of an unexplained death this time. You did kill that man."

After Radoff left, Sutherland sat and gazed out of his window at the low-hanging ceiling of gray clouds. It seemed obvious to him that the agent had come to satisfy himself and his superiors that the trail was dead. But he wondered whether it occurred to anyone in government that Baskin could have given his material to someone else or had more research waiting in Florida. The possibility prompted Sutherland to move up his plan to travel to Florida and find out for himself. All he needed was Baskin's daughters' permission to access his boat and condo.

On an impulse to tell Kelly about his latest visitor, he fished for the phone in his overcoat, and just like the other time, it didn't accept his pass code. Then it occurred to him that this could be Baskin's phone. He could have mistakenly picked it up and pocketed it during the confusion after shooting Rodolfo. If it was Baskin's, Sutherland had the password, because on one of their trips together, he needed to use Baskin's phone and was told it was year of his marriage: 1972. Sutherland entered the numbers and was in.

Sutherland scrolled down the names in the list, mostly people and companies he had never heard of. Then he checked recent messages, and sure enough, one was from Sutherland himself, when he'd called to say he was a few minutes late. Intrigued by the possibilities, he opened email and found that there were a dozen or so unread messages and several labeled folders, "Aguilar" and "Lawrence" among them.

Scanning through Baskin's most recent emails, Sutherland stopped when he saw an incoming one from an unusual domain name. The message said, "There's a photograph on page 26 of the book I sent you that strengthens my suspicions. It makes our story even more intriguing. I will let you know how we can continue."

Sutherland remembered that Baskin had mentioned how a photograph was supposed to add a sensational dimension to his story. But what photograph, and what book? He had to hope he'd find it in Florida.

CHAPTER 8

A t the end of the day, after everyone else had left the office, Sutherland called Marty Stevens, his real estate attorney, who'd negotiated the lease with Lawrence Laboratories' outside lawyers.

"Have you heard anything from your counterparts about our deal?" Sutherland asked.

"No word, no nothing," Stevens replied. "Not a surprise, with all that publicity they're getting. They've circled the wagons and battened down the hatches." Stevens was a great attorney, but he never knew a metaphor he couldn't mix.

"It's a good thing we spent so much time on milestones and indemnification. A lesson I learned in the Broadwell deal a few years ago. They agreed to indemnify us, but if they go bankrupt, which is a possibility, we'll see nothing."

"Let's not give up hope yet," Stevens said. "I'll let you know if I hear anything."

After hanging up, Sutherland shuffled through his mail, putting aside the usual invoices, invitations, résumés, and proposals for later scrutiny. With his project essentially on hold, where was the urgency? he asked himself. Besides, crucial as Lawrence's tenancy was for his company, it didn't have the same life-and-death gravitas as the other events of the last week. He loaded a briefcase with the rest of his mail, locked the office, and drove home.

A half hour later, Sutherland poured himself a scotch and slumped into the Eames chair facing the floor-to-ceiling windows. He watched the traffic on Lake Shore Drive, ribbons of flickering red and yellow trailing southward toward the Loop or north past his Lincoln Park neighborhood. Turning away from the window, he contemplated the ambience of his living room in the glow from the recessed ceiling lights. When he'd expanded and remodeled a year earlier, he followed his designer's advice. "Keep it simple, and select only the pieces that give you joy," she'd said. "Don't think you have to fill all this magnificent open space with stuff."

In a rectangular island in the center of the sprawling marbled floor sat a clean-lined leather couch, an outsize coffee table, two floor lamps with massive shades, and two pairs of upholstered armchairs on a hundred-year-old Tabriz carpet. The Eames chair and ottoman sat apart on another rug near the corner. Large abstract oils on either side of his flat-screen TV provided color, and the view of lake and city from three sides was spectacular. When Kelly first walked in and regarded the finished product, she couldn't help herself. "I see you went for the Mies van der Rohe look again. Very cozy," she'd said with a wry grin.

In the three months since Kelly's arrival at Lawrence as its corporate counsel, she hadn't seen much of Doc Castillo. He didn't spend time in the headquarters building. In fact, from what she could tell, he rarely visited any of the research centers, development labs, or production lines. Where he spent his time was a mystery to her, and whenever she asked Cheryl, Castillo's personal assistant, she said he was working at home, traveling, or in meetings out of the office. His whereabouts didn't seem to affect his ability to come up with product ideas, because history showed he frequently sent suggestions to the scientists, often with great medical and commercial results.

For the first time in a week, she saw Castillo's white Bentley in his designated spot as she drove into the executive parking garage. Taking the rare opportunity to see him, Kelly waited by Castillo's door until he ended a phone call. When she stepped into the office, he looked up and said, "Ah, Kelly. How are we doing? Keeping the lawyers at bay?"

"I wish I could say we had it under control. I've had to hire an outside law firm to help."

"Whatever it takes," he said. "We want this matter resolved and forgotten. Which reminds me … have Clark's separation documents been prepared?"

"You still think firing Clark is a good idea?" she asked. "He's innocent of all this."

"Maybe so, but it's Steve Underhill's call. You should know that he represents Morrow Partners, the venture capital firm that funded Lawrence. He thinks it will show the world we're taking responsibility."

"And we need a scapegoat. Are we blaming the attempted bribe on him too?"

"It might even have been Clark," Castillo said, shrugging with affected innocence. "Can't be proven one way or other. Besides, he'll be gone and with him our media problems. Our sales will rebound, and we can reconsider expansion and our IPO."

"We have to get past the lawsuits first," she said. "We're facing court orders for discovery, and we know there are damaging emails."

"That won't be a problem," he said nonchalantly. "I'm told there was a malfunction with the servers and some files were lost. So we won't face any criminal action. The civil suits will still cost us, but the worst will be over, and this all will come to nothing. Nada."

For a moment, Kelly was speechless, feeling like she was falling into a chasm. *Castillo must have ordered the destruction of the emails.*

Castillo turned his back on Kelly and began tapping into his computer, a clear message that the meeting was over. Five people dead and several dozen deathly sick from a faulty medication, an award-winning journalist and a whistleblower murdered, and Castillo had calmly declared it over. *That is one fucked-up nada.*

Kelly was fuming when she walked out of Castillo's office. He seemingly had ordered for the damaging emails to be destroyed, and she had to find out whether it had been done. What good was her position as the house lawyer if her best legal advice went unheeded? She tore down the stairs and entered the head of the company's technical-services department.

Instead of the manager, Jerry Arnold, a young man barely out of college sat at his desk.

"Where's Jerry?" Kelly said.

"He's been out," the young man said, recoiling from her intensity. "I'm Fadi Aziz, filling in for him." He looked as if he was of Indian or Pakistani descent, but his American English indicated he'd been schooled in the States.

Kelly was impressed. The technical-services department consisted of a dozen high-caliber technicians, so she figured Aziz must have been a real whiz to be filling in for Jerry as the manager.

"Do you know who I am?" Kelly asked, taking a chair in front of the desk.

"You're the new lawyer, right? Miss Matthews, the corporate counsel."

"That's correct. How long have you been sitting in for your boss?"

"A week now."

"He's sick? Is it serious?" she asked.

"No, I ah"—he hesitated—"I don't think he's sick. He may not be coming back."

"Really? Why's that, Fadi?" she asked. "That is your name, right, Fadi?"

"Fadi Aziz," he said. "He just walked out, and Dr. Ridgeway told me to take over."

Ridgeway's involvement wasn't a good sign, Kelly thought. He already was neck-deep in covering up the problems with BioVexis. She pulled out her smartphone, pressed a few buttons, and set it in front of Aziz. "I'm going to ask you some questions, Fadi. And I expect you to be truthful. OK?"

"Why wouldn't I be?" he asked defensively.

"Let's find out," she said. "I'd like to record this conversation. Do you mind?"

"What do I care?" Fadi said. "Record away, Miss Matthews. And while we're at it, why are you being so patronizing? I'm twenty-three, with a master's degree in computer science, and you're talking to me like I'm a delinquent kid."

It took Kelly a moment to absorb his remark. She had jumped to an erroneous assumption based on his youthful appearance. She swallowed hard. "I'm sorry. You're right. I'm a bit overwrought these days, so let's start over. And call me Kelly, please. OK?"

"Apology accepted," Fadi said indifferently. "Now how can I help you?"

"Are you aware that some emails have gone missing?"

"Let's say that has something to do with Jerry's sudden departure."

"How so?"

"He and Dr. Ridgeway had an argument. Shouting. Loud," he said. "Then Jerry stormed out without saying anything to me."

"Then Dr. Ridgeway told you to take over. What then?"

"He told me to delete a whole stream of emails, for a start," he said. "Probably the same sort of thing that Jerry refused to do and the reason why he left."

"That's what I figured. Let me guess. Dr. Ridgeway said it would be OK. They were mistakes or something like that, right?"

"A ten-year-old could've seen through that pretext," he said.

"So the question is … did you do it? Are they gone?"

"Yes and no," he said and grinned slyly. "To the technically challenged, they're gone—*poof.* But …"

"Aha! Then, to me, technically challenged as I am, they would appear to be gone?"

"Correct."

"But they're not gone."

"Correct again. I read a number of them first, and I didn't want to be accused of destroying evidence if it came to that. A push of a button, and voilà"—he snapped his fingers—"they could be back where they were."

"Very clever. You may get some more requests like that in the future. Even if it's Doc Castillo himself the next time, agree, call me, and do the same thing you did before."

"Up to a few weeks ago, I thought I was working for a great company. Now I've got grave doubts. I may be following Jerry out the door."

"Before you go, can I trust you to do something else for me?"

"For the right reason, sure," Fadi said.

"Believe me—it is. There was a funds transfer that went to an FDA inspector a number of weeks ago. I want to know who authorized it and what bank account it came from. I also want to know if any other funds were transferred from that account and where they were sent." Kelly paused, thinking of a way to end the conversation on a higher note. "I've got a feeling you're pretty good at hacking. Am I right?"

"We don't call it hacking," he said. "In cases like this, we consider ourselves truth seekers."

"Good. Our secret, OK?" she said with a knowing wink.

"I don't believe it," Sutherland said to Kelly over the phone. He had just walked into his apartment, and she was calling from hers. "Doc said that? No investigation?"

"I can't understand it," she said, "but that's what he said before cutting me off."

"What happened to the allegations of a cover-up? The bribery? FDA claims?"

"No details, just that it will die down to nothing. We'll settle any class-action suits, and that'll be all. If it's true, it should be a load off my mind, but I've got a bad feeling about it. It's like I'm entering the dark side."

"You? Just today, a federal agent pumped me about it. Like he was testing to see if I knew something. I think the government is a party in all this."

"As corporate counsel, I'd have to know about special agreements with the government."

"You're new. Arrangements may have been terminated before you arrived. If there was a secret program with Uncle Sam and it blew up, you think the powers that be want it publicized?"

"What am I supposed to do?" she asked. "Doc won't tell me anything. He's being very evasive."

"How much have you read since I gave you the flash drive?"

"Give me a break," she grumbled. "I've already got too much on my plate. The ship is sinking, and I'm the only one bailing."

"I know, but I've been slogging through it. My Spanish isn't as good as yours, so I've been reading through Jim Ridgeway's texts, the ones translated and sent by Doc. They're in English, and I'm starting to get paranoid reading them. I could tell you, but you'd better see for yourself."

"Give me a hint."

"Two words: *viral mutations.*"

Sam Baskin's memorial service was held in The Cliff Dwellers Club on South Michigan Avenue in downtown Chicago. Although both of Baskin's parents were Jewish, he had never been particularly religious and, with age and experience, had given up believing in any possibility of a divine presence. The only times he set foot in a synagogue were for weddings, funeral services, and the bar and bat mitzvahs of his children and grandchildren. The Cliff Dwellers was on the top floor overlooking Millennium and Grant Parks, Monroe Harbor, and Lake Michigan. The view was spectacular from the roof deck, but the twenty-degree temperature and a cutting north wind kept the attendees inside.

Sutherland and Kelly were among the hundred or so friends and family who had come to remember and honor Baskin. The program consisted of a slideshow presenting Baskin's life, beginning with his baby portraits and covering the majority of the noteworthy events and milestones, a skillful balance of humor and respect. The slideshow was followed by memorial speeches by his daughters, Nancy and Sharon; two of their children; and many friends and work colleagues. As close as he had been to Baskin over the years, Sutherland was disappointed that he hadn't been asked to add his sentiments.

After the service, Sutherland and Kelly were waiting for an opportunity to pay their respects to the family when Sutherland saw Castillo across the room. He was heading for the coat check, and when Sutherland waved, Castillo waved back and kept walking.

"Wait a minute," Sutherland said to Kelly. "I want to catch Doc Castillo for a sec. Get yourself a glass of wine, and I'll meet you at the window."

Castillo was slipping into his cashmere topcoat when Sutherland approached him, catching him at the elevator. "Hey, Doc," Sutherland called as he approached. "What's the hurry? You can't even say hello?"

"Sorry. I just hate these things," Castillo replied, adjusting his scarf.

"They serve a double purpose, Doc. People need to be reminded of what an exceptional man he was, as well as grieve. Sam was a good friend to both of us. We were lucky to know him."

"True. It was terrible. And you were there when it happened. Witnessed it. How are you holding up?"

"Can't get it out of my mind."

"Kelly must be worried about you, and so am I. All of this. Even the HQ plans. You know I'm against canceling our deal. It's in the board's hands, and I don't control it."

"I understand. Investigations and lawsuits, sales and profits off—head for the bunkers, right?"

"Very shortsighted, I agree," Castillo said. "It will all pass, but in the meantime …"

"That's what Kelly told me. No investigation, just settling the lawsuits. She's relieved," he said, not mentioning her growing qualms. "All this mess because of a research center's screwup."

Castillo stiffened with the comment. He stopped putting on his gloves and knitted his brow. "What do you know about that?" he asked warily.

"What Sam wrote in his column. Said it should be investigated."

Castillo shook his head and scowled. "Sam and his crazy ideas. I told him he was wasting his time. There's nothing to it. And now that he's died, his suspicions will die with him." He turned and poked the elevator button again, as if it were the period in Baskin's final article.

"If you say so," Sutherland said.

Castillo's head spun back, and he glared at Sutherland. "What's that supposed to mean?"

"Jeez, Doc, why so defensive?"

"I just don't appreciate being badgered about nonsense. We've seen enough trouble because of Sam's runaway imagination." The elevator door opened, and Castillo stepped in. "Déjalo morir," he said as the door closed.

Sutherland returned to the crowded room thinking about Castillo's last words. "Let it die." Or he could have meant "Let him die." Either way, it was clear the head of Lawrence Laboratories became very prickly when their research centers were mentioned. There was something there, no doubt about it.

Sutherland wended his way through the crush of Baskin's friends and relatives and found Kelly standing by the window, looking out over the park. A moment later, Baskin's daughter Nancy approached them with a stressed smile on her face. She was an attractive dark-haired woman in her late thirties. She hugged Sutherland, then Kelly, saying, "Thanks for coming, you two. Dad would have appreciated it. He thought a lot of both of you." She turned to Sutherland with a concerned look. "I heard about how it happened, Doug. You were nearly killed too. Is that from that night?" She reached and almost touched the bandage on his temple.

"Afraid so," he said. "But I was luckier than your father. I'm awfully sorry. He was a good man and friend. More like a father. He helped me more than you can imagine."

"Please accept my condolences," Kelly said. "I had a lot of respect for him."

"He was days away from retiring, and then some animal killed him. And for what?" Nancy said, wiping away a tear with a tissue. Then she put on a strained smile and said to Kelly, "Did you know that Dad tried to get Doug and me together ages ago?"

"Not very successfully," Sutherland added. "You had a crush on Dennis Kiefer, as I remember."

"That didn't work out so well," she said, shaking her head. "He turned out to be a louse." Then she turned serious again, her lips thinned and tight. "Doug, I have a favor to ask."

"Of course," he replied. "What?"

"Promise that you won't let them get away with this. Promise that you'll get the bastards. Kill them, whatever."

"The FBI, the police. They're on it, Nancy," he said, though he didn't believe a word.

"The same FBI that put Dad up in that hotel without protection?" Nancy said. "The same FBI that warned Dad off of the stories he was investigating? That FBI, Doug? Be serious."

"I want the bastards punished as much as you. I just don't know—"

"Don't be modest, Doug," Nancy said firmly. "A while ago, you brought down a future governor and an ex–police commissioner." It was true. Digging into his father's decade-old disappearance, Sutherland had uncovered video and audio recordings that implicated a cabal of corrupt officials and businessmen in a series of murders. In the process, he had nearly been killed and was framed for murder himself, an experience he didn't ever want to relive.

"I was only trying to understand how and why my father died. The rest just happened."

"And that's what I'm asking, Doug," Nancy said. "Find out how, why, and who. And then get them—make them pay. Promise me, Doug."

What could he say? Nancy was distraught and grief-stricken. She imagined him as a superdetective and an avenging angel, but here and now wasn't the time to disabuse her of that notion. As much as he wanted to avenge Baskin's death, it was unrealistic to think it was going to be easy or quick. "You know I'll do what I can," he said finally. "But you can do something in that effort yourself. Don't cancel your father's email or phone accounts. He's still getting messages that I want to follow up on. It might help us find who did this."

"Really? You'll do that? Thank you," Nancy said, sniffing and dabbing her eye again. Then she looked around as if to assure that she wouldn't be overheard. "One more thing, Doug. Word of warning. Avoid my sister today."

"What's wrong?"

"She's got a bee in her bonnet. Dad was murdered, and you were there. She thinks you could have done something."

"She blames me? That's unfair," he said.

"I know, but you know Sharon," Nancy said, rolling her eyes.

He did know Sharon. Baskin had tried matchmaking a second time, with the same results. But that time, Sharon, a stunning blonde, had turned out to be a conceited bitch. Sutherland couldn't run away fast enough.

"Did she hear how everything happened?" Sutherland asked. "The police tell her?"

"She hears what she wants to hear. Just stay away from her if you want to have another kid someday."

Paolo Aguilar hadn't arrived at his powerful station by acting rashly or out of unchecked rage, yet he neither turned the other cheek nor let any offense go unpunished. Each act of retribution in his turbulent life had been meticulously planned and, once executed, intensely enjoyed. So when he lounged in his mansion in Palm Beach, Florida, he focused on how to exact his due from the people involved in his grandson's murder.

Finding Matt Kirkland, *el hijo de la chingada* who'd supplied Rodolfo with a worthless firearm, might take some time. Matt had disappeared without a trace. But Aguilar had gambling contacts all over the world, and Matt was an addicted gambler. Sooner or later, his vice would expose him.

On the other hand, Doug Sutherland and Clark Kirkland were in plain sight. Each of them was responsible for Rodolfo's death in his own way. Sutherland had shot Rodolfo, and Clark must have encouraged Matt. He certainly benefited from Baskin's death and the disappearance of evidence. Patience wouldn't be necessary for either of them because they were still in Chicago. Aguilar just had to make certain that nothing linked him to their deaths.

Aguilar's daughter Renata was gathering information about both of the prospective targets with the help of his Chicago casino's security boss and a few of his *amigos oscuros*, as he sometimes referred to them. Thinking Renata had already taken too much time, he called out to Margarita, who was sweeping the floor outside his den. "Bruja, find Renata, and tell her to come in here."

"Sí, Tío," she said and shuffled away.

Several minutes later, when Renata entered, Aguilar said, "Well? What have you put together? Are we ready?"

"Almost," she replied. "I just need to confirm one detail with you. I think we should use Manny Vecino. What do you think?"

"Manny? No. He'd use a scope. I told you—I want this close up, and I want it recorded. Like I was there. What about the one in St. Louis?"

"Max?" she said. "He won't like it, but he can do close."

"Good. Is that it? We're on?"

"I'll make the arrangements," she said.

"One more thing," Aguilar said. "Rodolfo's birthday is in a few days. Thirty years old."

"What, you want a cake?" she cracked.

"No. I want that cocksucker who killed him dead that day."

CHAPTER 9

Max Patrón shifted position in his Ford Explorer and changed the radio to another country station. He was on the Edens Expressway on his return trip to Chicago after reconnoitering Clark Kirkland's house and neighborhood in the suburbs. He'd been on the highway for a half hour, his wipers sweeping away the driving snow and salty slush thrown up by the tractor trailers overtaking him. At the speed he was making, it would take another thirty minutes to arrive at his hotel in Chicago's Loop.

He had left his apartment in St. Louis at four o'clock the day before, leaving immediately after receiving the order from Renata Aguilar. It was a direct call using encrypted phones and circumventing the layers of management within the liquor warehouse where he worked as a part-time forklift driver. The manager and the others didn't need to know, and they would never find out, what he was doing. It hadn't surprised him that there would be reprisals for the death of Paolo Aguilar's grandson. He had heard about the fuckup in the Chicago hotel where the reporter and Rodolfo were murdered. It was just a matter of when—and who was chosen to exact justice.

Once in Chicago and situated in a hotel room under an assumed name, he had spent a day studying the material he'd been sent and then did some of his own reconnaissance. Through Renata, he had all the addresses, business clubs, car makes and licenses, phone numbers, personal photos, and floor plans of each of the pertinent domiciles and office buildings. Ordinarily, it would have been an easy assignment: find an advantageous location and window of opportunity, position the target in the scope's crosshairs, and pull the trigger. Even at a hundred yards, he'd never missed. This time, his orders made it complicated. No long distance between him and the marks, and no concealment when he pulled the trigger. His instructions were to video the scenes with audio as he informed each victim face-to-face on why he was going to die. And one hit had to be done on a specific day, or Max might become a victim himself. It was to be a postmortem birthday present, he'd been told.

⌘

After reading the summary of Clark's everyday movements and scouting the man's house, neighborhood, and office, Max had developed his plan. He'd quickly conceded that he couldn't gain access to Lawrence Laboratories' headquarters building because of the security the company employed and the number of company personnel he'd likely encounter. Intercepting him during his daily commute wouldn't work because he was being escorted to his home by a guard in a following car, a measure that had been begun after several threats over BioVexis. The guard would watch as Clark entered and closed the garage door and then leave until the following morning. That was the period where Max could be alone with his mark to video the hit. To succeed, he only needed to obtain the codes to the entrance to Clark's gated community and his home's security systems. Twenty-four hours after explaining the obstacles to Renata, he was given the codes. It seemed that Aguilar's tentacles reached into personnel in the alarm-monitoring business. And as another omen for success, Clark's wife had left town, leaving him alone in the house.

Max's other assignment was more frustrating because the target's movements were less predictable. Some days the mark drove, other times he took a taxi, and Max couldn't be sure what the destination might be. He'd go from his own building to the city hall, to an architect's or client's company, then to lunch at one of various restaurants. There were always a few employees in his office, the parking garage had valets on standby, and the restaurants were usually crowded at mealtime. Max's instructions necessitated a private face-to-face encounter in order to record the entire scene without interference. The only time he could be certain of the man's whereabouts and isolation was when he returned home for the evening. If it was going to be the apartment, he needed a trial run to see how he could get past the doorman and through the locked entrance doorway to the elevators.

Disguised with a mustache, glasses, and a knit cap covering his wiry hair, he approached the doorman at the front desk in the apartment building's lobby. He carried a pizza box.

"Can I help you?" the doorman asked.

"Delivery for Mrs. Delaney," Max said, using the name of the woman on the same floor as the mark's apartment. He knew that, once through the security door to the elevators and on the right floor, he could pick his target's lock and wait for him to come home. Max looked at the bill attached to the pizza box and read, "She's in 2005. Can I go up?"

"I have to call first," the doorman said, picking up his phone and running his finger down a list of residents. While the doorman waited, Max nonchalantly surveyed the lobby, mentally noting where the cameras were. After enough time for ten rings, the doorman hung up. "No answer. Sorry."

"Can I leave it at the door? It's been paid for."

"Sorry. Can't let you go without the owner's authorization."

"Then what am I supposed to do with this?" Max asked. "They'll fire me if I don't deliver it."

"Leave it here if you want. I'll give it to her when she comes in."

"Never mind—I'll take it back," Max said. "I'm supposed to get her signature."

Outside on the sidewalk, Max dropped the empty pizza box in the trash barrel by the curb and swore to himself. If a bogus delivery wasn't going to get him past the doorman, there was only one other way.

In her office at Lawrence Laboratories' Lake County headquarters, Kelly opened her laptop and was surprised when a video sprang to life. An animated image of a dozen reptilian creatures out of a sci-fi movie were circling a cowering princess dressed in a white toga. The attackers' yellow eyes were menacing slits, their mouths sharp-toothed snarls, their claws as sharp as scalpels. The young maiden's destiny seemed certain. As the predators tightened their circle, another figure appeared on the screen: a Jedi knight astride a horned biped that Kelly recognized from a *Star Wars* movie. The knight drew his light sword and spurred his lumbering steed forward into the swarm of waiting teeth and claws. He slashed through the attackers, each arc of his laser reducing another monster into an exploding green bloom. When the last attacker was vaporized, the Jedi brandished his light sword in triumph and raised his plasma force shield on high. Across the surface of his shield, the letters *PREVENIR* radiated in neon blue light. Then the screen faded to black, and after a few seconds, the vignette began again.

Kelly smiled for the first time in days. It was a corny animation, but it showed that the nerds from Lawrence's IT department hadn't lost their creativity in light of the BioVexis problems. She made a mental note to ask Fadi Aziz, her new collaborator, whether he had dreamed it up. This video was apparently an internal ad for a new vaccine, an experimental product meant to eliminate cancer from the planet. But Prevenir, the code name for the vaccine, hadn't lived up to its initial promise, and research on it had been discontinued. Evidently the techies hadn't heard.

Kelly had spent ten years in Chicago's legal department before accepting her position at Lawrence. But recognizing that she wasn't a scientist, she was determined to educate herself on the technical jargon and how to read the lab and clinical data. But many of the products in development were so confidential and siloed that only the science and medical teams working on them were privy to the information. Prevenir had been one such product, and Kelly only had access to Ridgeway's summaries covering its progress and ultimate lack of success. Ridgeway wrote that the research had been performed in Lawrence's clinics designated Alpha, Beta, and Gamma, which were part of el Centro, the entity Kelly assumed was part of Lawrence's research organization. But why the coded designation? And why were their clinics so confidential that Kelly couldn't know what state or country they were in?

Sitting in his office, Clark Kirkland received a phone call from Lawrence's reception desk informing him that an FBI agent named Jarret Sable was in the lobby with a request to meet him. Immediately after Clark told security to escort the agent to his office, he dialed his attorney, Victor Grossman, and put him on speakerphone.

"I had a feeling this might happen when you were falsely identified. You'll have to tell him I'm on the line," Grossman said. "We can't be accused of ambushing him."

A uniformed guard guided Agent Jarret Sable into Clark's office and disappeared as soon as Clark rose from his desk.

"I appreciate you seeing me without an appointment, Mr. Kirkland," Sable said as he shook Clark's hand. "But we're under time pressures, and you may be able to help. My name is Jarret Sable."

"Have a seat. But before you tell me the purpose of your visit, I should tell you that my attorney, Victor Grossman, is on speakerphone and will be participating in our conversation. Victor?"

"I'm here," Grossman said. "Agent Sable, if your visit is about Sam Baskin's murder, my client has already spoken to the Chicago police and has provided an airtight alibi."

"I'm aware of that," Sable said. "I'm here because we suspect Mr. Kirkland's brother, Matthew, could be the killer."

"Matt? Why is that?" Clark asked defensively.

"First, I understand he's your twin. He resembles you, and several people mistakenly thought they saw you there. Second, he works or worked for the family that owns the casinos Sam Baskin wrote about. In fact, he was with a member of that family, Rodolfo Aguilar, who was also killed the night of the murder. Finally, people familiar with him describe him as a fixer, a term that might encompass murder."

"My brother has faults and has had his troubles, but …" Clark began before he was stopped by a flicker of a childhood memory. "So what do I have to do with this allegation?"

"We thought you might know where he is," Sable said. "We can't locate him."

"I haven't seen or spoken to him in years, so I have no idea," Clark said. "None."

"Why is that, Mr. Kirkland? The estrangement, I mean?" Sable asked.

"You probably know. He has a gambling problem and was suspected of embezzling funds from his clients. I'm not sure how, but he avoided prison. Then he was employed by casino people and mixed up with the worst kind of lowlife. I couldn't bear to watch him ruin his life."

"So no phone calls, no emails, nothing?"

"Nothing," Clark said.

Grossman's voice cut into the exchange. "If you want to check the phone records or emails, my client will be happy to cooperate when you produce a warrant, Agent Sable."

"That's not necessary, Victor," Clark said. "They won't find anything—believe me."

"Don't forget what Hugh Trent did, Clark," Grossman said. "He sent emails in your name."

"I know," Clark said. "Why would Hugh be communicating with Matt, in my name or otherwise? Let's get this over with, Victor. I think it's a waste of time."

"I know your attorney disagrees with you," Sable said, "but it might clear up one more point …"

"What point's that?" Clark said.

"It would eliminate any speculation that *if*—and for your benefit, I say *if*—your brother is guilty of this, he did it for you. After all, Sam Baskin wrote that he possessed incriminating material on your company and, by extension, you."

"Unless my client colluded with him, it's immaterial, Agent Sable," Grossman said. "If his brother took it upon himself to do it, my client is innocent."

"That's my point," Sable said. "Lack of telephone and emails would help clear it up."

"Let's just do it," Clark demanded. "I'm sick of it all. There's no emails or phone calls to my brother—period. This is nonsense."

"Then where is he, Mr. Kirkland?" Sable asked. "He's disappeared. Why?"

"I don't know," Clark sighed. "Are we through?"

"One more thing," Sable said. "Would you accompany us to his apartment later? We plan to gather DNA and prints, and there may be something there that will give you a clue to where he went."

"It's a waste of time, but fine. Just tell me when."

Clark lumbered into Kelly's office shaking his head. "You won't believe what just happened," he said. "An FBI agent stopped by my office just now. They believe my brother killed Sam Baskin."

"They tell you why?"

"Mainly because the killer looked like me."

"Doug thought so after he saw you on the news," she said.

"The agent implied he might have done it for me to stop Baskin from publishing dirt on us."

"You don't even talk to your brother, do you?"

"Not since he swindled the hedge fund," Clark said with a frown. "The DNA will prove it one way or the other. But here's the scary thing: they question whether I was a part of it. You believe it?"

"Not that you had anything to do with it," Kelly said. "But someone in Lawrence might have. I just learned about a wire transfer for two hundred thousand dollars to a Cayman Islands bank." Fadi Aziz had found the transfer details and informed her earlier that day. "It was from a secret company fund. We're still looking into who the sender was, but I have my suspicions."

"I don't get it," Clark said. "What's that have to do with this?"

"That secret transfer took place the day before Sam Baskin was killed."

Clark let out long sigh. "Some coincidence. Baskin writes he has dirt on us; someone inside has him bumped off."

"Pure speculation, but plausible," she said. "But no one's going to believe you had anything to do with the murder if I can help it."

"You think Trent knows about the wire transfer? He so much as admitted he was responsible for wiring the bribe money to the FDA inspector when he said no one could trace it."

"As much as it troubles me, I think so," she said. "He'd deny it, of course. An attempted FDA bribe is not as serious as a payoff for a murder, if that's what it was. I've got someone taking a deeper look into it. A techy that I can trust."

Kelly thought for a moment before reaching in her drawer for an old draft of the company's annual report that had been prepared for the IPO. "Speaking of the FDA bribe and inspectors, I have a question you can help me with." She turned to a dog-eared page of the report. "This states that BioVexis was first tested overseas, then domestically, before being approved by the FDA. Where was it developed?"

"Good question," Clark said, shrugging. "Never dealt with those things. By the time BioVexis or any product came to my group for marketing, it was all packaged and ready to go."

"Aren't FDA arrangements usually made through us in the headquarters labs? Here?" she asked.

"That's what I thought. This time, the FDA approval was handled from somewhere else for some reason. I didn't hear a thing about it until it was approved."

"Strange," Kelly said. "Where was the original development done? Puerto Rico?"

"Beyond me," Clark said. "I just marketed the stuff. Could have been China, far as I was concerned."

That evening, Agent Sable drove Clark Kirkland to his brother Matt's apartment to join the evidence team looking for clues to Matt's whereabouts. After an hour of searching, it was clear that there was nothing there that could help them track Matt down.

"I still don't believe he did it," Clark said with more conviction than he felt. He couldn't dismiss a nagging mental image.

"We'll know soon enough. Blood from the murder scene will match the DNA we got from you and his hairbrush. You see anything that would help us find him?"

"That's just it ... nothing," Clark said, taking in the spartan living room. "No memorabilia, photos, files. It's like he didn't live here."

"He lived here all right. Neighbors saw him come and go with different women all the time. We got some good prints," Sable said. "We'll see if any turn up on the system. Maybe one of the women can tell us something."

"He was divorced years ago. Maybe his wife could help you."

"Already talked to her. She gave us an earful," Sable said and chortled. "Said the cocksucker fucked every hooker in the casinos and she was hoping he'd die of syphilis—her words."

"She always had a mouth," Clark said. "And he always had an insatiable appetite."

"A fixer working for the casinos—probably comes with the territory," Sable said. "Anyway, we're packed up and leaving. Can we give you a ride back to your office?"

"I'll stick around and see if we missed anything. I'll leave my car in the company garage and take a cab home from here."

After the agents left, Clark sat at Matt's desk and thought. All the drawers and closets had been searched, and many had been left open with little or nothing inside. Clark was mystified. His brother had always lived large and surrounded himself with the best of everything. He also had an enormous ego and used to openly display all his trophies, awards, and prizes. So where did he keep all that old junk? Clark couldn't explain it, so he put on his coat and called a taxi to take him home.

Fifteen minutes later, in the taxi, he remembered that Matt had rented a storage garage years earlier, before their falling-out. Clark had accompanied Matt the day it was rented and hadn't been there since. Curious, he ordered the cab driver to drop him off at the storage facility and was amazed to find that the original combination, their birth date, still worked after all the years. The temperature inside the unit, more like a single-car garage, felt colder than outside. Clark turned on the hanging fluorescent light fixture and made a quick assessment of the space's contents. Matt's BMW motorcycle was leaning against the left wall, next to an old armoire containing a collection of shirts, jackets, and shoes. A long workbench lined the right side of the space. Seeing an electric heater beside the bench, Clark switched it on high and began examining the top of the workbench.

He was initially alarmed to find several tiny video cameras and what he assumed were dime-sized microphones. But then he conceded that security equipment could be part of legitimate work for someone employed by a casino operator. But what Clark noticed next gave him a real shock. Iron pipes, coils of wire, mercury switches, and digital timers were neatly lined up, seemingly in preparation for assembly. And Clark couldn't explain why a legitimate gun owner would need the silencer attached to the semiautomatic pistol. Clark had suspected that Matt was involved in questionable activities since his fall, but not this. It added a new dimension to the FBI agent's use of "fixer," and it made Clark question his fading hope that Matt wasn't the assassin. He would notify the agent about his findings first thing the next morning, but now he was too troubled.

Clark spotted an opened bottle of bourbon on the shelf. He grabbed it, removed the top, and slugged down a mouthful to calm himself. Reflecting on what he'd discovered made him wonder what else he didn't know about his brother. He shivered as he looked around the cold garage and fixed his gaze on a metal-framed shelf containing several large cardboard boxes. Angry and saddened at his own naivete and curious about what other secrets Matt would be hiding, he pulled down and opened the first box. It was filled with file folders, and he began to sort through them. He found high school and college yearbooks, diplomas, newspaper clippings about football exploits, SEC certificates, accommodation letters, and several awards. Surprisingly, Matt had also held on to several articles about the investigations into the fraudulent misuse of client funds and his ignominious departure from the hedge fund.

But as Clark sorted through the second box, he recognized a disturbing trend. It seemed that for years Matt had been collecting clippings concerning a wide variety of crimes. There were newspaper accounts of arson, murder, disappearances, and bombings that had taken place in cities across the Midwest. Few of the articles mentioned suspects or arrests, and Clark inferred that the authorities had been baffled. He also surmised that his brother's interest in these crimes meant he either was involved or knew who was.

With the evidence amassing around him, Clark realized what he should have conceded from the first: that his brother was indeed capable of killing the reporter. In Baskin's last article, he had alleged criminal negligence, corruption, and a cover-up at Lawrence Laboratories. So if Matt's motivation had been to protect Clark from criminal charges, it was another case of his well-meaning but ill-advised actions backfiring and causing problems for Clark. Sometimes mistaking one twin for the other played a part in the screwup, like the time Matt roughed up a boy who was bullying Clark, an act that resulted in Clark being punished. Another time, Matt punched a junior high gym teacher who was tormenting Clark with gratuitous sets of push-ups, a futile attempt that led to suspensions for both brothers. In a high school practice game, Matt, the best linebacker in the league, disabled his own team's quarterback, expecting that Clark would assume the player's position. Instead, Clark was accused of having conceived the scheme and was bounced from the squad.

Matt's attempts at help might have painted Clark as a problem teenager, but Clark's grades were exceptional, and he was accepted into several colleges. Then, in the winter of their senior year of high school, the boys' father, an undistinguished ex–pro football player, was fired from his used-car-salesman job. That night, he informed Clark that he wouldn't be able to help finance his college as promised. Clark was devastated, but Matt wasn't affected because he had just been awarded a full football scholarship to Northwestern University. Then, a few months after Clark received the bad news, his admission to Northwestern was miraculously made possible by the sudden death of both his parents.

Near the bottom of the last box, Clark unfolded a large schematic that stopped him. It was the floor plan of a house, with every room laid out denoting placement of electric outlets, toilets, baths, sinks, and light fixtures. The two-story plan also depicted the entry point for the main power line; where water and sewer lines entered and exited; and the path of the gas lines leading from the meter to the furnace, stove, and fireplace. At points along the natural gas path, someone had circled the fireplace connection, an outlet behind the stove, and the point where the line exited the meter.

Despite the cold, Clark began to sweat and felt short of breath. He snatched the bourbon bottle and took a deep swallow, trying to slow his racing heart. Several minutes passed as he sat with his eyes closed, letting the whiskey settle him, trying to deny what he knew must be true. Finally, he opened his eyes and picked up a clipping from the *Chicago Tribune*. It was an old account of a residential fire in Evanston, and of course he recognized the address. According to the fire inspector, a gas leak in the basement had been the cause of the explosion. Clark started to read the old obituary, and his eyes welled up before he could finish. It didn't matter; he knew the story too well. He took another long pull of bourbon, finished the bottle, and threw the empty across the room.

CHAPTER 10

Sutherland imagined Kelly needed a break from all the pressure she was under at Lawrence Laboratories. Rather than taking her out to dinner after her long commute from the office, he decided to surprise her by entering her apartment with a grocery bag filled with the makings of a poached-salmon-and-pasta dinner, along with a salad and a chilled bottle of sauvignon blanc.

Her loft was part of a converted warehouse. Kelly said she loved the openness, the high ceilings, the exposed-brick walls, and the south-facing view of the city. It was a practical size for a neat person who disliked maintenance and cleaning. It contained a master bedroom, bath, and walk-in closet. It also had a modern kitchen with adjacent dining area, a den with a second bathroom, and a living room with a large balcony and fire escape.

By the time Kelly came home, Sutherland had the dining-room table set with her good china, a floral arrangement, and new candles in her silver candelabras.

"This deserves a special reward," Kelly said as she walked into the kitchen. She gave Sutherland a hug and a wet kiss on the lips as he stood holding tongs, preparing to slip the salmon into the water.

"Take it easy, tiger," he said. "Danger. Hot stove and knives."

"I see that," she said, stepping back from the pot-and-pan collection on the range. "This will have to be continued later."

"I'd hoped as much," he said. "Get yourself comfortable. Have a glass of wine and relax while I put all of this together. You deserve it."

An hour later, as Sutherland was cleaning up the kitchen, Kelly's intercom buzzed. She sighed, took a sip of wine, and said, "Probably someone forgot their key. Happens all the time."

"Or a burglar," he said.

"True."

The intercom sounded again, this time a long piercing buzz, implying the person in the lobby wasn't giving up.

"Shit," she said, stomping across the room to the intercom speaker. "What? Who is it?"

"Clark Kirkland, Kelly," a voice crackled. "Gotta talk to you."

"Clark," she said. "It's late. Can't it wait?"

"No," he said. "Gotta talk. S'important."

"He sounded drunk," Sutherland said. "Last thing we need. Get rid of him."

"Be all right," she said to Sutherland. "He's having a tough time. All this BioVexis publicity. Getting pressured to resign by the board." She said into the intercom, "I'll open the door for you. I'm on the fourth floor. Four C."

A few minutes later, Clark knocked on the door, and Kelly ushered him in. He plopped a leather briefcase on the floor, took off his cashmere overcoat, and let it fall to the floor after a botched attempt to hang it on the entryway coat hook. "Shorry to bother you so late," he slurred to Kelly. "Was in the city—needed to talk to you."

Clark's suit coat was buttoned in the wrong holes, making his broad body look cockeyed. His shirt collar was open, and the tie pulled down at an angle. Kelly got a whiff of whiskey and noted that Clark's pale blue eyes were bleary.

Seeing Sutherland come out of the kitchen, Clark said, "Oh, see you got company." Squinting at Sutherland, he said, "Who are you?"

"That's my partner, Doug," Kelly said.

Seeing Clark teeter, Sutherland said, "Can I get you some coffee, ol' buddy?"

"Naw," Clark replied. "Got any scotch?"

"Let's get to why you're here," Kelly said. "Have a seat on the sofa."

Clark moved unsteadily to the sofa and fell onto the nearest cushion, the weight of his body knocking the sofa backward a few inches. Settled there, he raised his index finger and said, "I've decided. I'm resigning."

"We talked about this," Kelly said, taking an armchair in front of him. Sutherland stood behind her. "Why be a martyr? Why give up a quarter-million-dollar salary when you're not responsible?"

"Money's not a problem. Company's buying me off," he said with a hiccup. "Anyway, that's not the reason. It's time I settled things with my brother."

"That agent convince you that Matt killed Sam Baskin?"

"Wasn't the FBI did it," Clark said, blinking and looking around as if wondering where he was. "You sure you don't have any scotch? Bourbon, maybe?"

"How about some coffee instead?" she suggested.

"Nah." Clark shook his head stubbornly. "I find Matt—get what he deserves. I just went through his storage garage. Found old papers—surveillance stuff and bugs, wires, timing devices."

"Bombs," Kelly said, shocked. "Better let the police know."

"Evidence in there," he said, pointing to the briefcase where he'd dropped it. "There's more …"

Clark's eyes began to well up, and he took short fitful breaths between hiccups. For a moment, he stared blankly at the darkened television screen, confused, a few tears beginning to spill down his cheeks. Then he began to weep, silently at first, but building to choking sobs, his body heaving, his fists pressed against his temples.

Kelly hurried to the kitchen, drew a glass of water, and placed it in front of him on the coffee table. He sat there sobbing for a full minute while Kelly and Sutherland looked on helplessly. When he stopped, he looked up and whimpered, his voice cracking, "My parents weren't bad people. Dad had a temper—drank too much—but he'd had a tough time after his football career ended. Mom was just a sad woman. I don't think it was payback for the bullying or the beatings. It must have been for my benefit. But he shouldn't have done it."

Kelly and Sutherland were silent while Clark sat with elbows on his knees, head in hands, sobbing. Unable to stand the suspense any longer, Kelly gently asked, "What did he do, Clark?"

Clark looked up, eyes streaming tears, and slurred, "It was the insurance."

"Insurance?"

"So that I could go to college. He burned down the house. Mom and Dad were asleep inside."

"Jesus," Sutherland said under his breath as Kelly exhaled an agonized sigh.

After the weeping subsided, Clark gradually slumped sideways on the couch and started snoring. Kelly and Sutherland agreed it must have taken a lot of liquor to get a man as big as Clark to slip into a stupor. Realizing there was no alternative but to let him sleep it off, they lifted his legs onto the couch, took off his shoes, covered him with a blanket, and left the room.

As he climbed into bed, Sutherland said, "Just when you think you've heard the worst …"

Kelly added, "An even more heinous creature slithers out of the mire to crush your belief in humanity."

Max Patrón waited in Clark Kirkland's darkened living room wondering how long he had to wait. Entering Clark's house had been easy. After getting past the gated community's entrance with the keyed code, he'd parked several houses away, jimmied open a patio door, and disarmed the alarm with the code Renata had obtained for him from the security company. It was nearly midnight, and still no sign of Clark. If matters had gone as planned, it should have been done by now—he'd have delivered and videoed the message and finished the job. He punched in a phone number and waited until Renata answered.

"Is it done?" she asked.

"I'm in his house, but he didn't show. What now?"

"This can't wait. You have another job for tomorrow."

"Tell me what you want. I saw Kirkland leave his offices in a government car. I lost them in traffic, and I have no idea where they went or where he is. He never came back to his office for his own car."

"Then get into the company garage tomorrow, and plant a package on his car. I'll send you what you'll need to enter. You have the right material with you?"

"Yeah, but I thought you wanted me to record everything face-to-face."

"No time. Install it tomorrow, and finish off the other mark with the video tomorrow night. Paolo insists it can't wait."

"Right," Max said. "The birthday."

Kelly leaned back in her chair and stretched, looking out the window at the nearly empty company parking lot. It was snowing again, the asphalt had begun to turn white, and the lot lights were haloed with swirling flakes. Most of Lawrence Laboratories' employees had gone home for the night, but she had stayed to churn through the pile of work in her in-basket.

She checked her watch. Almost eight on a Friday night. Normal people would be at a movie, in a bar, dining out, or watching television with their family. But for months, Kelly had known nothing but late nights and weekends in the office, and Sutherland was beginning to feel like a work widower. Although she had always had long days in her city job, it was nothing like the load she had taken on since arriving at Lawrence.

Tired from a long workday and cranky for missing her morning workout, Kelly finally left her office at eight o'clock. The day had started early, with Clark awakening from passing out on her couch the night before. Hungover and remorseful, he apologized profusely and took a taxi to his Lake Forest home, where he planned on taking a few days off. As she walked to her car in the executive garage, she noted that Clark's BMW was still there.

Sutherland had left Kelly a message saying he had a meeting that evening and couldn't meet her for dinner as planned. Instead, he suggested a rain check for the next night. While crawling south in traffic along the Edens Expressway, she considered what to do with what little remained of the day. Go to the gym, veg out with a glass of wine and a bath, or settle for some needed sleep. *Working too hard*, she thought. When she'd accepted the position at Lawrence, it was understood that her predecessor would stay on while she acclimated herself. But with the first whiff of the BioVexis problems, he had abandoned her. Despite Doc Castillo's contention that there would be no federal charges, she hired two law firms to defend whatever might come, including the settlement of a number of emerging suits. Even with a formidable team of defenders on her side, she felt like a quarterback about to be sacked.

Because of the pressure of the new job, her private life was suffering. While working in Chicago's law department, she had rarely missed a day of exercise, usually consisting of a long run. Lately, she managed only one or two workouts a week, and they were shortened and hurried to the point of causing more anxiety than relief. Then there was the effect of her job on her love life. Not only was her time with Sutherland being curtailed, but when they were able to be together, she was often so distracted with work-related issues and worry that he had begun to be noticeably resentful.

They'd been together off and on for long enough to recognize when fractures began to show in their relationship, when the sense of intimacy began to dwindle. They had been estranged a few years earlier because of a disagreement about development versus preservation on one of his office-building projects. She had been an activist for the preservation of Chicago's dwindling number of historically significant buildings, and because he was a practical, profit-driven real estate developer, they were publicly at loggerheads. Time and a series of difficult and nearly fatal experiences brought them together again. And despite the fact that they maintained their separate homes, the relationship had been sailing along smoothly since the reconciliation. At least until she'd begun working for Lawrence Laboratories. She couldn't even remember the last time she had one of the incredible orgasms that she used to experience with Sutherland.

As she recollected the last few months and the declining frequency of their sex, she felt her nipples harden and suddenly knew exactly what she needed most that night. The sensation grew like an itch, and as she arrived at the Fullerton exit of the Kennedy Expressway, she swerved off the ramp and pointed her Volvo toward Sutherland's apartment. She had her own key and planned to stop for some champagne to surprise him. Forget exercise, sleep, or vegging out. A ripping good roll in the hay was what she needed.

It was nine o'clock when Sutherland took a taxi to his apartment after the meeting with his bankers and attorneys, where they discussed what steps were needed to clean up the financial and legal mess Lawrence Laboratories' cancelation would cause if it came to that. Sutherland's firm owed significant design fees to the architects and engineers, and he would lose the substantial sum he'd paid for the option on the building site. If Lawrence definitively canceled, his attorneys would be submitting all the incurred costs as part of his damage suit. It was going to take time and litigation to resolve, and in the meantime, Sutherland didn't have any new projects in mind, much less the desire to pursue any.

When he entered his condominium-building lobby, he waved to Jacob, the evening doorman, a balding, overweight man who always seemed to be on a new diet. With each new attempt, Jacob swore it was working despite ample evidence to the contrary. The phone rang as Sutherland passed the doorman's desk, mercifully allowing him to retrieve his mail without engaging in conversation about carbohydrates, sugar, protein, or the latest weight-loss fad. More than once, Sutherland felt like blurting, "Keep it simple, and get rid of the cookies and chips you stash in your drawer!"

Once inside his twentieth-floor condo, Sutherland was surprised to find the hall and kitchen lights on. It wouldn't be the first time that building maintenance had come in and forgotten to switch off the lights. He hung his coat in the hall, tossed the bills and junk mail on the kitchen counter, and grabbed a beer from the refrigerator. From the freezer, he selected a frozen enchilada dish and put it in the microwave. It would be a poor substitute for the dinner out he'd planned with Kelly before his late meeting interfered. Normally, before Kelly became consumed with her new job, the two of them would have eaten out or cooked something together at the end of their workdays. The recent frozen-dinner habit he was living with was getting old fast, and Sutherland wished Kelly had never accepted Doc Castillo's offer. To some extent, it was Sutherland's own fault because it was only through him that she even knew Lawrence's president. There were plenty of less-demanding opportunities out there if leaving the city law department was so important to her. But she'd been lured by the stock options she was given, believing that after the IPO, they would be worth a great deal.

While he was waiting for his enchiladas to be ready, he turned on the TV in the living room and searched the menu for something worth watching. Before he could finish surfing, his doorbell rang. He walked over to the door and looked through the security peephole, expecting to see Kelly smiling back. But it was Jacob the doorman, holding up an envelope.

Sutherland opened the door, and before he knew it, Jacob was bull-rushed through the opening by a stocky mustached man wearing a ski jacket and a black stocking cap. Sutherland was knocked backward, barely maintaining his balance while trying to understand what was happening. The second man closed the door behind him and pointed a gun at Sutherland. "Back up," he said.

"I'm sorry, Mr. Sutherland," Jacob cried. "I didn't have a choice. He made me come up with him."

"Shut up," the intruder said. "Both of you"—he pointed to the living room—"on that couch."

So this is it, Sutherland thought. He'd been warned and hadn't wanted to believe it. "What do you want?" he said, though he knew the answer well enough. The guy wasn't there to rob him. This was how you died.

Jacob and Sutherland sat next to each other on the living-room couch, and the intruder picked up the remote and flicked off the TV, all the time keeping his eyes on his captives. Then he fumbled in his jacket pocket and pulled out a smartphone and held it up as if taking a picture. "Not enough light," he said and turned on the floor lamp at the end of the couch.

"Mister, please," Jacob pleaded. "I did what you asked—now let me go. You don't need me. Just get what you came for, and I'll forget the whole thing. Mr. Sutherland will too. Won't you, Mr. Sutherland?"

"You're right," the intruder said. "I don't need you." With those words, he fired his silenced pistol, and a dark hole appeared on Jacob's forehead. The doorman's head was flung backward, and a shower of blood and brains spattered the window behind.

Sutherland, taking in the gore and the enormity of what he'd witnessed, reflexively bellowed, "Jesus! You didn't need to ..."

"Sorry for the mess," the intruder said and smirked. "Now as soon as I figure this thing out"—he fingered the smartphone with his left hand, his eyes flicking back and forth between Sutherland and the device—"it'll be showtime."

Kelly awoke with a start. As soon as she arrived at Sutherland's apartment, she had gone to the master bathroom, taken a long shower, and slipped between the sheets naked, where she expected to surprise Sutherland when he arrived. She hadn't intended to fall asleep.

The cry that awakened her had come from the living room, and its anguished tone set off alarms. What on earth was going on out there? Had Sutherland fallen or cut himself? She jumped out of bed and ran down the corridor. Stopping by the dining-room table, she was shocked by the scene in the living room. A man with a gun was standing facing the couch occupied by Sutherland and the very dead doorman. The man, his back toward her, was fiddling with something in his left hand while holding a gun in the right. She knew she didn't have much time before Sutherland met the same fate as the doorman. What could she do against a man with a gun?

The man lifted the device, a phone or a camera, as if to take a picture of Sutherland. Holding it there, he began to speak, as if moderating a movie. "Douglas Sutherland, you have been found guilty of the murder of Rodolfo Aguilar, a man who would be turning thirty today. Having been found guilty, you have been sentenced to death. Do you have anything to say before the sentence is carried out?"

Kelly frantically looked around for a weapon and fixed on the brass candelabras on the glass dining-room table. She grabbed the closest one and dashed across the oak floor on tiptoe, raising the heavy bludgeon as she ran.

Sutherland's eyes glanced at her and quickly darted back to the shooter. "As a matter of fact, I do," he blurted. "Tell the Aguilars—"

Before he could finish, Kelly swung the heavy candelabra, smashing the gunman on the temple, producing a loud chunking *thwack*. The man staggered for one step before crumpling in a heap, his pistol and phone skittering along the Tabriz carpet. Kelly dropped the candelabra and stared openmouthed and wide-eyed at the fallen assassin.

Sutherland jumped up and threw his arms around her. "Not a minute too soon," he gasped, catching her as her knees gave out. "Unbelievable." After rushing her to an armchair, he ran to the kitchen for a glass of water.

A splash of cold water was all it took; her eyes shot open, and she stiffened as if still in battle mode. "Doug," she cried. "Are you all right?"

"I am—are you?"

"He was going to kill you," she said. "I was frantic."

"You were beautiful."

The hit man was on his back, wheezing and gasping, signs that didn't seem promising. Blood oozed from his crushed temple, and his eyes where open and fluttering wildly. Sutherland picked up the phone and called 911. Damned if he was going to do anything else for the bastard.

Max Patrón's smartphone had captured the last scene in vivid color and crisp audio. After the police and FBI viewed it, Sutherland's signed statement of the events in his apartment was hardly even necessary. The image of the doorman's dead body slumped backward on the couch, the gunman's voice announcing Sutherland's death sentence, and the wet clunk sound when the brass candelabra cracked open his skull told most of the story. The before and after events seemed unimportant in the light of that video, but the involuntary role of the doorman and the timely arrival of Kelly were easily added on.

Yet there was one sequence of the video that went largely unnoticed. These scenes chronicled the action after the gunman lost his grip on his phone, sending it spiraling from his hand. The recording had continued until the device clattered onto the carpet, moments after his temple was bashed in. The last whirling images flashed by so quickly that most viewers ignored them. Later, a police technician slowed the recording so that the scenes were recognizable. The final stop-action image revealed a wild-eyed woman wielding a candelabra in both hands, her muscles corded, flexed, and strained, like a pro tennis player following through on a vicious backhand. Anyone seeing the picture would be struck first by the ferocity blazing on her face and the obvious force unloaded in the blow. But the fact that wasn't mentioned in any of the sworn statements or reports was that she was stark naked.

CHAPTER 11

C lark Kirkland heard the news of the attempted murder the next morning while he ate breakfast alone in his home in Lake Forest. The newscaster didn't offer many details, only that a gunman had forced his way into Douglas Sutherland's apartment, killed the condominium's doorman, and was himself killed before he could murder Mr. Sutherland. The gunman, one Max Patrón of St. Louis, had died before he reached the hospital.

It was ten o'clock in the morning when Detective Demming telephoned Clark in his home. "Mr. Kirkland, I tried you at your office, and they gave me your home number. Are you ill?"

"Just taking some time off," Clark said.

"I would have preferred to discuss this face-to-face, but this is too important to wait. Did you hear about what happened to Douglas Sutherland last night?"

"It was on the news."

"The attempt seems to be because he shot Rodolfo Aguilar. We found the gunman's files in his car. Along with details about Mr. Sutherland and his movements, he had information on you. We believe that you were to be the next target, Mr. Kirkland."

"Something to do with BioVexis?"

"Apparently not. Being party to the death of Rodolfo Aguilar. Or at least that's someone's opinion."

"Doug Sutherland shot him. How am I involved in that?"

"Mr. Kirkland, your brother's DNA is solid evidence that he murdered Sam Baskin. He may not have killed Rodolfo Aguilar, but someone thinks he's responsible. The people behind these attempts may believe that you were part of your brother's scheme. Let me read the script that the hit man was prepared to recite: 'Clark Kirkland, you are guilty of conspiring with your brother to kill one Sam Baskin and, as a consequence, guilty of the death of Rodolfo Aguilar. Do you have any last statements before your death sentence is carried out?' That little paragraph was to be recorded along with the video of your murder."

"Then whoever sent him is connected to this Aguilar guy. Find and arrest him, then."

"That's beyond the reach of the Chicago PD, Mr. Kirkland. That's in the FBI's court now."

"What should I do with this information? Dig a hole and crawl in? You going to give me protection?"

"All I can do is give the same advice that I gave Mr. Sutherland. Be careful, and maybe get a bodyguard and a gun."

After dealing with police and local FBI interviews into the late hours, Kelly Matthews took the next day off to come down from the events of the previous night. She was relieved and thankful for arriving in time to save Sutherland's life, and that should have been enough. But all the images, sounds, and sensations kept looping in her mind—the doorman's slumped corpse, the ruthless gunman, the heavy candelabra, and finally the wet thwack of brass splitting flesh and shattering bone. A thoroughly justified act, so why was she troubled? Was it that she couldn't deny the thrill and exhilaration she had experienced, if only temporarily? Panic followed by an explosive release of adrenaline when she swung the candelabra and hit the man. It had amazed and electrified her at the same time. Almost better than the sex she'd missed.

It took Clark Kirkland overnight to process the news that Detective Demming had passed on. The fact that Clark may have been targeted by the Aguilar family for what his brother had done only made his anger and thirst for revenge against Matt more intense. Sutherland had miraculously warded off the threat that night, but that didn't mean either of them was out of harm's way. Because the attacker's death had probably saved Clark's life, he felt he owed Sutherland a personal thank-you, as well as an apology for his drunken visit to Kelly's apartment.

He called Sutherland's office and arranged a meeting for the next day. Clark told him he had an appointment with his attorney in the Loop and would stop by afterward. Then he said, "You know what people say about the happiest two days of a boat owner's life?"

"It's an old cliché," Sutherland said. "The day he buys a boat and the day he sells it."

"I got a better one. Best two days of a man's life are the day he gets married and the day he gets divorced. That's why I'm seeing my attorney."

Jim Ridgeway was sitting in his office at Lawrence Laboratories when he received an email from Dr. Castillo asking him to call. Ridgeway reached Castillo while the latter was presumably attending a biotech conference in San Diego. Ridgeway never knew exactly where his boss was, only that he wasn't in the office very often. It didn't matter; for years, he had been the conduit, though not the real source, of the discoveries that provided Lawrence Laboratories' profits.

"I received the word this morning," Castillo said when he answered Ridgeway's call. "The CIGB has announced that it is completely closing down its operations."

"That's not good news," Ridgeway said.

"In fact, it is merely relocating to a more remote site."

"I don't understand. Why the subterfuge?"

"They're worried that the BioVexis could be traced back to el Centro's activities, so they're making a show of closing it down and arresting the fictitious leaders in a sham move. Then the government will disavow any knowledge of secret clinical activities."

"How would it get traced back to el Centro? You said there wouldn't be an investigation. What are our friends in Virginia saying?"

"Not much, but I think they had something to do with the decision. The need for deniability and distance at every level in case it does leak somehow," Castillo said.

"How will it affect us?" Ridgeway asked.

"Possibly a pause in communication and results, but nothing to worry about. It's not going to make General Mitchell very happy. He's still pushing for his pet project."

"Can't he understand that a mutated virus without an effective vaccine or cure would be a catastrophe of the worst kind?" Ridgeway said. "He's got to be more patient. He's too used to giving orders and having everyone salute."

Hours had passed, and Aguilar's anger and frustration over Max's botched attempt had not abated. The only consolation was that Max hadn't survived, because you never knew when an underling would talk when he faced prison time. But his death still counted as another black mark against the *cabrón*, Sutherland. Max's video recording of his sentencing speech to Sutherland would probably bring the FBI to Aguilar's door. Fortunately, there were dozens of family members who might have mourned Rodolfo's death and ordered the hit. Aguilar would claim innocence, of course, and then drop the names of several senior government officials who he considered close friends. He was confident that nothing would come of the matter; his phone calls to Matt couldn't be traced.

Renata entered his office and sat down with a sigh. "Still no news," she said.

"You sure he planted it?" Aguilar asked. "He didn't fuck that up too?"

"He said he did," she replied. "Clark hasn't been in the office. A matter of time is all."

"That's what you always say. What do you have on Matt?"

"Like you said, he can't stay away from the tables for long."

Sutherland was just leaving the University Club locker room after a squash game when his cell phone rang. He didn't recognize the number but answered, ready to disconnect if it was another robocall. A woman's breathy voice said, "Doug? Is that you?"

"Who's this?"

"Sharon Pietrazak. Don't you recognize my voice?"

Sutherland racked his memory but couldn't place the name or voice. "Sorry. Do I know you?"

"You sure do, dummy," she teased. "Don't you remember? We went to the Stones concert together before getting stoned ourselves in your apartment in Evanston."

Shit, he thought. It was Sharon, née Baskin, one of Sam's two daughters. The one who, according to Nancy, blamed him for Baskin's death by not doing anything to stop it. If she had called to harangue him about that, it would be short call, because he wasn't going to listen to her bitching. "Sharon!" he said, trying to sound enthused. "I didn't recognize your married name. What a pleasant surprise." Surprise, yes; pleasant, not so much.

"You didn't say hello at my father's memorial. That wasn't very nice. I know you were there. I saw you and your friend."

"There was a crowd, and you looked busy with other guests. Anyway, please accept my condolences. Sam was a good man and a friend."

"That's what I'm calling about, among other things," she said.

Here comes the blame, he thought. But he was thankfully wrong.

"You've been on my father's boat, right? It's in Florida—the Keys somewhere?"

"Key West," he said. "He told me he was planning to spend some time on it, not to go anywhere, just to do some research and writing. That was before it happened."

"You know where it is? How to operate it, drive it or whatever you do?"

"Sure. It's a motor cruiser—twin screws—easy to handle. Why?"

"He kept a lot of things on the boat and in his condo there. I want to clear them out and sell the boat. I may keep the condo if it's any good."

"Won't you have to wait until his estate is settled? Probate and all?"

"Dad put the boat and condo in Nancy's and my names, so we don't have to wait for all that probate and trust bullshit. We own them, and that's where the favor comes in. I don't have a clue about boats, and I don't want anyone else going through his personal things. They could be valuable. Wouldn't you help me do that for your old friend? *Pleeease?*"

This was just like the Sharon who Sutherland remembered. The wheedling, the needy and manipulative pleas, the knowing which buttons to push. As a rule, Sutherland ran the other way when the word *favor* was introduced into a conversation. It always involved money, time, or trouble. But this time, the invitation couldn't have been more welcome. Baskin had left information about Lawrence Laboratories in Key West he wanted to share, but he was killed before it could be arranged. His research files were probably still on his boat or in his condo. Since Sutherland was looking for an escape from the cold and the threat of another attempt on his life, he didn't need more encouragement.

"I suppose I can move some things around. Maybe a day or two," he said, implying it was a great inconvenience. "For Sam."

"Terrific, Doug. Let me make our plane and car reservations, and I'll call you tomorrow."

She hung up leaving Sutherland with one thought: *Our* reservations? Was she going too? If so, this wasn't going to be just a favor; it could turn out to be punishment.

⇝

"You're really leaving town?" Kelly asked as she slipped into bed beside Sutherland. It was past ten o'clock, and she had just arrived at his apartment from her office. "For how long?"

"A few days," he said, placing his laptop on the bedside table. "If Sharon hadn't asked, I was planning on asking her sister and going to Key West anyway. I have to get my hands on the rest of Sam's files."

"We haven't even finished going through the material he already gave us," she said.

"I know. So far, we still have no clear idea of the whole picture. The Aguilar family, Castillo, Matt Kirkland, the government … all too vague. Mushy." He clasped his hands behind his head and grimaced from the pain from his flesh wound.

"And you're hoping to find the answer in Key West," she said.

"We're missing a major piece. Sam said so himself. But listen to this: I told you I accidently picked up Sam's phone and asked his daughter to keep his email and phone accounts open. Sure enough, Sam's other informant—not someone inside Lawrence, but closer to the source—has tried to reach him with more information. He obviously doesn't know Sam's dead."

"You're talking to him?"

"Just one message that hasn't been returned. He wrote Sam that the photo in the book he sent Sam proves his contentions and makes the story more sensational—whatever that means. If I can reach him, he'll probably be suspicious. I'll have to convince him that I want to finish what Sam started. I'll start with the book he sent. Sam probably left it in Key West when he was there a little while ago."

"You're staying on Sam's boat?"

"No. Sharon has reservations at the Hyatt. Hey, why not quit and come with me?" he said, rolling over to face her. "You've uncovered corruption and cover-ups, and Sam said it was even worse. Fighting to guard dirty secrets you don't yet know about."

"But I'm learning," she said. "I just uncovered an email about a failed antiviral drug test coordinated with the Department of Defense. The army yet. It was handled by Ridgeway, and he's got his files locked up. He just blows me off. Just like Doc."

"Gaslighting you."

"At least no one's trying to kill me. I asked Fadi Aziz to help you get technically invisible. Did that go all right?"

"Fadi got me in touch with a helpful geek. I have a new email account and a burner phone so no one can locate me. Sharon made the flight reservations. I should be out of reach of Aguilar's men."

"Burner phones, security—man, is this creepy," she sighed. "I'll be glad when this is over."

"Truth be told, when this is over, it's only the first step," he said. "I'll have some serious thinking to do."

"About?"

"What I'm doing. The future, my company. It's not just the uncertainty over Lawrence's headquarters but whether I want to undertake another development. The entire business—dishonest contractors, corrupt city bureaucrats, unreasonable clients—it's gotten oppressive. And then there's this fucking weather. I knew it would happen sooner or later, but this may have pushed me over the edge."

"What do you expect?" she said. "Sam's death, your development, now someone trying to kill you. No wonder you're down. And all because you were at the wrong place at the wrong time."

"I almost wasn't there," he said, ruefully remembering the fateful coin flip. "I could've left when Sam went into the other room."

"But you *were* there, and nothing to do now but pass it off as a bad case of luck."

"You don't know how true that is," he said, visualizing the quarter with George Washington's stern profile resting on the table. "It could easily have gone the other way. Sam would still be dead. Possibly that Rodolfo asswipe too. All because of a supposedly inconsequential notion to let chance decide. A reminder that even random decisions can have consequences."

"Huh?" she said, knitting her brow.

"Nothing. Just tired and rambling," he said, turning over on his stomach. Why admit that the wrong side of a coin had nearly gotten him killed? He already felt foolish enough.

"If you hung it all up, what would you do?" she asked. "You tried practicing law. What's next? Pig farming?"

"According to everything we've learned so far, it couldn't stink as much as what's going on at Lawrence. Wake up and smell it."

Agent Radoff sat in the second row of a morning flight to Key West and studied a series of surveillance videos on his laptop. Several times, he paused the recording, reversed it, and started again in slow motion, as if he were scrutinizing every pixel on the screen. The videos contained scenes taken at different locations and times, all with Douglas Sutherland as the targeted subject. It captured him descending Baskin's town house's stairway the night Baskin was wounded, entering the Royal Suites lobby bar to meet Baskin, and leaving the hotel after the reporter was killed. Other segments followed Sutherland driving into his condo-building garage, walking through his condo lobby, and entering his downtown office building. Each of the grainy snippets had been patched together and sent to him by his operations center.

Sitting next to Radoff was the new partner who operations had foisted on him over futile objections. Radoff liked to work alone, and it wouldn't have mattered who he was assigned as a partner—there was bound to be friction. Alejandro Hernandez, who liked to be called Alex, stood six feet tall and had long, shaggy black hair and a dark complexion. Radoff judged him to be in his midtwenties, but he had never cared enough to ask.

Hernandez looked up from the Google map of Key West on his smartphone. "Baskin's boat is about a ten-minute drive from the airport. Condo's twenty minutes from there."

"Still think it's a fucking waste of time," Radoff said, closing his laptop. "We won't find anything there."

It was to be a day trip, enough time to search Sam Baskin's boat and condominium, find any leaked material from Lawrence Laboratories, and bring it back to operations for inspection and destruction.

"How do you know, *viejo*?" Hernandez said insolently. "Anyway, those be the orders."

"Which is bullshit," Radoff said. "You know how many years I've been doing this?"

"Maybe in the bureau, but this is a new game, a new mission. No room for dinosaurs. Like blowing that hit on that reporter on the stairs. What you gonna fuck up next? My grandmother could have made that shot," Hernandez said and chuckled.

"You were there too," Radoff said, trying to tamp down his annoyance. "Look at your video, asshole. Not my fault he slipped and did a cartwheel just as I fired. What did you want me to do then? He was behind the fucking bushes."

"Save your excuses," Hernandez said. "Ops doesn't buy them. That's why they wanted me to take out that Lawrence whistleblower. That Wright character didn't know what hit him. *Pan comido* when you you're on top of your game."

Radoff had told operations he and Hernandez wouldn't get along. *Goddamn Puerto Rican spic thinks he's a hot-shit secret agent. Straight from the DEA, wears nothing but jeans and sloppy shirts, like he never heard of a suit and tie or getting a haircut. Maybe that works playing a narco agent, but we're supposed to be and look like professional agents.*

"And you think they'd take my advice?" Radoff said. "We should be focusing on this Sutherland character. He tried to put me off, insisting that Baskin's murder had to be about the casinos investigation he was conducting. Maybe he believes that, but Baskin wanted to warn him about problems at Lawrence, and I'm betting he gave Sutherland evidence to document it. Why else would Baskin be taking his briefcase if they were just going to dinner that night? Sutherland was given something, and he's shared it with his lawyer girlfriend, who's been asking the kinds of questions that prove it. I've already asked Colonel Lansing for electronic surveillance on both of them."

"Now *that's* a waste of time. How long you think it's going to take for Paolo Aguilar to send a man to whack him?"

"Could still take a while. Sutherland could upload Baskin's material any day now. It would be all over the internet. We shouldn't wait for Aguilar's move. Take him out ourselves, if you ask me."

"But they didn't ask you, old man," Hernandez said.

It was true. Despite being a veteran agent in the regular FBI, Radoff found that his opinions didn't hold much sway in this clandestine spin-off. Besides having a law enforcement or military background, the most essential criteria for admission to the unit were blind and undying patriotism, the belief that the administration wasn't doing enough to keep America safe, and the willingness to disregard any legal or ethical rules to do something about it. Radoff fit into that template perfectly.

"Permission or not, if it comes to that, I'll take him out myself," Radoff said. *And maybe Hernandez as well if he keeps it up.*

The temperature had fallen to below zero, the sky clear and sunny, when Clark Kirkland left his house and took a metro train downtown. After meeting with his attorney regarding his divorce and the sale of his house, he caught a taxi to Sutherland's office building, where Sutherland met him at his reception desk on the thirtieth floor.

"You look a lot better than you did the other night," Sutherland said as they shook hands.

"Sorry about that. Doesn't happen very often."

On the way to the conference room, they passed a half dozen vacant cubicles, the computer screens black, the desktops free of paperwork.

"Everyone at lunch?" Clark asked.

"I had to put some staff on temporary leave until we know what's going on with the new headquarters. Killed me to do it, but what else could I do?"

"Shortsighted, but the board didn't ask me. We're both victims of this BioVexis fiasco."

"Kelly, too, if she's not careful," Sutherland said, taking a seat across from Clark at the conference table. "It must be a relief that you're out of that snake pit, but you're not out of danger. Neither am I. Whoever ordered the hit on us won't be giving up."

"The thing is, Matt has to be in as much danger as we are. I'm counting on him to settle it for us."

"If he's smart, he's on a tropical beach somewhere, drinking margaritas. Unless you know something different."

"I don't know where he is. And it's not likely either of us would be able to find him. But I know Matt, and he won't want to live like a hermit, so whoever ordered the hits would eventually hunt him down, and Matt must realize that. If that's not motive enough to kill that person, there's another reason. He's bound to learn about that gunman sent to kill me and want to go after the man who sent him."

"If you and Matt are so alienated, why would he care about an attempt on your life?"

"I don't have a good answer except that it's a fact, strange as it is," Clark said. "Matt's always had this thing about helping or protecting me. In this Baskin case, I believe he killed the reporter to stop the stampede to hang me for the BioVexis disaster."

"If Matt does kill the bastard, hallelujah, but how does it avenge your parents' deaths, if that's still on your mind?"

"It's still my plan, and here's why. I have all Matt's files and newspaper clippings from his storage unit. The contents cover some events I'd heard about, others that I'd forgotten or was too obtuse to see. Like the arson that killed my parents. Or the drowning death of my first fiancée, a woman he'd once dated and later maligned. He was the only witness and swore he couldn't save her, but now I have to wonder."

"Your parents and fiancée too," Sutherland said, shaking his head. "That's one coldhearted son of a bitch."

"Many of the news clippings on murders, bombings, and fires bore his scribbled comments, underlinings, and notes, contradicting the published accounts as if he was there and knew the truth. On an item about a car bomb in Minneapolis, he scribbled, 'Take that, motherfucker.' The article mentioned the victim was on the board of Matt's hedge fund that almost had him jailed for fraud."

"How does that help? Giving it all to the police won't add anything. He's already wanted for murder," Sutherland said.

"And not just for Baskin's. The FBI told me once they had his DNA, they matched it to several unsolved murders, and they think there's more."

"And I was nearly another," Sutherland said. "But how does more evidence of his crimes help? Wanted for one or a dozen, what's the difference?"

"There's a better avenue than the police. I copied all of the articles, added my comments, and sent it all to the *New York Times* and the *Tribune*. Knowing that the DNA proved Matt killed Sam Baskin, and with DNA matches to several other murders, they each agreed the material could spice up one of their columns. It's a brother's condemnation of a psychopath. He'll read it and find me, though I'm not sure whether he'll want to beat me up, kill me, or seek absolution. You can never know with him. Whatever his intent may be, I'll be waiting—and be thanked for removing a proven murderer and fugitive from the world."

"Your brother sounds like a complex man. An assassin on one hand, your guardian angel on the other. Is that because he was the older brother?"

"Only by fifteen minutes, but that has little to do with it. We were always black and white, hot and cold, volatile and calm. Opposite sides of the same coin, you could say. But I think his protective behavior toward me throughout our teens really began when we were eleven or twelve. We were attending a summer camp, and there was a shocking death—an adult counselor who was overly friendly to young campers. It was eventually ruled an accident, but not before we were interrogated for hours—days, even."

"Let me guess. You didn't squeal on him. He owed you."

"We never talked about it, and I put it out of my mind. Until now. It might have been his debut performance."

Sitting at her desk at Lawrence Laboratories, Kelly closed down her email, knowing there was more than enough work there to keep her busy all weekend. She had been puzzling vainly over a few new entries Fadi Aziz had uncovered. Lawrence had been wiring millions of dollars to a company named Arcon International without any documentation on what the payments were for. What did they do for Lawrence? One more unanswered question to the growing pile.

Giving up for the night, Kelly grabbed her briefcase and switched off the lights, planning to stop at the East Bank Club for a workout before meeting Sutherland for a late dinner. He would be leaving the next day for Key West.

On the way to the elevator, she noticed Steve Dixon's office light on and peeked in. He was one of the company's top accountants, and since the CFO was sick, Dixon was Kelly's best bet at getting answers to several of her financial questions. He was just hanging up his phone, sitting with his back to her. She knocked and entered without waiting.

"Still here, Kelly?" he said as he turned in his chair to face her. He was a forty-five-year-old man with balding gray hair and a matching mustache. On the corner of his desk, there was a portrait of him in an army uniform with golden oak leaves on his epaulets.

"Catching up on administrative stuff and talking on the phone with our lawyers. The water's still rising."

"I know, but Doc tells us not to worry," Dixon said. "We'll get out of this, he says. Something I can help you with?"

"I hope so. Going through our accounts, I found a couple entries I don't understand," she said and sat in front of his desk. "What's Arcon International do for us? We paid them over thirty million last year alone, and I can't find any explanation. Payments labeled 'consulting' without any further explanation were sent to a Panamanian bank account. Then there's the test clinics. There's no accounting information on them. There's none of the expected contracts or entries for the clinic's expenses—no doctor's salaries, no supplies, materials, travel—no nothing. How can that be?"

Dixon nodded, digesting the question. "Arcon International," he said thoughtfully. "You may have answered your own question. I think those Panamanian payments are for Arcon's expenses to run those clinics and collaborate on some research. But that's just a guess."

"You mean Arcon and the clinics are independent contractors?" she said, incredulous.

"I don't know the details, just the payments," Dixon said, shrugging with his hands palms up as if he was embarrassed for not knowing more. "Doc or Jim Ridgeway signs off on them."

"What about our auditors?" Kelly asked. "Or the IPO? If we ever go public, it won't look good that independent contractors are developing and testing our products. Contractors don't have to live with the consequences if they screw up. Like our BioVexis mess, for example."

"I agree, but I couldn't tell you whether they're independent or just another cost center."

"Then why the Panamanian bank? Isn't that strange?"

"I have to admit it's a little different. But it's Doc's company."

"Does the board know about it?" she asked.

"No idea. Sorry," he said with another shrug.

Shaking her head in frustration, Kelly stood to leave. "I'll let you know if I find out more. Thanks."

"Glad to help," he said as she walked out the door.

On the way to the garage and her car, she thought, *What help?*

CHAPTER 12

The next afternoon, Kelly was still mulling over Lawrence's millions in unexplained payments to the mysterious Arcon International, when Clark stuck his head into her office and waved. "This is it, Kelly. Cleaned out my personal things and taking off."

"So soon?" she said, surprised. "We haven't even had time to organize a farewell party."

"None of that for me, thanks," he said. "I couldn't take it. Better I sneak out without a peep. No one will miss me."

Kelly came out from behind her desk, walked to the door, and gave him a hug. "I will, damn it. I told you not to be a martyr. You don't deserve this."

"Martyr? Leaving with my hide and a bag full of money. You should be so lucky."

"I'm beginning to think so too," she said. "I've just been learning more about this place. About to find Doc and get some answers."

"Good luck with that," he chuckled. "Doc? Answers? Come on! You ever find out about that center?"

"Not much. Now I've got more questions, like, Where are the test sites and clinics we use?"

"I was just a marketing guy. Guess I should have paid more attention. Might have prevented all this."

"Don't blame yourself," she said. "And stay in touch, will you?"

"With you, sure. The only honest one in this organization." Clark turned around to face Ridgeway, who had just come down the corridor. "Oh, hi, Jim. I was just about to stop in and say goodbye."

"I saw your boxes on your desk. Leaving now?"

"Yep. Lug the stuff down to my car. Hope it starts—it's been sitting there a couple days."

"Those boxes look like more than a one-man job," Ridgeway said. "I'll give you a hand. Come on."

❧

Minutes after Clark and Ridgeway left Kelly's office for the garage, she hurried down to Castillo's office, meaning to catch him before he left again. She entered his office as he was putting on his suit jacket, preparing to leave.

"Doc, I need a minute," she said, standing in the doorway.

"A minute's all I have," he said, gathering papers into his briefcase. "By the way, Clark just left. You say goodbye?"

"No need. He's got a seven-figure check, which says it better than I could. Now what's so important?"

"Tell me about Alpha, Beta, and Gamma."

Castillo stared at her a moment, as if trying to read her thoughts, see what she knew. He took off his reading glasses, shook out the handkerchief from his suit breast pocket, and wiped the lenses, a clear case of stalling.

Impatient, Kelly finally added, "They have to do with the test clinics—part of el Centro, which I assume is our research organization."

Castillo raised his hand and snapped, "I know what they are. But how do you know, Kelly?"

"I can't defend what I don't know about or understand. I read it in correspondence to you. I've seen emails and research material, test results, protocols, all highly scientific and over my head. But I do know they were testing vaccines and antibiotics in those clinics."

"Well, that's what we do," he said, warily choosing his words. "How else would we know if they're effective? But I'm very interested in learning how you found this correspondence. It's highly sensitive."

"I'm not surprised, under the circumstances. What subjects do we test on?"

"Guinea pigs, rats, fleas, depending on the particular virus or bacteria," Castillo replied, an edge of irritation in his tone.

"What about on humans?"

114

"Only if all the animal trials justified it and under extremely controlled conditions, blind studies with placebos," he said. "What are you getting at? This is not an area you are qualified to delve into. Especially since that correspondence you somehow got your hands on is highly confidential."

"I can understand why. I know what blind tests with placebos are, and that's not what they're doing in those studies. The overall success rate in the clinics is abysmal, and the mortality rate is high. It's as if the attitude is 'Maybe we'll get lucky,' showing little respect for the patients, or, as some might consider them, the victims," Kelly said. "And you're saying your corporate counsel shouldn't know what's going on?"

Castillo's face turned a shade darker as he glowered at Kelly for several seconds. Then he took a deep breath and exhaled slowly, an audible sigh, as if he realized it was no use to resist further. "First of all, it is el Centro, not Lawrence Laboratories, that is responsible for what you're suggesting. Those clinics were part of el Centro's research organization. What happened was terrible and indefensible, something that we neither condoned nor overlooked. That's why we have ceased using el Centro."

"Because they were responsible for BioVexis or the fatal tests?"

"Both. They have become an unreliable partner. So you don't have to worry about it anymore. And since government is taking a hands-off attitude, so should you. Forget you ever heard of it."

"How? As soon as the class-action attorneys begin their discovery, the existence and involvement of el Centro will be at the center of the litigation. No pun intended."

Castillo furrowed his brow, seemingly surprised and suddenly apprehensive. He thought for a moment before pasting on a plastic smile. "But I thought tech services purged all those communications. How did you get to see them?"

"They weren't destroyed," she said, mentally thanking Fadi for his cleverness. "The head of tech services quit before it was done."

"Then have someone else do it," he said gruffly. "And get rid of everything in your possession too. All of it. Understood?" He looked at his watch and huffed. "Now you and your meddling have made me late."

Before Kelly could find the words to object, the building trembled for a second, the horizontal blinds rattled, and Castillo's framed awards and photos fell off the wall. A moment later, a deafening explosion pierced the shocked suspense between them. As they stared in bewilderment at each other, the fire alarm began a high-pitched warble.

Sutherland had to hand it to Baskin's daughter—Sharon knew how to travel. First-class air to Miami, a limo to the Hyatt hotel in Key West, and chilled champagne waiting in his suite. Either her husband was a big-time earner or Sharon was already spending her inheritance. The lavish treatment only partially compensated for the fact that he'd had to listen to the woman's incessant chatter for most of the trip south. She had exhausted him with tedious details about her personal life, from her children's high school and college grades and sports activities to her workout regime and tennis game. Then, at the end of her monotonous discourse and fortified by her third glass of wine, she shifted into interrogation mode.

"So how long have you been divorced, Dougie? How old is your daughter? Are you and that woman I saw at my father's service serious? Pretty sexy looking—hope you can handle her." Sutherland managed to satisfy her by being sufficiently responsive to most of her factual questions and sidestepping the matrimony-related probes. Then she began to reminisce about their short-lived dating history, wondering what had gone wrong.

"You know we never did it," she giggled. "How come? I gave you enough hints. Creamed in jeans every time I saw you. You were one good-looking dude. Still are. So what happened?"

How could he tell her that she was his good friend's daughter; that he'd gone out with her in the first place only at the insistence of Baskin's wife, who had no idea about Sharon's dubious standing on campus; and that he couldn't stand her? She was self-centered, manipulative, needy, and peevish. For the sake of peace, Sutherland said, "Simple, Sharon. You were, and are, the daughter of a very good friend and mentor. I couldn't have looked him in the eye."

"Such a prude, such a shame," she said before slurping a mouthful of wine. "Are you still that way? Ever step over the line a little? You're a man of the world now."

He could guess where this conversation was going and decided to cut it off.

"Still a prude, I'm afraid. One woman at a time."

Undeterred, she said, "One at a time is good enough for me, as long as I'm the one. I'm not such a bad lay. Been a long time, though. Husband doesn't turn me on. Christ, he even has man boobs."

"Two children are enough," he said. "The all-American family."

"Easy for you to say. You aren't climbing the wall all the time," she said, pouting. With that, Sharon closed her eyes and drifted off for the rest of the flight, allowing Sutherland to regain his equanimity.

While she napped, Sutherland reflected on his many visits to Key West over the years. When Sutherland was a teenager, his father had taken him there to sail and fish, and sometimes Baskin and his wife would join them to cruise along the chain from Key West to Key Largo. Later, Sutherland and his then wife, Margo, celebrated their first anniversary on Key West. Besides drinking in the most popular bars and visiting the obligatory historical sites, Margo, a decent swimmer, swam laps in the hotel pool or along the shoreline while Sutherland went for long runs around the island. But between babysitting Sharon, collecting Baskin's files, and organizing the sale of Baskin's boat and condominium, Sutherland doubted he'd have time for any fun this time.

Magnífico Enterprises' headquarters offices filled seven floors of a downtown Miami office building. But most of the time, Aguilar's expansive corner suite remained empty, as he preferred working from either of his two sophisticated home offices, which were equipped with electronic links to all his company's holdings. Despite his seventy-eight years, he still liked to be involved in his broad business empire. It was only recently that he had begun to relinquish partial control to a few relatives and qualified professionals. Though he had five children by two now-deceased wives, as well as fifteen grandchildren, twelve great-grandchildren, and more grandnieces and grandnephews than he could keep track of, the majority of the younger generation had decided on careers and professions that had nothing to do with his businesses. They considered his hands-on management methods old school and oppressive, his politics too conservative, and his principles questionable at best.

The casino business and its spin-offs were Aguilar's first love and remained his bailiwick alone. It was one of the most lucrative of his companies, and he continued to study the monthly profits and losses of every operation, knew the top people in every casino by name, and visited each at least once every six months. He also knew and, for the most part, respected his competition. Staying on friendly terms was essential if they wanted to keep their golden goose laying twenty-four-karat eggs.

After Matt Kirkland disappeared, Aguilar had circulated his photo to all his own casinos and those around the world that he was on good terms with. It wasn't an uncommon practice, and Aguilar was certain that Matt would show up at one of their tables before too long. And he was correct.

The call came from the general manager of the Atlantis Casino in the Bahamas. Matt, now with a shaved head and sporting a beard, had been spotted at the blackjack table, betting large. Aguilar considered three approaches for avenging Rodolfo's death. He could advise the Nassau police of Matt's presence and have them extradite him, but that might implicate Aguilar himself. Besides, prison wasn't punishment enough. He could have his men locate and kill him, which would be cleaner but would deprive Aguilar of the satisfaction he thirsted for. He wanted to participate in Matt's death, to make it slow and painful. So he sent two of his men to Nassau from Miami on a fifty-foot powerboat and arranged for his grandnephew Marco to join them by plane. Aguilar's instructions were for Matt to be abducted and returned to Miami. Alive.

Sutherland learned of the deadly explosion at Lawrence Laboratories minutes after walking into his Key West hotel room and turning on his TV. According to accounts, the explosion had killed two Lawrence executives and injured another employee. The sheriff had already called in the FBI, and neither organization had any initial suspects or leads. But the channel's talking heads had plenty to say about the possible motive being retribution for the BioVexis deaths. Information about Max Patrón's assignment to kill Clark Kirkland had not been publicized. But Sutherland certainly knew, and it didn't take much imagination to realize he was still at risk of an identical end by the same hidden hand. Although Sutherland was in Florida with Baskin's daughter, he reasoned that his sudden departure provided only a temporary shelter from the threat. That someone was bold enough to risk a bombing in Lawrence Laboratories' own headquarters indicated that the man behind the murder would stop at nothing. Where did that leave him?

Sutherland was still considering his situation when his hotel-room phone rang. It was Kelly.

"So you're all right?" she gasped. "I was worried they'd come after you again."

"How about you? The news just said two executives."

"Ridgeway and Clark," she said, sobbing. "Awful. Nothing left of them. A car bomb is all we know. Jim was helping Clark with his things."

"You sound like you're a mess. Go home. Have a stiff drink."

"I can't. Have to talk to the police and FBI," she said. "Had to call you first. Gotta go. Be careful. Love you."

CHAPTER 13

Sergeant Daryl Durant was an hour into his regular shift in the monitoring center, reviewing video of unusual activity on a chemical company's loading dock in Indianapolis, when his phone rang. "Sergeant Durant here."

"It's Colonel Lansing, Sergeant. Fill me in."

"You know about the bomb?" he asked. "At the drug company?"

"Already spoken to the agent in charge. Losing Ridgeway will be a major problem."

"Who's responsible? They know yet?" Durant asked.

"Just keep your sights on the Matthews woman," Lansing said. "She's stumbled onto some sensitive information, and we need to find out where she's getting it. Another whistleblower, maybe?"

"We've only been monitoring her emails for a week. All her messages were about that BioVexis matter with different lawyers. We've only had the mic in her office since yesterday, and we haven't heard her talking to anyone about anything else of interest. Then, too, she could be meeting somewhere else in the building, and we wouldn't know it."

"How about phone calls?" Lansing asked. "You're recording them?"

"Yes, ma'am. Like I said, lawyers, insurance, finance people. Nothing you wouldn't expect," Durant said. "A few personal ones but nothing interesting."

"Who to? The personal ones."

"A relative in the suburbs. Her aunt, I think. And a few minutes after the bomb, she used the lobby security phone to call someone in Florida. She sounded like a wreck—telling some guy about the bomb."

"The lobby phone? How do you know it was her?"

"You need to enter your ID code on that phone. Got a lobby video too."

"Have a name, this guy?" she asked.

"She asked for a Mr. Sutherland. The Hyatt hotel in Key West."

"Sutherland?" she snapped.

"That's it. He important?"

Sharon Pietrazak, somewhat refreshed from napping on the plane, made an appointment for a manicure and pedicure in the spa. Grateful to get away from her, Sutherland changed into shorts, a T-shirt, and flip-flops and rented a car through the concierge desk, charging it to Sharon's room. He drove to the marina on Stock Island, where Baskin's boat was docked. He told Sharon he planned to start the engine, verify everything was functioning, and schedule repairs if needed. But his ulterior motive was to find Baskin's journal and files on Lawrence Laboratories without having Sharon around.

Stock Island was the second-to-last island in the archipelago and the closest to the actual island of Key West. When the commercial shrimp boats were driven from Key West's harbor by rising docking costs, they had settled in one of the many harbors on Stock Island. Although there were many upper-end homes on the island, a large percentage of residents were there because they couldn't afford the elevated housing prices in Key West. In many ways, Stock Island was Key West's poor relative. Trailer camps or parks had never been a part of Sutherland's living experience, and what he knew about them he'd learned years earlier when he'd visited in the Keys. Articles in Key West's daily newspaper the *Citizen* often reported fights, murders, arrests, and drug busts involving the denizens of one or another of the trailer neighborhoods. But that was slowly changing for the good as new affordable housing, hotels, and marinas were replacing the trailer communities.

Sutherland parked in Baskin's marina's lot, walked along the dock to the water's edge, and listened. The sound of gulls screeching overhead and halyards pinging against masts reminded him of his Chicago marina in the summertime. If he closed his eyes, he could imagine himself casting off on his sloop and gliding through the gap toward the lighthouse on a broad reach. But the sight of brown pelicans squatting on the pilings and the smell of brine on the heavy ocean air persuaded him that he wasn't anywhere near his own sailing yacht or Lake Michigan. He was on an island between the Atlantic Ocean and the Gulf of Mexico.

Minerva, Sam's motor cruiser, was a forty-two-foot Chris-Craft Catalina built in 1985. It remained in the same slip Sutherland remembered, and as he climbed from the dock onto the stern platform, he heard a voice shouting from two boats down, along the pier.

"Hey there!" a man said, walking toward Baskin's boat, looking down at Sutherland from the dock. "What are you doing?"

"I'm a friend of Sam Baskin," Sutherland said. "He died, and I'm here to help his family with his boat."

"Sam died? Can you prove you're a friend of his?"

Sutherland held up Baskin's key ring. "Got the keys to his boat."

"Lot of good they'll do," the man said, pointing to the aft door to the salon.

Sutherland turned and saw that the door had been jimmied open. "When did that happen? Who?"

"Two days ago. Saw the guys that did it, but they were gone before I could do anything. Took off in their rental car," he said. "I reported it to the dockmaster, but I haven't heard anything."

"What they look like, these guys?" Sutherland asked.

"That's the surprising thing," the man said. "One's in a dark suit and tie; the other was Latino in jeans and a tropical shirt. Not bums."

"Did they take anything with them when they left?"

"Empty-handed, as far as I could see. By the way, my name's Charlie Little."

"Doug Sutherland, Charlie. Sam's daughter is at the hotel. She wants to sell Sam's boat and condo."

"It's a shame. He was just here a couple weeks ago. Stayed on the boat a couple nights because his condo air-conditioning wasn't working. You need anything, just ask. I'm just two boats away," Charlie said.

Sutherland climbed down the steps to the salon, where he surveyed the aftereffects of an obvious search. The contents of the chart table were on the cabin sole, books were strewn across the seating, and the drawers had been opened and emptied. Despite the disorder, it looked like a haphazard job by men in a hurry, looking for something obvious.

Beginning to believe he might be too late, that anything resembling research files had been found already, Sutherland remembered Baskin's lockbox. Baskin had bolted the steel box under the forward bunk and covered it with loose anchor chain. One of Baskin's keys opened it, and Sutherland retrieved a stack of personal files, several flash drives, two journals, and a well-worn Spanish-language paperback book. Sutherland assumed the book was the same one Baskin had mentioned that had come from his newest source. Under the papers, he was surprised to find a nine-millimeter semiautomatic pistol in its holster, two full magazines, a box of shells, and a recently dated receipt for all of it. Evidently, even before the first attempt on his life, Baskin had had serious apprehensions about someone trying to silence him.

Sutherland meant to sort through the research files by himself when he returned to the hotel, but once he saw Baskin's journals, his curiosity took over. He leafed through the first dog-eared leather journal and stopped on a bookmark indicating an entry from decades earlier, when they'd discovered Doc Castillo adrift on the raft. Sutherland had been a teenager at the time, and he remembered the morning well. But the journal entry intrigued him, and he sat down and read it.

Like all the entries in the journal, this one was dated, but it was also titled: "Castillo Saved." Baskin's account of that morning was just as Sutherland remembered it—he, his father, and Baskin sailing through the storm, the two bodies sprawled on the sinking raft, the one shoved off, and then the three of them hauling Castillo onto the sloop as the man held on to his treasured suitcase. The text of the entry ended with "The survivor identified himself as Dr. Jorge Castillo, and later that day, we discovered why he'd been so determined to save that suitcase. While he slept, we opened the case and found research papers from an organization titled CIGB. Bernard and Doug spoke some Spanish but gave up in the face of all the special terms and esoteric language."

That was the extent of the original entry, but Sam had recently slipped in a loose page with an addendum to the text: "Over the years, we came to believe that those research papers in the suitcase were to be the foundation of Doc Castillo's reputation in the US and ultimate success with Lawrence Laboratories."

Made sense, Sutherland thought. It hadn't taken Castillo very long to get a job at a pharmaceutical company and make enough of a splash that he soon had an offer to start his own business. Sutherland closed that journal and picked up another, but he decided he'd read it later.

Matt Kirkland awoke late in the morning after a night of gambling at the Atlantis Casino in the Bahamas. His room in Nassau's Sandy Shores Hotel overlooked the swimming pool, and the sunlight reflecting off the water made him squint and look away. It had been a late night, and he'd had too much to drink after spending the first night at the tables in a long time. Since he'd left Chicago, he'd limited his gambling to online poker in order to avoid detection by anyone associated with Aguilar. Adding to the tedium, the lack of attractive and obliging guests at the pool and bar had severely inhibited his accustomed success at getting laid. So after days of internet gaming and a few rendezvous with call girls, he found the lure of the nearby casino too tempting. It took only a few minutes at the tables before the old buzz lifted him out of his monotony. He hadn't realized how much he'd missed it.

Matt had chosen the low-budget hotel, figuring that, because Aguilar knew Matt's expensive tastes, he would initially limit his search to higher-end destinations and resorts. The Bahamas was the closest alternative outside of the United States, and might be obvious, but Matt needed a location near enough to Florida to be reached quickly by a short boat ride. He was growing a full beard and had shaved his head, but even with his new passport and credit cards, getting through airport customs would be impossible. So as soon as his revised plans to dispatch Aguilar were finalized, he would prevail upon the same fisherman he'd used to arrive in Nassau to transport him to a small marina in Key Largo.

Matt didn't generally watch television or read newspapers, but he frequently signed on to the *Chicago Tribune* website to follow the stories about Lawrence Laboratories and see whether the authorities had made any headway on the Baskin case. It had been nearly a week since he last checked, and when he paged through the most recent editions, he was stopped by the headline "Suspect Identified in Lawrence Laboratories Bombing."

Matt hadn't even finished scanning the article before he kicked the wastepaper basket, sending it into the mirror, cracking the glass. "Son of a fucking bitch," he bellowed and then punted the basket across the room. *Of all the goddamned shitty luck*, he thought. *Just because that Sutherland faggot put a round in me and screwed up everything. Clark would be alive if I'd killed Aguilar when I planned.*

The explosion had occurred a day earlier, but the FBI had already claimed they identified the bomber as one Max Patrón. Their theory was that the two Lawrence Laboratories executives were killed as payback for the deaths that the BioVexis drug had caused.

"It was Aguilar, you dumb fucks. FBI couldn't find their ass with …" Matt growled in exasperation. He had tried to help his brother only to get him killed, as if Matt had planted the bomb himself. He pictured his brother as a teenager, right after one of Matt's ill-advised plans had misfired, consigning a mortified Clark to take the blame. Though guilt was an emotion foreign to Matt, he couldn't prevent the wave of regret from rolling over him as Clark's innocent likeness morphed into a mocking Aguilar, the aging fuck who had ruled Matt's life for years.

Like a lumbering madman, Matt stumbled across the salon and retrieved the semiautomatic he'd smuggled onto the islands on the boat. He screwed on the suppressor, chambered a round, and opened the window, looking out on the pool deck. Twenty people lay scattered about on lounge chairs, and others floated around in the water, every one of them unaware that they could be dead within seconds if Matt obeyed his darkest instincts. Instead, he aimed at a woman in a bikini strutting seductively past a few men by the pool. "*Bang*—you're dead, babe," he said as his imagined round struck the center of her deep cleavage. Then he envisioned his next bullet wasting an obese man toweling himself, followed by an old man asleep on his lounge chair. In the next minute, he had decimated the entire pool population, and with each fancied death, he began to feel better and back in control.

Then he tossed the gun on the bed and glared at his own face in the shattered mirror. *No more delay. A bullet in my gut isn't going to stop me from killing Aguilar this time.*

❧

Aguilar and Renata were finishing breakfast on his penthouse balcony when the phone rang. Aguilar listened for a few moments; said, "Muchas gracias"; and hung up. He wiped his mouth with a napkin, carefully folded it, and placed it beside his empty plate.

"Qué pasa?" Renata asked.

"Rodolfo's murderer is in Key West," Aguilar said with his raspy, cigar-abused voice. "Downtown Hyatt hotel."

"Can we trust the intelligence? Who's the source?" she asked.

"Our friends—who do you think? Send some men right away, and tell them we want him alive. Have the crew sail *Buena Suerte* there too. We'll go there in a helicopter later. The yacht's the perfect place for that *pendejo* to die."

"What about the girl?" Renata asked. "We already scheduled her, but if the mother has to take her to Key West, she may change her mind."

"Until she sees the money," he said. "She meets us in Key West. Take care of it."

Sutherland woke up early and sat outside on his hotel-room balcony sipping bitter coffee and watching as a few charter fishing boats headed for deep water. It was a beautiful morning, with a cloudless sky and a light breeze rippling the water beyond the hotel's marina. To the north, the ragged tree-lined silhouette of Wisteria Island served as the backdrop for the dozens of boats anchored off its shore. *Too nice a day to laze around*, Sutherland thought as he dumped out his coffee in the sink. He pulled on his running shorts, slipped on a singlet, laced up his running shoes, and exited the hotel onto Front Street, where he began his first outdoor run since the last warm day in October.

Forty-five minutes later, after completing a random route around town, reacquainting himself with streets and parks and neighborhoods, delighting in the flaming poinciana and blooming frangipani trees, he finished the last hundred yards in a triumphal sprint. It felt as if he had been set free of the cage he'd been locked in since November, when he'd decided that running in the cold and gloom was for martyrs—or best left for people with thicker blood than his. On days when the mercury dipped below forty and he couldn't find a squash game, he settled for the University Club's indoor treadmill. Running outside with the warm ocean air kissing his bare skin was almost erotic. He hadn't felt so good in months.

><£

Baskin's daughter had never seen her father's condo, so after breakfast, Sutherland escorted her on a walk through downtown Key West to an area called Truman Annex, named for former president Harry Truman. Baskin's condo building was a white four-story structure on Front Street overlooking the harbor. Paradise Realty Management's offices were on the ground floor of the building, and the manager was a middle-aged blonde woman with hair and skin that had seen too many hours in paradise's unforgiving sun. The nameplate on her blouse said Vickie, and she must have thought her two visitors were potential buyers, because she was oozing charm and helpfulness until Sharon introduced herself as Sam Baskin's daughter. Vickie swallowed hard; blurted, "Oh my"; and pressed the palms of her hands on her cheeks.

"Oh my *what*?" Sharon asked.

"I'm so sorry," Vickie said. "I just learned about it the other day. Terrible."

"Well, thank you. It's been a few weeks, and we're getting on with life," Sharon said. "Now we need the keys to his place."

"I imagine you can you prove who you are," Vickie said. "I mean, the others had a court order."

"Wait," Sutherland said. "What others?"

"The two men. Agents," Vickie said. "Investigating his murder."

"That's news to me," Sharon said. "They haven't done shit, as far as I've heard. Anyway, I've got the goddamn deed back at the hotel. You gonna make me go get it? I just want to see the place. We're thinking of selling it."

"Oh," Vickie said brightly. She must have sensed a commission. "Well, as you'll see, your father hasn't used it much lately. He needed to make arrangements for the crane to replace the old condenser on the roof. After one night, he left and turned off the water and the main circuit breaker."

"Well, if you'd let us in ..." Sharon said.

"Let me get the keys," Vickie said. "I'll take you there."

Minutes later, with keys in hand, Vickie led them through the condo-building lobby and up two floors to Baskin's unit. When she unlocked the door and saw the hall light on, she said, "Darn it. They left the electricity on. I specifically asked them …"

Sutherland stepped into the living room, and after surveying the result of the living room's thorough ransacking, he said, "Seems those agents weren't housebroken. You get their names? What did they look like?"

Vicki stared slack-jawed in disbelief at the scattered books and papers, the torn-open cushions, and upturned furniture. Meanwhile, Sharon was edging toward the door, ready to bolt.

"The older, white one was pretty intense," Vickie said. "Suit and tie. Professional looking and super serious. The other was Hispanic looking, younger, with long hair and casual clothes."

"Sounds like the same men that broke into Sam's boat," Sutherland said.

"I've seen enough," Sharon said, her hand on the door handle. "Nothing but junk in here."

Vickie stooped down and picked up a set of car keys and handed them to Sutherland. "These are his car keys. An older Buick in the garage. Space 52. The upstairs neighbor starts it now and then."

"That old Buick?" Sharon scoffed. "My dad registered it in my name, but I don't want the damn thing. A BMW or Benz, maybe …"

Sutherland pocketed the keys.

"I'll see what I can get for it," he said, reasoning that with the car in Sharon's name, it wouldn't attract unwelcome attention if he drove it. "What about this mess in the condo? Can you get it cleaned up?"

"Cleared out, cleaned, and painted, if it's really going on the market," Vickie said.

"What will it sell for?" Sharon asked.

"The last one that closed in the building was just under a million," Vickie said buoyantly.

"Sell the fucker," Sharon said as she walked out.

CHAPTER 14

That evening, after eating a grilled mahi-mahi sandwich at the hotel bar, Sutherland took a taxi from the hotel to the marina where Baskin's boat was docked. He wanted to investigate why the head wasn't flushing properly, a messy job he was sure wouldn't interest Sharon. She was napping in her room when he left, so he'd slipped Baskin's car keys under the door, along with directions to the boat, in case she wanted to drive there after she'd eaten. If she opted to hang out in the hotel, that was just fine with him.

Two hours later, he was in the boat's forward cabin, studying a schematic of the head's plumbing system, when he felt a subtle rock in the boat's motion.

"Anybody home?" Sharon shouted. "Permission to come aboard?"

He didn't bother to answer. She had to know he was on board because all the salon lights were on.

"Doug, darling," she crooned from the cockpit. "It wasn't nice of you to leave me like that. I thought I'd come down and we could check out one of those beds or berths, if that's what you call them. If the boat's a-rockin' …"

Then Sutherland felt the boat shift hard to port and heard Sharon shout, "Hey! What are you doing? Ohhh."

The sound of scuffing feet was followed by a thud and the muffled voices of men speaking Spanish. Aguilar's men again? Who else? And nowhere to hide.

"Señor Sutherland?" a man shouted. "We know you are in there."

Sutherland slipped behind the bulkhead, where he couldn't be seen from the salon.

"We just want to talk." A different voice this time.

"I'm calling the police," Sutherland shouted.

Sutherland heard footsteps—leather soles on the deck—and felt the boat's weight shifting again. They were coming down the companionway into the salon.

"How you gonna call, amigo? Your phone is on the table," the first voice teased.

There was a foredeck hatch over Sutherland's head. If he was quick enough, he could open it, climb out to the foredeck, and jump on the dock before they knew he was gone. He edged away from the bulkhead and had one hand on the overhead hatch's handle when the man said, "Come out now, or we come in. We have guns and will use them."

No time to escape. Sutherland had left Baskin's semiautomatic in his hotel-room safe. He scanned the cabin for something to wield as a weapon—an anchor, a chain, anything. Then he saw Baskin's pole spear on the shelf. The five-foot spear had three six-inch barbed prongs meant to penetrate flesh and remain embedded. With the shaft in both hands, Sutherland readied himself beside the cabin door and wondered what his chances were. The door was narrow, and only one man's body would fit through the opening. When the door flew open all the way, Sutherland swung the spear in an arc at the shadow filling the gap, plunging the prongs deep into the man's windpipe. The assailant dropped his pistol, clutched the shaft with both hands, and fell backward, gurgling and sputtering blood. Sutherland sprang and scooped the gun off the cabin sole, and when he looked up, the other man was roughly shoving the dying man aside. Once free of his collapsing companion, the attacker raised his pistol and fired. There was a *pppphht* sound, and Sutherland felt a sharp pain in his shoulder before he pulled off three rounds from the fallen assailant's pistol. He saw a hole appear in the man's cheek, then another in his forehead, and the man crumbled backward. Still in his crouched stance, Sutherland stared for a moment in disbelief at the two bodies sprawled on the salon sole, the first man twitching and gurgling with his hands clenching the shaft. When Sutherland tried to stand, he lost his balance, and his vision began to blur. The last thing he remembered was seeing the dart dangling from his shoulder.

❧

Sutherland spent the night in the Lower Keys Medical Center on Stock Island and awoke in the morning nursing a headache and a general feeling of malaise. He didn't know whether he was being considered a suspected murderer or victim, because there was a sheriff's officer outside his room. He was told that Sharon was in the hospital with a broken nose from a punch, and a concussion from where she'd been bashed in the back of the head. Fortunately, she was recovered enough to corroborate Sutherland's version of events up to the time where the men boarded the boat and attacked her. But it was only after Sutherland convinced the sheriff's department to contact the Chicago police that their attitude improved. Detective Demming recounted the details of the previous assassination attempt that had taken place in Sutherland's apartment and explained how Sutherland had originally become a target: by defending himself against another hit man when Baskin was killed.

"Who were the men I killed?" Sutherland asked the deputy as he was getting dressed to leave.

"Some asswipes from Miami, they tell me. Got sheets going back years. They were seen waiting around your hotel lobby and probably followed you to the boat."

"Any connection to a man named Aguilar?"

"Hell if I know. Talk to the sheriff or those FBI big shots calling and asking all the questions. Pretty soon, we'll be having a Fantasy Fest for feds."

The link with the Aguilar name was one thing. The bigger question on Sutherland's mind was how anyone, especially someone from the Aguilar family, knew that he was in Key West, much less that he would be on Baskin's boat.

Sutherland called a taxi from the hospital lobby and had the driver let him off at the Hyatt. After he returned to his hotel room, he called Kelly on her condo phone.

"I can't believe it," she said breathlessly. "Another attempt to kill you? Are you all right?"

"Yeah. Just a hangover from the tranquilizer dart," Sutherland said. "Sharon wasn't so lucky. They banged her up pretty bad, but she'll live."

"And you shot them? You don't even have your gun."

"It was their gun. For a while, the deputies wouldn't allow me to leave the hospital. Two men killed, a woman injured, and I'm in the center of it. Didn't matter that I had a tranquilizer dart hanging from my shoulder."

"Any proof of who sent the hit men?"

"They're checking their phones and emails, but no connection yet. Same ol' shit."

"And you're left out to dry. Two attempts on you, and three dead men trying. You think it's going to stop there?"

"Not likely. And don't forget—someone killed Matt's brother, which indicates that the madman behind this goes after people close to his primary targets. That puts you in the crosshairs too. Have you considered that? We're both vulnerable, and no one seems to give a damn. It's up to us if we're going to live to see our next birthdays. My fortieth is coming up."

"We could always disappear. Any ideas on where?"

"Right here wouldn't be bad," he said as he glanced out of his open balcony door at the swaying palms. "End of January and seventy-five degrees today. Never again would I ruin a pair of expensive shoes stepping into a slush puddle. Hell, I wouldn't even need shoes."

"Can't disappear there now. Someone knows where you are."

"And that's the thing that bothers me. The only people who should have known I was down here and on Sam's boat were you, Sharon, and, I suppose, her husband. So how did two badasses from Miami know where to find me?"

"No one else knew?" Kelly said.

"Unless you said something."

"I'm trying to think ..." she said tentatively.

"Who?"

"I remember now," she blurted. "Doc Castillo asked me how you were doing. I said you went out of town, but not to Key West or even Florida."

"You're sure?"

"Yes, I'm sure," she snapped. "Because he pressed me. Just out of town, I said. I don't trust anyone in this company anymore."

"OK, OK. Don't get mad. This is serious. Someone knew. We already have enough conspiracies to write a spy novel."

Seconds of silence passed between them before Kelly spoke again. "I'll give you another conspiracy to think about. After the bomb, I used the phone at the building lobby security desk while the guard was clearing the building."

"So?"

"That's when I called you in Key West to tell you I was OK. What if?"

"Anybody could have made that call," he said.

"Nope. It's a special line. For security, I had to enter my ID," she said. "From that call, you'd know the city, hotel, even the room number. Voilà!"

"Someone's monitoring your company's phones?" he said. "Jesus, this gets more sinister by the hour."

The explosion that killed Clark Kirkland and Jim Ridgeway had made the executive garage and several floors above it temporarily unusable. The next day, the police were still sorting through debris for evidence, and engineers had been called in to assess the structural integrity of that wing of the building. Given the turmoil, the board had ordered employees of Kelly's section to take time off until further notice. Kelly stayed in her apartment trying to settle her troubled thoughts. The world she'd thought she knew was gone, and it seemed that havoc reigned. Sam Baskin, Clark Kirkland, and Jim Ridgeway were dead. Her closest friend and lover had been attacked and was still in jeopardy. Unnamed and covert forces were working to keep secrets. And in the last few days, she had killed a man, and Sutherland had killed three.

Unable to relax, she paced around her apartment, did her laundry, cleaned the kitchen, vacuumed the living room, and washed her windows. But the distractions were in vain. She couldn't ignore the irrefutable fact that the source of her upturned world was Baskin's investigation and that she possessed the product of that research. She had still only scratched the surface of the contents of the flash drive Baskin had given Sutherland. It was evident to both her and Sutherland that there was a cover-up and the government was involved. Otherwise, she could have given the feds Baskin's files and relied on them to seek justice. Failing that option, and in light of the latest deaths, she knew it was up to her and Sutherland.

She dug out the drive from its hiding place, plugged it in, and began where she'd left off. Two hours into her scanning, she uncovered a file labeled "Department of Defense" and learned that Ridgeway was the company's liaison for products used by the military. Many of the drugs involved had code names without their chemical designations, identified opaquely as Antibiotic XYZ and Vaccine ABC. No mention was made of the FDA's involvement, and Kelly assumed that was because the medications were still experimental. It seemed the program was an expedient approach to provide treatments that wouldn't be available if the government had to wait for its own imposed FDA regulations. In another agreement between the Department of Defense and Lawrence, the company was released of liability in the event of adverse effects of the products the military used. That provided a shield for Lawrence, but it was also a license to be careless and irresponsible—a scary prospect considering that lives were at stake.

Kelly had heard about vaccines and other treatments in the past being tested on prisoners and people who didn't know they were part of experiments. She'd also learned of the unscrupulous practice in which unknowing victims were intentionally given diseases to test aspirant cures and treatments. But she believed that the practice had been vehemently and universally discredited and outlawed years earlier. Yet here in black and white was a secret program to supply unapproved medications to military personnel.

The documents showed that the Department of Defense program included arrangements with Veterans Affairs, the Pentagon, and a string of military hospitals. If products in the program were effective, they would be given a brand name, receive FDA approval, and be made available to the general public. But burrowing deeper into Ridgeway's files, Kelly found the negative side to the pre-FDA arrangement. Two schizophrenia treatments and a vaccine for dengue fever had been withdrawn as a result of poor results, including several deaths. Success or failure seemed to be a crapshoot, and the unknowing victims were sick or injured military personnel.

Kelly knew she had only part of the picture. Ridgeway was the liaison with the Department of Defense, and since she had never heard of this program, she doubted that Ridgeway would have opened up about it. But he was dead. Everyone had been sent home immediately after the blast, and now his office and all the other offices in the wing were vacant. What was she waiting for?

⁂

It took only twenty-five minutes in sparse traffic on the Kennedy and Edens Expressways for Kelly to drive to Lawrence Laboratories' headquarters campus. It was nearly midnight when she parked in front of the main entrance and entered the lobby. She normally would have parked in the executive garage, but the bomb had made the area unusable, and the police had declared it a crime scene. She walked to the security officer's front desk, where she entered her ID code into the digital pad and placed her fingertips on the glass scanner. A light blinked, and the word *PASS* appeared on the screen.

"The executive wing is off-limits, Miss Matthews," the security guard said as he read her clearance information on his own screen. "There's structural damage, and the engineers haven't OK'd it."

"I know," she said. "I won't be going there. I left some papers with the graphics department that I need for a meeting downtown tomorrow. Only be a few minutes."

She took the elevator to the second floor, where the graphics office was located, climbed the staircase to the third floor, and hurried down the corridor to the executive offices. Then she ducked under the yellow tape past the nonfunctioning security pad and through the unlocked door to the offices. Ridgeway's door hadn't been locked after the bomb blast, and she entered using her iPhone light to survey the space. The explosion had knocked books and mementos off the shelves and framed photos and certificates off the walls. Wasting no time, she focused on the file cabinets and was thankful that no one had locked them after the explosion.

She filled her big law briefcase with every hanging folder that looked promising, including those labeled Department of Defense, BioVexis, and el Centro. Satisfied that she had what she needed, Kelly swept her light over Ridgeway's desk and saw his open laptop. She touched the keys, and the screen sprang to life. Pleased with her luck and preparation, she dug a flash drive out of her pocket and plugged it into the USB slot. Following the instructions she had obtained from Fadi, she downloaded Ridgeway's email files, slipped the flash drive into her pocket, and left the floor and the building the same way she had come in.

In a lounge chair on the Sandy Shores Hotel pool deck, Matt Kirkland pulled up another day's issue of the *Chicago Tribune* on his laptop. He was interested in learning of any discovered links between Clark's death and Aguilar. Instead, he was stunned to find the posthumous publication of the excoriating material Clark had sent the newspaper about Matt's psychopathic history. It was titled "Murder in His Blood," and it was crowned by Clark's newly acquired evidence that Matt had murdered their parents for the insurance money.

Matt barely breathed as he skimmed the piece the first time. When he finished, he banged the laptop closed and raised it over his head, ready to pitch it into the pool. He stopped at the last moment and took a deep breath before opening the laptop and reading the article again. This time, a humiliating burn ran through him as he fumed at the words that exposed him as a monster. Then, after pausing to calm himself, he read it once more, gradually smiling as he exhaled a soft chortle. *It doesn't fucking matter*, he thought coolly to himself. *None of it.* He was already a wanted man, and nothing in Clark's disclosures could make it worse. It was regrettable that Clark had to learn about the arson before he died, but it was not as tragic as the fact that his death had been caused by Matt's last attempt to help him after so many years. It was intended to be Matt's final way to pay Clark back for his long-sustained silence about that bloody day at the summer camp—Matt's first murder.

Matt's gunshot injury had thwarted his original scheme of ambushing the Aguilars and their bodyguards as they arrived in their mansion. The approach would have worked only if he was lying in wait to surprise them, because if Aguilar, Renata, and the guards were already there, they could have barricaded themselves in one of the rooms and returned fire.

His best alternative now was to wait for Aguilar's next excursion on his yacht, where his defenses would be down. Rafael, Aguilar's alienated son, might provide the timing of that event if it suited him. But since it was known that Matt was responsible for the death of Rafael's son, Rodolfo, the question was whether Rafael's loathing for his own father would outweigh his understandable antipathy toward Matt. The only way to find out was to ask.

Matt had met Rafael Aguilar several times before the man's estrangement from his family, and Matt had run into him once since Rafael had established a new hedge fund in Boulder, Colorado. Matt looked up the number, placed the call, gave his name, and asked to speak with to Rafael.

A moment later, Rafael came on the line and said, "Aren't you worried that this call might be traced?"

"Not a problem," Matt said.

"My father once said you were smart. But now everyone knows you killed the reporter. You got shot and left your DNA, so not very clever, Matt."

"Yeah. A fluke. A wild card."

"A wild card that killed my son. Saved you the trouble."

"He was sent to kill me—you must know that," Matt said, still wondering whether Rafael would help.

"And that's why you called, I'll wager. Because my father's not going to give up."

"A year after you left your father's business and we met in Boulder, you implied you still had inside knowledge about what he was up to. Is it your sister?"

"Not Renata. She's as despicable as my father," Rafael said. "No, my little birdie is Margarita. Maybe you met her on one of your visits."

"Latina woman. Kind of a servant?"

"More like a slave, but that's her. Despises my father and my sister— and with good reason. I chat with her from time to time."

"Will she know when Paolo is planning one of his adventures on the yacht?"

"Ah, so that's what's on your mind," Rafael said, seemingly intrigued. "She'll know. They don't even realize Margarita's there half the time."

"So here's the key question: Do you despise your father more than me?"

Rafael paused for several seconds before answering. "My father is an odious man. A murderer, a rapist, a sadist, a pedophile, racketeer, and a corrupter of everyone and everything he touches. He corrupted my son from the very beginning. Taught him to be like him—to hate, to cheat, to steal, to kill," Rafael said. "He's responsible for Rodolfo's death, not you or your wild card Sutherland. Rodolfo was already dead to me. Does that answer your question?"

"Loud and clear," Matt said.

"I'll let you know when the time's right. It will take place on his yacht, as it usually does. This time, I was told it will be in Key West."

"I can be there in a few days."

"Shouldn't take that long. You're in Nassau," Rafael said.

Matt flinched as if he'd been slapped. "Ah, how—"

"You've been spotted," Rafael said. "The casino. A careful man would've known better."

"Shit," Matt said as he jumped up and quickly scanned the pool deck, thinking he could already be in someone's crosshairs.

"One more thing," Rafael said. "When you came to Boulder to see me that time, I already had been warned that it wasn't really for a peace offering and truce. He sent you to kill me, and I had already taken serious precautions. So what happened? I know you don't have a conscience."

"I got a call from Renata at the last minute. Told me it was off. Go figure."

"Yeah. Go figure," Rafael said. "We'll never know how that would have turned out."

A moment after Rafael disconnected, Matt called the front desk, told the clerk he was checking out, and asked her to prepare his bill. He knew that Aguilar had connections everywhere and would be notified immediately of Matt's appearance at the casino. And after taking part in hunting down and killing other deserters from Aguilar's world, Matt knew that Aguilar wouldn't waste time sending his henchmen after him. He stuffed a few articles of clothing, cash, his laptop, his semiautomatic, and toilet accessories into his backpack and left for the maids what didn't fit from his suitcase. As an afterthought, he added Baskin's laptop, thinking he could extort Lawrence Laboratories with what it contained at some point. After paying his bill with cash, he headed to the pool bar to have a drink while he decided on his next move.

He was roused from his thoughts when he felt the presence of someone standing next to him at the bar and then heard someone whisper his new assumed name. "Hey, Greg."

He turned toward the voice and squinted at a man silhouetted against the tropical sun. It took several seconds for him to recognize Raymond, a blackjack dealer at the Atlantis Casino. In shorts and a singlet, he seemed out of place, because Matt had last seen him dressed in a tux at the blackjack table. The night before, Matt had won a few thousand dollars and tipped Raymond with a stack of chips.

"This really where you stay?" Raymond asked as he looked around the run-down bar, frowning in disapproval. "Couldn't find a nicer place?"

"It's OK. Want a drink?"

"I gotta work later. Rules."

"Sit down. You look like you got something to tell me."

Raymond was from Liverpool, England, a detail Matt had learned from periodic chats while the cards were shuffled. He'd been in the Bahamas for ten years, a dealer for four. He spent his evenings in the casino and, from the look of his dark tan, his afternoons lying in the sun. His hair was bleached almost white, and the tattoos on his arms and legs were barely readable against the dark skin. A new tat on his shoulder was still red and swollen: "Raymond Rocks."

"You got a problem, man," Raymond said, taking a seat on an adjacent stool. "Some guys are looking for you."

"What guys?" Matt said, already imagining Aguilar sneaking up behind him.

"Two from Miami. Thought you were staying at the Atlantis hotel, but when they found out you weren't there, they started asking around. Came to see me this morning on the beach, knew you were at my table last night. Slick guys. Puerto Ricans or something."

"What did they want?" Matt said, waving at the bartender, signaling for another drink.

"Called you by a different name but described you right down to the beard and shaved head. Wanted to know where you stayed. I told them I didn't know, which I didn't. Offered to pay me a couple hundred if I found out for them."

"And you said?"

"Said I'd do what I could, just to get rid of them. But they won't give up easy. Said they'd meet me on the beach before my shift tonight."

"And how did you find me?"

"I know the blonde next to you at the table. The one you were hitting on. She told me where you were staying."

"My luck. She never showed up," Matt said. "Anyway, these guys give a reason?"

"Friends of yours, they said, but neither of us believe that."

No doubt they were Aguilar's men. And they'd keep looking until they found him. Matt realized he'd been stupid and careless. He'd told himself that a few hours couldn't hurt. Just a few hands and a few throws—what would be the harm? Yet Aguilar had gambling connections all over the world, and even though he had changed his appearance somewhat, it was impossible to hide his size.

"They offered you a couple hundred to find me?" Matt asked. "Not very generous of them."

"That's what I thought," Raymond said, lighting a cigarette with a Zippo. "You, on the other hand …"

"Would be much more generous." After all, Raymond had seen what stakes Matt played for and how much he'd won. "What do you say I give you five hundred?"

"That's more like it," Raymond said, his eyes half-open, calculating. "But this is serious business we're talking about, Greg. These guys …"

"You're saying it's more like a grand? That what you're saying, Raymond?"

"That would be about right."

"Do you know where they're staying?"

"I think they're sleeping on their boat in the Atlantis Marina. Figured you'd be near the casino."

"I know that marina. The boat I arrived on dropped me off there." He rattled the ice in his glass while he contemplated his next move. Undecided, he scribbled a phone number on a bar napkin and handed it to Raymond. "Here's what I need you to do. Tell them you talked to this hotel and that I checked out, which is true. Call me on this number, and we'll pick a place to meet. I'll have the cash ready."

"Hey, I just figured it out," Raymond said and grinned. "Why you're living in this dump. Guys looking for you … a low profile, right?"

"You're a genius, Raymond."

❧

140

The sun was about to set, and the beach was deserted except for a barefoot couple strolling at the water's edge while their black Labrador frolicked through the surf. The tide was out, and the waves moved in and out lazily, lapping and sucking at the wet sand. A wave smacked against an isolated rock, and the Lab barked and snapped her jaws at the spray. Her masters called, and she raced to them and sent them retreating when she shook off the seawater.

After walking by her masters' sides for a while, the Lab ran off again and scouted out the shoreline ahead, sniffing at seaweed, sun-bleached logs, boulders, plastic bottles, a detached mooring buoy, stray fishing line, and then crabs. For the next few minutes, the Lab gamboled around in a frenzy, bounding after and missing one scurrying crustacean, then whirling around and chasing another of the dozens that had left their holes, only to disappear when they sensed the barking monster descending on them. When her amused masters finally called, she trotted over and lay down at their feet, panting.

"Good girl," the woman said, squatting to pet the animal's wet head. "Now take it easy."

The couple continued along the water, now and then letting the approaching wave wash over their ankles. The Lab roamed higher up on the sand near the line of coconut palms, smelling and nuzzling the ground, digging, then taking off again. Suddenly, she stopped about ten feet in front of a mound, as if on a point during a bird hunt. The Lab crouched and started to growl, then got up and circled to the other side and growled again.

"What is it, girl?" the man asked as the couple approached.

"Something alive," the woman said. "Look at it."

"Crabs," the man said, pulling a flashlight from his pocket. "Swarming over something, probably a dead bird or turtle. Come here, girl. Get away from that."

"Wait!" the woman said. "For heaven's sake, be careful."

The man turned on the flashlight and inched closer, the dog barking at the mound of rapacious crabs. As he shined the light on the teeming mass, he had to turn away and fight back a need to retch. "Oh Jesus," he said.

"What is it?"

He gathered himself, turned to face the animated mass again, and took a few steps closer while swallowing back the rising bile. In the halo from his flashlight, he could clearly see what was under the ravaging scavengers—the empty eye sockets and gaping mouth of a blond-haired man in a bathing suit. A tattoo on his right shoulder read "Raymond Rocks," and the garrote around his neck looked like fishing line.

It was getting dark, and three hours had passed since Matt had spoken to Raymond. The fact that he hadn't called was a bad sign—ominous for Matt, probably much worse for Raymond. If they'd gotten the truth out of Raymond, which was what Matt suspected, he didn't have much time. Finding another hotel on the island would only delay the inevitable, and if Aguilar's men couldn't find him right away, they might engage the local police. After all, Matt was a wanted fugitive.

Matt believed that humankind consisted of two types: sheep and wolves. After paying for his drinks, he boarded a taxi for the marina at Atlantis Paradise Island. All his life, Matt had been the wolf.

CHAPTER 15

Matt was familiar with Nassau's Atlantis Marina layout from the night he'd arrived by boat. He didn't know where Aguilar's boat was located, so he waited in the evening shadows by one of the gates. His patience paid off when he recognized a man adjusting one of the spring lines on a fifty-foot Sea Ray powerboat. Matt had seen the same muscular, dark-haired man on Aguilar's yacht in Miami years earlier. A moment later, another man appeared in the cockpit and caught up with the first man as he walked toward shore. Both men wore tight T-shirts and jeans, meaning they weren't carrying. If they'd come to the Bahamas armed, which was surely the case, the weapons were hidden on the boat.

Raymond had said that there were two men, so Matt figured the boat should be vacant, affording him the opportunity to board. Fortunately, the gate combination hadn't changed since Matt's arrival days earlier, and there was no one on board the yacht on either side of Aguilar's boat. Boarding, he noted that the aft swim platform held a strapped-in Jet Ski, and the absence of outboard engines meant that inboards provided the power.

From the cockpit, Matt climbed through the unlocked hatch to the salon below. In the semidarkness, with the light from his phone, he slipped into the dark forward stateroom and prepared to wait, his suppressed Beretta nine-millimeter resting on his lap.

An hour passed before he heard murmured voices speaking Spanish approaching, and he readied himself behind the bulkhead that separated the salon from the forward stateroom. The boat shifted with the weight of the men coming aboard, and one shouted to someone else on the dock.

"Dame tu maleta," the man said curtly. "Apúrate. Tenemos prisa."

Now there were three men Matt had to take out.

The man Matt had recognized stepped into the salon from the cockpit, went to the chart table, and flicked on the salon lights. After the other two were in the salon, the first man held up a dart gun and said, "Mira. Un tranquilizante. Un tiro y el cabrón estaría inconciente. Entonces, llevámoslo a Miami."

"Donde espera don Paolo," the third man replied with a cruel laugh.

Matt understood enough Spanish to know that they intended to tranquilize him and take him to Miami. It would be a long, cruel execution, like the one Matt had witnessed years earlier. All three stood in the salon within fifteen feet of Matt, oblivious to his presence in the dark. It had to be clean and fast to avoid any noise. The suppressor on the semiautomatic would stifle most of the gunshot noise, but he was worried about shouts or cries.

The newest arrival looked around the cabin and asked, "¿Dónde están las pistolas?"

"En la proa," the first man said, turning and pointing to the bow. The surprise on his face at seeing Matt lasted only an instant before it was wiped away with a shot in his left eye. With two more head shots, the other two dropped like gallery props, and only one man managed a truncated groan. Matt stepped out of the forward cabin and surveyed his work. So much for Aguilar's Shanghai attempt.

Matt stood in the boat's salon, the three dead would-be assailants sprawled like potato sacks on the cabin sole smelling of shit and urine. He held his breath and rummaged through their pockets retrieving wallets, keys, and phones. He stuffed the cash into his backpack and found the boat keys.

After firing up the Sea Ray's engines, Matt cast off the mooring lines, slipped out of the marina, and was safely away before opening the throttle wide on the boat's twin diesel inboards. Eyes glued to the GPS and radar, he made good time around Andros Island and was well past Bimini before he hit the Gulf Stream and had to slow down. The waves were pitched high and seemingly random, and for another hour, the boat was pounded and tossed around until the Gulf Stream was left behind. By the time he saw the glow of Miami far off to starboard, Matt was able to cruise at speed again. Soon, shore lights from Key Largo and Islamorada appeared, and he slowed to consult the GPS charts. Soundings beyond the reef approached eight hundred feet, an appropriate depth for three dead shitbags. The waves were down to two feet, calm enough for the Jet Ski. He manhandled the machine off the swim platform and into the water, started and idled the motor, and tied it off while he finished his work on board the Sea Ray. He emptied two fuel cans over the dead bodies and throughout the salon and cockpit and down into the engine area and fuel lines. Then he disconnected the propane tank line, opened the valve, and set it next to another full tank. After pulling the Jet Ski close and mounting it, he lit a fuel-soaked rag, threw it into the cockpit, and motored to a safe distance to watch the fireworks.

Straddling the idling Jet Ski, Matt watched the flames spread and grow, lighting up the dark midnight sky. Then the boat's fuel tank ignited, the propane exploded, and it was time to leave. The fire would be seen from Key Largo's shore miles to the north, and soon, boats or even a helicopter would be coming to the rescue. Matt ran parallel to the Keys without lights, aiming for landfall near Islamorada.

It was nearly three in the morning and dark when Matt made out a stretch of white sand between a resort's pier and a patch of mangroves. He idled the machine, let the surf carry it among the mangrove roots, and turned it off. As he'd sped along shore, he'd spotted several rescue boats heading in the direction of the destroyed boat. He doubted anything would be salvageable by the time they arrived.

Dismounting the Jet Ski, he waded along the shallows to the beach. All he had with him was his heavy waterproof backpack holding everything he'd brought from his hotel in Nassau. Every other asset to his name, including his large stash of money, was safely and judiciously distributed in various Caribbean Island banks.

The resort he'd landed on covered acres of prime Atlantic waterfront. He circled the tennis courts, casitas, and tiki bar and found a row of beach-cruiser bicycles on a rack. He grabbed the closest bike and rode past the vacant gate house onto a deserted road. After a half mile, he came to a mature blue-collar neighborhood and found a one-bedroom house with a scruffy littered lawn and advertising flyers lying by the front-porch steps. The windows were shuttered, and the porch screen door was half off its hinges. He parked the bicycle out of sight, kicked open the rear door, and, with a sweep of his phone light, confirmed that the house had been empty for some time. It was unfurnished except for a ratty couch, a wobbly coffee table, and a single bed frame without a mattress.

He sat on the bed frame and dialed a number he hadn't used in months. It rang six times before a sleepy voice answered. "It's three o'clock. Who the fuck is this?"

"Your old buddy Matt. How they hanging, Flaco?"

"*Chingada* …" Flaco mumbled. "You know the whole world's looking for you? What you calling me for?"

"Same as always—business. You never turn that down," Matt said.

"I do when it's too hot. And you are hotter than hot, motherfucker."

"That just means the price goes up, Flaco. I know your game."

"But I ain't in this game, so don't call me again," Flaco said before hanging up.

"Shit," Matt said. He stared at his phone a moment, then redialed. It went into voice mail, and Matt left a message. "Here's the deal, Flaco. I could drop a dime on you with the FBI, letting them know about your warehouse, or I could just stop by and kill you and your family, which you know is not beyond me. But I'd rather do business."

A minute later, Matt's phone rang, and as soon as he picked up, Flaco cried, "Jesus, Matt. This is no way—how many times I fix you up, huh? Now you're threatening me? That's not right."

"Now I got your attention—let's talk business," Matt said. "And cut the chickenshit about being too hot. You got asbestos for hands, man. Your little enterprise made more widows than Capone."

"Fuck you," Flaco said. "Just tell what we're talking."

"Let's start with plastic," Matt said. "Semtex. C-4."

"Oh, maaan," Flaco groaned.

In her apartment and unable to sleep, Kelly Matthews continued with her systematic digging into Sam Baskin's files, determined to find out more about the company's research facilities. Days earlier, Doc Castillo had sidestepped her question about clinics Alpha, Beta, and Gamma. Yet from what she'd learned so far, the problems with BioVexis stemmed from the practices of those very clinics, a belief that made her redouble her efforts to learn more.

A five-year-old memo from a doctor referencing "Alpha" was her first clue. It had been sent to Castillo explaining that the latest Angolan violence and politics were interfering with the clinic's research there. The doctor suggested that the sensitive work of the Angolan clinic be moved to their operations in either the Dominican Republic or Venezuela. From that remark, Kelly speculated that if Alpha was an Angolan clinic, Beta and Gamma could be the Dominican Republic and Venezuela. It was a start, but why these three countries? Why not the United States, Mexico, and Puerto Rico, an island that had hosted pharma labs for years?

While reading through another file, she had to consult her Spanish-English dictionary to verify that ADN in Spanish meant DNA, a discovery that meant el Centro's labs were experimenting with gene sequences. It was clear that el Centro was playing on the threshold of scientific knowledge, and while that was the way progress was achieved, there was always the risk of unintended consequences like BioVexis.

The most troublesome surprise came when Kelly translated a year-old report from the Gamma clinic that documented an experiment where twenty men and five women had been given a new vaccine for a virus that was coded RNV-22, without any description of its origin. Of the small vaccinated population, sixteen contracted the disease, and of those, eleven died. Kelly wondered whether the participants lived in a high-risk area where a new epidemic had suddenly appeared—or had the virus been introduced deliberately? Her question was answered when she read the IDs given to the participants in the trial. They were all given numbers, but rather than designating them as *pacientes* 123, 124, and the like, the report used the terms *presos* and *presas*, meaning they were prisoners. It also meant that they probably hadn't volunteered.

After Matt Kirkland's early-morning phone call with Flaco, ordering his supplies, he spent the rest of the night on the dilapidated couch in the abandoned house. He woke up with a kink in his neck and a sore back and spent fifteen minutes stretching and massaging until he felt close to normal again. It had been two weeks since the doctor had removed the bullet in his side, and after examining the wound, Matt decided it was time to remove the stitches. He'd done it before, and in just a few minutes, he cut them out with the scissors on his Swiss Army knife, leaving a bright red scar to add to his collection. Then he rode his stolen bike to the Overseas Highway, rolled it into a ditch, and made a call to Uber.

Fifteen minutes later, in the back seat of a Subaru heading south, Matt considered everything he needed to succeed in killing Aguilar. His plans revolved around Rafael's promise to advise him of the time and place of Aguilar's next bout of sexual debauchery, a hunger that needed feeding every month or so. Matt was counting on that, and when he looked at his phone, he saw a text and smiled. It was from Rafael, and it was short: "In a few days on *Buena Suerte* in Key West. Be ready. Won't be much notice."

It was all the information Matt needed. He had enough time to take delivery of Flaco's ordnance and finalize his plans for his strike. Having been a guard on previous trips, he knew the layout of *Buena Suerte* and was familiar with where she would anchor off Sunset Key. He just had to decide on a stealthy approach to the yacht by water.

In the meantime, he had the Uber driver drop him off at a motel in Looe Key, twenty-seven miles from Key West. After paying several days advance in cash and downing a hamburger at the bar, he called Flaco with directions for the motel where he wanted his supplies delivered.

Since arriving in Key West, Sutherland hadn't spoken to his office, so he called his assistant to see whether anything needed his attention. When Eileen answered his office phone and heard his voice, she said, "Are you all right? I saw what happened. It was on the news."

"I'm OK. Thanks for asking," he said. "Nothing serious. Just had to spend the night in the hospital."

"It still sounded terrible," she said. "When are you coming in?"

"Not for a few more days. You can hold down the fort. Anything going on?"

"We received an emailed document from your law firm, and I sent it on to your new email address. You should have it in your in-box by now."

"What's in it?" he asked, opening his laptop.

"Stuff about Lawrence Labs. Research for a lawsuit in case they cancel," she said. "Something else—a man named Rafael Aguilar called. It's the same last name as the one I saw in the document I just sent you. Aguilar."

"What did this Rafael guy want?"

"He already knew you weren't in town and wanted a number to reach you. I wasn't going to give him your new cell phone number, so he left his number and said it was in your interest to call."

"He knew I wasn't in Chicago?"

"Before I said a word. He must have read about that attack on you or something. You want his number?"

"Might as well send it. What's one more Aguilar in my life?" he said before hanging up.

After disconnecting, Sutherland sat staring at the handset wondering why Aguilar's name would appear in research his attorneys were doing on Lawrence Laboratories. The only connection between that name and Lawrence that Sutherland could think of was in the verdict Max Petrón had planned to read to Clark Kirkland before he was to be executed. Aguilar's name had also appeared on the statement Max had read to Sutherland, but that judgment was for killing Rodolfo, not for anything to do with Lawrence.

Sutherland began reading his lawyers' report, and his question was answered straightaway. Kelly had told Sutherland that Morrow Partners, a venture capital company, had funded Lawrence's start-up and still held a majority interest in the company. Sutherland's attorneys had also discovered that Morrow Partners was founded by Rafael Aguilar years before Lawrence was capitalized and that Rafael was the son of Paolo Aguilar, the patriarchal head of the family and of Magnífico Enterprises.

Once the connection among Lawrence Laboratories, Morrow Partners, and an Aguilar family member was uncovered, digging deeper became a priority for the attorneys. Sifting through news articles and court records, Sutherland's attorneys learned that the Aguilar family conglomerate Magnífico Enterprises had been involved in a wide range of litigation, both civil and criminal. It was while searching through case summaries that Sutherland's attorneys came upon an article about the conviction of three Magnífico Enterprises executives for blackmail and bribery of Illinois, New Jersey, and Florida politicians. One of the convicted men was an Aguilar family member, but that wasn't the highlight of the trial; the star prosecution witness was Paolo Aguilar's son Rafael. Apparent in the court proceedings was the intense mutual enmity between Rafael and his father, and several acrimonious exchanges between them had resulted in contempt charges against the senior Aguilar.

Rafael's testimony had fractured his relationship with most of the family. After the breach, Rafael left Morrow Partners and moved with his wife to the Rocky Mountain foothills near Boulder, Colorado, where he launched another venture capital company several years later. Sutherland's attorneys believed Rafael could be a way into the Aguilar family secrets, but then they learned that Rafael was the father of three sons. One was a doctor in Boston, another a professor in Los Angeles, and the third and youngest was Rodolfo, the man Sutherland had killed in Baskin's hotel room.

The attorney's research, thorough as it was, didn't shed much light on who was ordering the assassinations. Given the animosity between Rafael and the rest of the family, he could be a valuable source. The question was, Would a man help someone who had killed his son? Sutherland studied the phone number Eileen had given him, took a deep breath, and punched in Rafael's number.

The company receptionist answered, asked his name, and connected him.

"Mr. Sutherland. Returning my call, I presume?" Rafael's tone was gracious. "If you're calling to offer your apologies or condolences, save your breath. Rodolfo was there to murder the reporter. He would have killed you. Don't be sorry."

"I'm not," Sutherland said. "But it's not over."

"I know. I could have warned you about the attack in Key West, but I learned too late and didn't know how to locate you."

"Someone in your family is behind it. Who?"

"If you want the details and who's involved, we can't do it on the phone. You'll need to come to Denver. We can meet at the airport."

Sutherland had been advised to remain in Monroe County until the medical examiner and sheriff had finished their preliminary investigation on the killings. But this invitation was too important to turn down. Finally, he would have a peephole into Aguilar's secretive world.

CHAPTER 16

Baskin's daughter Sharon Pietrazak suffered a concussion from the blows she received on her father's boat. Her husband planned to fly into Key West and make the arrangements to have her flown to Chicago. He'd been in Singapore on business and wouldn't arrive in Florida for another two days, allowing Sutherland enough time to meet with Rafael in Denver before he arrived. He caught a multileg flight to Denver and met Rafael in the Denver International Airport's club room.

Rafael was a well-built, handsome gentleman with thick black hair, a trimmed mustache, and a friendly smile. Sutherland guessed he was in his midfifties and had taken good care of himself. He wore a blue sweater, jeans, and Italian loafers. Sutherland shook his hand and sat across from him in one of the lounge's chairs.

"You've had a rough several weeks," Rafael said. "I've followed it closely. The attempts on your life, and the death of your friend Sam Baskin. How are you holding out?"

"Hanging on," Sutherland said. "Your interest is understandable. It's all about your family."

Rafael shrugged. "Former family. After I blew the whistle and testified against my father and his cohorts, I became persona non grata. That's not a complaint, by the way. I feel a lot cleaner these days. But let's get to why you're here. I didn't want to discuss any of this on the phone because you could be monitored."

"Is your family capable of that?" Sutherland asked.

"They've always had contacts in high government circles, and now I understand they have secret associates that probably tracked you to Florida," Rafael said. "But let's start at the beginning. My guess is that your first impression was that Sam Baskin was murdered for the dirt he'd uncovered in my family's gambling casinos. Am I right?"

"Initially, yeah. Lately, I'm not so sure."

"Your doubts are justified," Rafael said. "In fact, Sam Baskin called me for information a few weeks before he was killed. He had no real interest in the gambling story—only in what was going on in Lawrence Labs. I couldn't help him other than saying Paolo, my father, was very angry about the articles covering the Lawrence investigation."

"No wonder," Sutherland said. "I just learned Morrow Partners was funded with Magnífico's capital, a connection my girlfriend, Lawrence's corporate counsel, wasn't even aware of until now. Then, when you were head of Morrow Partners, you supplied Lawrence with the start-up financing. So your family controls Lawrence."

"You've done your homework," Rafael said. "That relationship isn't known, because Morrow and Magnífico are both private companies. When I ran Morrow Partners, it operated independently, but my old man's part of the business stunk so bad I couldn't help smelling it. Apparently, the stench has now spilled over into Lawrence's activities, and after Sam started writing about it, he was ordered off the story."

"But not to be deterred, he contacted two newspapers and proposed they collaborate. I've already contacted them."

"If you're implying that you have material from Sam's investigation, I'd discreetly give those papers whatever you have and forget it."

"Not going to happen," Sutherland declared firmly. "Those newspapers could be gagged just like the *Tribune*. There's no way I'm seeing Sam's research suppressed."

"It seems pretty personal to you," Rafael said.

"It's Sam's story, a good friend and mentor. What's going on in that company killed him, screwed up my partner's life, is damaging my business, and nearly killed me. Getting that story out can't get any more personal. Just like exacting retribution, a life for a life."

"That may be a bigger ask than publishing Sam's story."

"Then let's be clear," Sutherland said. "The FBI justifies its inaction for the attack on me and Clark Kirkland by saying it's a big family and any Aguilar member could be responsible. That's bullshit. Am I right?"

Rafael nodded. "The only one who pulls the strings is my degenerate old man."

"If you're not on speaking terms with him, who's your source?"

"Margarita. She works as my father's nurse, secretary, and, for all practical purposes, slave. She was an illegal immigrant, and she was pretty much grabbed off the street at nine or ten years old. If she ever tried to escape from my father's clutches, he'd make sure she'd be sent back to Guatemala. She's a clever woman who keeps me informed."

"What else has she told you?" Sutherland asked. "Another attack on me, for example?"

"Not out of the question. And you should be concerned about your girlfriend because her name came up in a conversation," Rafael said. "They'll use her to get to you."

"That makes getting to your father all the more urgent."

"That's where Matt Kirkland may come into the picture," Rafael said. "A few days ago, Matt called me, just like you did. He asked for information about my father's plans. He didn't need to tell me why. He obviously intends to kill him."

"He set up your son to be killed," Sutherland said. "No doubt would have shot him if I hadn't."

"True. But my thinking was this: Both Matt Kirkland and my father are monsters. If Matt goes after my father, I could be sure at least one of them will die."

"When would Matt attempt this?"

"The next time my father indulges in his disgusting pedophilic sickness. Little girls. He pays off the parents through a middleman. But I don't think Matt's arrangements will do you any good," Rafael said. "You've survived a number of my father's attempts, but you have to admit you were lucky. That's not to say I doubt your talents. I spoke to an acquaintance of yours recently, and he gave me an impressive account of your resourcefulness."

"Who was that?"

"Alfonso Rivera," Rafael said. "He and I shared some minor business interests a few years ago, and I had occasion to call him the other day. He sends his regards."

Don Alfonso was a legend and hero in parts of Chicago's Mexican community, but his enterprises sometimes blurred the recognized legal boundaries. He and Sutherland had found themselves on the same side against a brutal smuggling ring several years earlier, and each owed the other for the positive outcome. But Sutherland never liked to be reminded of the resulting body count, or his own narrow escape from joining the list of the dead.

"But here's the bottom line," Rafael said. "Matt Kirkland is a psychopath and a totally amoral animal, as proven by the picture his brother, Clark, recently painted for the newspapers. He's a cold-blooded assassin, pure and simple, and notwithstanding Alfonso Rivera's glowing testimonial, that's the difference between you and Matt. There's a wide moral chasm between self-defense and outright murder. I'm not telling you what to do, but I don't think you're up for that."

"I just want the chance to prove you wrong. Sam's murder will not go unavenged."

"I'll see what I can do. But in the end, it's you who has to live with yourself."

Back in her office, disheveled by the bomb but deemed structurally safe, Kelly locked her door and began scanning through the material she'd copied from Jim Ridgeway's computer. It didn't take long to locate the file she'd been hoping to find. It was labeled "Military Contracts," and it elaborated on what she had read earlier about how Lawrence Laboratories supplied medications and treatments to the military, much of which had not yet been submitted to the FDA for approval. But the more she read, the more troubled she became. She couldn't understand how the program could have been approved by Lawrence or the military in the first place. By circumventing the drug administration, it broke the law. Worse yet, it had caused unnecessary service personnel's deaths, an unpardonable outcome no matter what specious rationale the military might advance.

But her legal and moral antennae got another shock when ten minutes later she opened a folder with the label "Gen. Mitchell" and found several emails using the *.gov* domain suffix. The first email Kelly opened had an attachment with a scanned magazine clipping containing a sensational, paranoid theory that the latest flu strain was a Chinese plot to use biological warfare against American citizens. Kelly had never heard of the magazine or the author, but it was apparent that neither was an accredited source. The author seemed to be a member of some fringe element on the extreme Right or Left. Still, the notion that a nation could develop a new strain of virus or bacteria, inoculate its population and troops against that disease, and then launch an epidemic in enemy territory was hardly new. And as spurious as the given example was, Kelly was disturbed that Ridgeway had seen a reason to save the article. Minutes later, she opened an email from the same *.gov* domain and sender, with an attached newspaper article describing a new outbreak of the Ebola virus that had sprung up in West Africa. The text of that email sent her pulse racing: "Jim, what's the progress with the mutated viruses and vaccines? Just look at what's happening in China now. We're falling behind. How much more time and additional funding is it going to take?"

The email was simply signed with the letter *J.* Maybe Kelly was adding two and two and getting five, but she didn't think so. She immediately thought of Fadi Aziz, who had already performed several favors for her by tracing funds to and from Lawrence's secret accounts. She had a good feeling her new request would be a day at the beach. But after someone had discovered Sutherland's whereabouts in Key West, she didn't trust her phone or office security. She walked down to Fadi's office with the flash drive of Ridgeway's files and found the tech at his desk.

After the two exchanged a few pleasantries, Kelly handed Fadi the flash drive. "I have some new research I'd like you to do. I need the name and office of the sender of an email. Take a look. It's dated two days before Jim Ridgeway died."

Fadi plugged it into his private laptop, and Kelly directed him to the email correspondence she'd just read.

"This one?" Fadi asked. "About mutated viruses?"

"Yes. How long would something like that take?" she asked.

"I can work on it tonight, if that's OK. Good thing you didn't email it, because I think someone's been monitoring our mail lately."

"I was worried about something like that," she said with a sinking feeling.

After Fadi examined the email, his face lit up and he chuckled. "Dot gov. This should be fun. Seeing that Doc Castillo is the recipient of the message, I can use his address to do some phishing."

"I don't want you to get in trouble for this," she said, having a second thought about using him.

"Don't worry. They'll never trace it to me," Fadi said. "Anyway, I won't be staying here much longer. Every day, I'm learning more about what goes on in this place. Call you tomorrow, Miss—I mean Kelly."

Jim Ridgeway's memorial service was held in a large Episcopalian church in Winnetka. The pews were almost full—friends from Ridgeway's church, his graduate school, Lawrence Laboratories, his golf club and the professional societies, and even a small contingent from a military hospital lab where he'd worked before joining Castillo.

After the service, Kelly piled into the wide back seat of the company limo with Castillo and Hugh Trent. It was still early afternoon, and they were headed back to the Lawrence Laboratories campus. Two inches of wet snow had fallen, and the Cadillac hissed down the expressway's passing lane through a cloud of spray and slush. Kelly was steeling herself, knowing she had to confront Castillo about everything she'd learned.

Once Rafael had confirmed to Sutherland that it was his father who had ordered the murders of Baskin and Clark, and that Lawrence Laboratories was indirectly controlled by Aguilar, everything had fallen into place for Kelly. Any claim that Aguilar was guilty of the murders could also be made about Castillo himself. He, like Aguilar, had a lot to lose if Baskin's story was published. Whether his involvement was active or passive, he had to be complicit in Baskin's murder.

In a matter of hours, Castillo would be leaving for a trip to San Juan, Puerto Rico, so Kelly couldn't afford to wait. But she had to be careful because she realized she might be tackling a dangerous man.

"Nice service, don't you think?" Kelly said.

"A big loss for us," Castillo said as he pulled out a cigar and plugged it into his mouth.

"Jim would have liked it," Trent said.

For the next fifteen minutes in the limo, Castillo had nowhere to run. It was Kelly's opportunity, and she wasn't going to miss it. She took a deep breath and began her assault.

"Doc, I've got a problem," she began. "With all the secrets, denials, and evasions I've been faced with, I can't do a proper job as corporate counsel."

"There you go worrying again," Castillo sighed and waved his cigar dismissively.

"Worry doesn't begin to describe it," she said. "It's not enough that we tried to cover up our BioVexis defects, but the research center that developed it is using inhuman practices to test vaccines against virulent viruses. People died. Sam Baskin got wind of all this and was murdered for it."

Castillo scoffed. "Sam could have been killed for a dozen reasons. And as for the tests you're so concerned about, I told you we stopped using that organization. It's over."

Kelly debated whether she should expose the lie, divulge that she'd read an email from el Centro dated several days earlier. She decided against it and instead added it to a long list of his fabrications. "It's over, all right. Over for Baskin. Over for Clark and Jim. But not over for everyone. And have you forgotten that Doug Sutherland was attacked as recently as this week?"

"What does the attack on Doug have to do with us?" Castillo asked defensively. "It was revenge for Doug shooting Sam's killer."

"Exactly. Revenge for the death of Rodolfo Aguilar, grandson of Paolo Aguilar, the man who effectively funded this company and had a lot to lose if Baskin's story got out."

"This has nothing to do with him," Castillo snapped.

"See? That's what I mean—secrets and denials," she said. "Can you deny that Paolo Aguilar capitalized Lawrence and, through Morrow Partners, still controls it?"

Trent, who had been looking back and forth between the two, finally interrupted. "What?" he sputtered.

"Never mind now. We'll finish this discussion in my office," Castillo huffed. "Enough!"

When Castillo's limo arrived at Lawrence's headquarters building, the driver dropped Castillo, Kelly, and Trent under the entrance portico. The three of them took the elevator to the top floor and walked down the corridor to Castillo's office without saying a word. Inside the office, the effects of the car bomb were everywhere; the window blinds were askew, Castillo's framed photos and certificates lay broken and piled in the corner, and books from the shelves were stacked on the table.

Castillo eased behind his desk and began to pile folders and papers into his briefcase. Kelly and Trent took off their coats and sat on the facing guest chairs.

"As I was saying in the car," Kelly said, "Paolo Aguilar's company financed Morrow Partners twenty-some years ago, and Morrow is still our major stockholder. That means Paolo Aguilar is the ultimate boss of Lawrence Labs."

Castillo tried to appear calm, but the venom in his voice couldn't hide his anger. "Whatever you're doing, it is far beyond your authority. Do you hear me? Stop it right now, or ... or—"

"Sam Baskin had all the background on the BioVexis cover-up," Kelly said, "and he also found damaging evidence on the secret clinics—the ones using dangerous and unethical practices that often ended with fatalities. As a stakeholder in Morrow, and therefore of Lawrence, Paolo Aguilar had plenty of reason to silence Baskin. As did you."

"That's insulting and libelous. You have no evidence of that," Castillo said defiantly. "We're well-respected citizens. We have many friends in the government. They'd laugh at these speculations."

"Ah, yes, the government. Like our arrangement with the Department of Defense, providing experimental medicine to the military, exposing servicepeople to the same fatal complications as BioVexis did. I read the reports—a number died. The DOD preferred that el Centro do the politically dangerous and unethical work while allowing Uncle Sam to appear squeaky clean."

"You're making it sound dirty and illegal," Castillo said. "We're doing good work. These drugs are curing our military personnel. FDA approval takes years, and some injuries and diseases won't wait."

"Does that explain why el Centro is testing the effects of viral mutations on humans? And don't give me that crap that we're not using el Centro anymore. I've seen Jim Ridgeway's latest emails."

Trent was speechless watching Kelly confront Castillo so forcefully. Finally, with a confused expression on his face, he said, "Is this true? I thought this was just about BioVexis."

"Kelly's being hysterical—that's all," Castillo said, glowering at her. "Jim's replacement will be arriving tomorrow and settle all this talk down. I want everyone to give Colonel Lansing their full obedience. Is that clear?"

Kelly had a good mind to resign then and there, but she wasn't finished with the final touches on the story Baskin had unearthed. But as for Colonel Lansing, if they thought she was going to salute, they'd better think again.

❧

Kelly stood and walked out of Castillo's office thinking, *Full obedience? You have to be kidding me. This isn't the fucking army, goddamn it.* She returned to her office and plunked down in her chair with an exasperated groan. Then she noticed that she had a text message. It said that her prescription was ready.

Perplexed, she looked at the sender and saw that it was the private number Fadi had given her, and she hoped it meant he had the information she'd asked for. When she arrived at Fadi's office door, he was slipping his personal laptop into his briefcase. His desk was free of any of the items she'd seen earlier, as if he'd cleared it to leave for the day. She was about to speak, but he put his index finger to his lips and gestured for her to follow.

In the hallway, he turned and said, "They bugged your office. I don't think they did mine, but let's play it safe."

Kelly let out a long sigh. "I was afraid that might be the case. Who could have done that?"

"Not tech services. It had to be our own security department."

"This is so fucking creepy—I should be running for the door."

"That's what I'm doing," he said. "I already thought of leaving after they told me to delete those emails and files. Now I'm definitely quitting. You should too."

"I can't disagree. But you said you got my *prescription*," she said. "So tell me."

"Tougher than I thought. I had to wend my way through some clever diversionary servers to an organization calling itself X-ops, a name that may or may not mean something. Then I used Castillo's email address to do some phishing. A couple of the organization's users bit, and now I have access to pretty much everything."

159

"Fadi, you're a magician. Who are they?"

"I spent hours reading through my downloads, and the best I can tell is that it's a small group of current or former members of the military and intelligence agencies. The person who sent that email to Dr. Ridgeway is John E. Mitchell, who is or was an army major general."

"He's the man interested in el Centro's progress on the development of mutated viruses and vaccines," she said.

"Yeah," he said. "You can guess what for."

"Unfortunately, I can," she said. "What else?"

"It's not just Lawrence Labs they're involved with. They work with all types of companies that provide products or services of a defense or support nature. We're talking chemicals, munitions, medical supplies, surveillance equipment, food, drugs—all kinds of strategic material, collected from companies like Lawrence and secretly shipped all over the world. Sufficient quantities to have an effect, but minor enough to go unnoticed. But bottom line—on a small scale, they're messing with the internal politics of allies and enemies alike, helping to topple or buttress foreign governments."

"I don't think Sam Baskin had any idea," Kelly said, amazed. "His research dealt only with the secret relationship between Lawrence, the Cuban medical centers, and their unethical practices. I don't think he knew anything on what Lawrence had going with the DOD or this X-ops group. He only had the tip of the iceberg."

"It's all in here," Fadi said, handing her a flash drive. "Another function of the organization is to monitor the communication of companies they work with, like Lawrence—an obsessive fear that their operations could be exposed. You'll be interested in the name of the person in charge of the monitoring—Colonel Catherine Lansing."

"That's the person replacing Dr. Ridgeway," Kelly said uneasily.

"That's why I mentioned it. Her center has been tracking phone and internet transmissions in and out of Lawrence and has even gone further, planting bugs in some areas—like yours."

"Are you safe?"

"They'd never follow the route I took or the servers I used. That's all I'll say about it. Anyway, in a few days, I'll be far away."

"I'll be out the door behind you, but keep that to yourself."

Fadi took a deep breath. He looked as if he had something more to say, but he vacillated, uncertain and guilty.

"What is it, Fadi?"

He bit his lip, seemed to muster his courage, and said, "I have a confession to make. I screwed up. I don't want what happened to Ken Wright to happen to you."

"Ken Wright? The scientist who was murdered?"

"Yeah. He asked me to show him how to retrieve controlled files and send them using encryption and compression software. At first, I thought he was involved in corporate espionage, stealing company secrets. But he showed me some of some of emails he was after, and it convinced me he was a conscientious whistleblower sending material to that reporter who also was killed."

"Sam Baskin," she said.

"That's why I was so careful hacking that X-ops organization. They've got technology and tentacles into everything. I'm thinking that Catherine Lansing's group traced those transmissions to Ken Wright."

"And had him killed."

"That's just another reason to get the hell out. She's going to be here soon."

A light on Sergeant Durant's phone console indicated that Colonel Lansing was calling. He punched the button and held his breath. She probably wanted results from the latest phone taps, and he didn't have anything new to report.

"Sargent, what's going on?" Lansing said.

"Everything's quiet, ma'am. Nothing new happening," he said, bracing himself for what might come. You never knew with her.

"Then you better wake up, soldier. Do you know what happened here in the last twenty-four hours?" she demanded.

"No, ma'am," he said, glad to be a few floors away.

"We've been hacked—that's what. And you don't even know about it? The hacker got into everything. Right through the firewalls, identified everyone on the team, got our emails—we don't know what else. You didn't see any of that?"

"Not a thing. How could someone do that?" he asked, seriously puzzled.

"No activity in or out of Lawrence? No unexplained incoming data stream?"

"None, ma'am. Why would it be Lawrence, anyway?" he asked.

"Because that's the center of a major clusterfuck. Now get moving and dig into what's going on in there. Especially what that Matthews woman is up to. I doubt she has the tech savvy for that kind of hacking, but she could be involved. Anything unusual, get back to me right away. I plan to be there personally tomorrow."

CHAPTER 17

The next afternoon, Kelly met with investment bankers to discuss the postponed initial public offering. The mood in the room was very negative, the consensus believing the IPO couldn't go forward until sales improved and the lawsuits were settled. If Kelly had told the bankers everything she had discovered, they would have bolted for the door in fear that their white-shoe reputations would be sullied. The meeting was interrupted when Kelly's assistant, Melinda, knocked on the conference-room door and stuck her head in.

"A Miss Lansing is at the front desk, Kelly," Melinda said. "She claims she works here and asked for you. What do you want me to do?"

"Shit," Kelly said under her breath. She had dreaded dealing with Ridgeway's replacement. Lansing's mission at Lawrence was bound to be nothing more than damage control and suppression of any more news about BioVexis, el Centro, the DOD relationship, and the latest surprise to surface, the X-ops group of shady characters.

"Take her to Human Relations, and have them get through the paperwork," Kelly said. "I'll meet her after my meeting."

"She insisted on seeing you right away," Melinda said. "She was a little pushy, if you don't mind me saying."

"Tell her I'm in a meeting, and take her to HR. After she's through, she can wait in Jim Ridgeway's office for me."

"Is she really working here?" Melinda asked. "Replacing Jim?"

"That's right," Kelly said. "Might as well get used to it."

Twenty minutes later, after the investment bankers left, Kelly walked down the corridor, entered Ridgeway's former office, and got her first look at Catherine Lansing. The colonel had wide green eyes, a button nose, and short blonde hair. Upon seeing Kelly arrive, she stood up and held out her hand. She was at least eight inches shorter than Kelly, maybe five feet one or two.

"Kelly Matthews, I presume. Finally," she said with an acerbic sigh. "I thought I was expected. Didn't Dr. Castillo inform you I was coming?"

Kelly shook her hand and got a whiff of strong soap. "He wasn't very specific about when. Anyway, welcome to Lawrence Laboratories. Did HR finish with all their paperwork? I hope it wasn't too painful."

"In the army, one gets used to paperwork," Lansing said. "Though I hadn't thought it was necessary, considering my background."

"Like the army, we have rules and regulations. Did someone show you around?"

"I don't need a tour. Before you came aboard, I visited two or three times to meet with Jim Ridgeway and Dr. Castillo on different matters. I know the terrain."

"Good," Kelly said, relieved that she didn't have to shepherd her through the offices and labs. "So how do you like to be addressed? Colonel? Catherine, Ms. Lansing?"

"Catherine will work fine. Now I have a question," Lansing said, sitting down and gesturing to the disorder around her on the floor—the books from the shelves and the photos and certificates that had once hung on the wall. "Things are a mess. Are all of Jim Ridgeway's files the way he left them?"

"Obviously, no one's been in to tidy up after the bomb," Kelly said, sidestepping the question. "He didn't have a secretary, just lab assistants, and I don't know how his files were organized. His computer's still there, I see. Tech services can give you his password."

"Doc informs me you seem to be privy to a lot of confidential information. Have you looked through his files?"

"Some of them," Kelly said. "Enough to make alarms go off, truth be told."

Lansing arched her eyebrows. "Alarms? Why?"

"Come on," Kelly said. "Let's be honest with each other. As corporate counsel, I'm more than a little nervous with Lawrence's secret relationship with el Centro and the DOD. Not to mention el Centro's unethical practices and research on viral mutations that could indicate a biological-weapon program. How can I not be alarmed?"

"You're jumping to conclusions," Lansing said. "Biological weapons? *Puh-lease.*"

"You sound like Doc," Kelly said. "He brushes everything off as if everything's peachy."

"With good reason. Because Washington has a lid over everything. State, federal, everyone. Nothing gets out—no government entity will be investigating what went on here. All of us are under the strict constraints of the US secrecy acts. Any leaks would be deemed treason."

"Does Washington's gag order cover disclosures in the class-action suits? We've already been hit with court orders for release of our files. The plaintiffs have barely even begun with the discovery process, and when they do, it's bound to come out."

"My understanding is that Lawrence Laboratories will settle all BioVexis cases before any damaging information is uncovered."

"That would bankrupt this company," Kelly said. "It will be hundreds of millions, possibly more."

"Washington will stand behind anything you and your attorneys negotiate. It's a private corporation, and no one will notice the infusion of government funds necessary to settle the cases. It's all settled. So no more questions. Those are my and your orders. Clear?"

"And Paolo Aguilar with his hit men and secret friends? He gets a pass? Doc too?"

Lansing's eyes flashed with menace. "Doc warned me about your meddling, your insubordination."

Kelly turned to leave. "Forget I asked. I didn't expect an honest response—I haven't gotten one in three months. As for my orders, I'd better take a few days off to let them sink in." And she walked out.

For Dr. Silvio Delgado, a senior microbiologist for el Centro de Ingeniería, Genética, y Biotecnología, sometimes referred to as el Centro, it was to be the first time he would set foot on US soil. He had worked for the Cuban organization for three decades and had often dreamed of this moment. His assignments had allowed him to travel to the center's clinics in the Dominican Republic, Venezuela, and Nicaragua, but it was always on a Cuban flight with strict controls. It was only because of a senior colleague's illness that he had been allowed to join the country's medical and educational delegation for the cultural exchange forum in Miami.

Delgado was one of twenty delegates chosen from university medical schools, the national education hierarchy, the national health service administration, el Centro de Inmunología Molecular, and, in Delgado's case, el Centro. The rest of the visitors were so-called assistants, though in reality they were sent to keep an eye on the participants and their activities.

Delgado's stomach was revolting against his rice-and-beans breakfast in Havana, and his emotions were flying in a dozen directions, bouncing from wild hope to abject fear. The days that loomed before him were rife with potential obstacles, and he knew it could end in either his freedom or death. As a reminder of the dangerous road he was treading, he couldn't stop thinking of the contents of his suitcase—decades of el Centro's secret archives, going back to the era of Dr. Luís Delgado Ortega. The files Silvio Delgado had stolen would give Sam Baskin all the ammunition he needed to expose the corrupt activities of Lawrence Laboratories and his own organization, el Centro de Ingeniería, Genética, y Biotecnología.

He still wasn't certain how he was going to manage to slip away from his Cuban babysitters when he arrived in Miami, a city that was totally foreign to him. Baskin had promised to arrange a diversion that would help him escape, but Delgado hadn't heard anything from the reporter in days. Now it seemed that he was on his own.

☿

After a long run in the snow, Kelly entered her condominium apartment in time to hear her phone ringing. It was a land line, and she had to run across the living room to pick it up. "Hello," she answered.

"Kelly Matthews? It's Barbara Ridgeway, Jim's wife."

Kelly had met Barbara only once, and that was during Ridgeway's memorial service. In the days since, Kelly's impression of Barbara's husband had depreciated considerably.

"I need to talk to you," Barbara said.

"I'm kind of busy, but what did you have in mind?"

"Not just to chat. This is serious. I've been avoiding going through Jim's papers in his office at home, but I needed to find some financial records. So I finally worked up the courage, and I found some things you should see. You *are* the company lawyer, right?"

"As of now," Kelly said. "Things are up in the air here after what happened. What do you have?"

"Reports about vaccines and the field studies in Africa and South America. Lots of medical statistics that I can't understand."

"Neither will I, but I'll send someone over to pick them up."

"But that's not all." She sniffled, and Kelly could hear her blowing her nose. "I'm torn between telling you and being loyal to Jim."

Kelly sat down at her desk. "Tell me."

"It's about that reporter that was killed. Jim had something to do with it. He was in a bar with a man called Matt and another Lawrence executive named Hugh Trent. It's all recorded."

Paolo Aguilar's broad empire, Magnífico Enterprises, was booming, but business success was hardly enough to offset all the bad news he'd been receiving recently. His grandnephew and two of his most trusted men had vanished during their mission to capture Matt Kirkland, and Doug Sutherland had somehow killed two more of Aguilar's men in Key West. Now that Aguilar had demonstrated his reach and determination, Matt was bound to go underground, and Sutherland would make himself scarce as well. Further attempts against either of them would entail employing less-dependable underlings, or calling on X-ops, an act that he would prefer to avoid because it would reveal his organization's recent ineptitude.

One positive note was that Clark Kirkland had been killed by the car bomb Max had installed before his attempt on Sutherland. Aguilar still believed Clark was complicit in Rodolfo's death, and besides, Aguilar believed that if you couldn't strike back directly, you needed to seek retribution through someone close. That principle could apply to more than one adversary. Sutherland's girlfriend was asking too many questions, and several days earlier, Aguilar had asked Renata to look into her life.

"Rita!" Aguilar shouted from his penthouse office.

A moment later, Margarita stepped into the room. "Sí, Tío?"

"Tell Renata I want her reconnaissance on that lawyer at Lawrence Labs. We have to do something."

"You mean Kelly Matthews?" Margarita asked.

Aguilar glowered at her. "How do you know her name, puta?"

"I heard you talking about it," she muttered sheepishly.

"Maybe you hear too much, eh, Rita. Do you hear too much?" he teased. "Maybe Renata will have to cut off your ears. Be careful, puta."

Sutherland realized that since Aguilar knew he was in Key West, he had to move out of his hotel and lose himself. He located a low-key motel and made a reservation under an assumed name. When he was packing to move, he found Baskin's latest journal entry, which was dated two weeks before his death. Sutherland had put it aside to look at later when he'd read Baskin's journal account of Castillo's rescue.

In the entry, Baskin wrote that he'd received a package containing a box of cigars and a note explaining that the sender was an American doctor who preferred to remain anonymous. The doctor had recently visited Havana on a medical exchange, and while there, he'd been asked by a Cuban scientist to forward the package to Baskin at the *Tribune* upon his return to the United States. Under the top layer of cigars, Baskin found a news clipping of his article about Lawrence Laboratories and BioVexis, a slender paperback, and seven pocket-size notebooks chronicling medical experiments. A note from the original sender explained that he'd seen the name el Centro in Baskin's column on Lawrence Labs and thought the reporter seemed to be sincere about getting to the bottom of a conspiracy.

Baskin had the book translated from Spanish and read the history of a Dr. Luís Delgado Ortega within el Centro de Ingeniería, Genética, y Biotecnología, known commonly as el Centro. Dr. Ortega created a unique and gruesome specialty for himself and his team, secretly experimenting on prisoners and other unfortunates of the Cuban state, a supply that never was a problem in the Castro era. When the Cuban military became involved in the war in Angola, prisoners of war were used as guinea pigs for his research on viruses, and Ortega's appalling undertakings earned him the sobriquet Dr. Muerte. For a time, Ortega was one of Castro's heroes, but he fell from favor after one of his purported cures ended the life of a close friend of Raúl Castro. Soon afterward, Dr.

Ortega disappeared, and it was assumed he was either incarcerated or executed.

The notebooks in the package contained entries for experiments on unnamed patients in various clinics, each recording reactions, progress, or regressions that rarely ended in success, and often in death. Many of the charts had been signed by Dr. Ortega.

The sender ended by writing that these old reports documented practices that were still in use today at el Centro and that he would provide Baskin with more information when he found the opportunity.

This unexpected gift of supercharged material was what had convinced Baskin that the story had to come out regardless of how strong the resistance was. So he reached out to David Hurly of the *New York Times* and Francis DeMarco of the *Washington Post* and asked whether they would be willing to pick up the story for their papers. Even though he didn't divulge much of the story's substance, they'd agreed.

Baskin ended his entry by writing that besides validating and expanding on the material he received from Lawrence's whistleblower, the book added a name that he'd seen in Castillo's precious suitcase the day he was rescued: Dr. Luís Delgado Ortega.

"Wow," Sutherland said to himself when he finished reading Baskin's narrative. What a perfect villain Ortega made, a monster following the model of Mengele. No wonder Baskin had wanted to establish him as the first link in a long chain leading to the BioVexis deaths. A monster like that made great copy.

Since Sutherland learned he had Baskin's phone, he'd been charging it every night along with his own. Baskin's daughter had agreed to keep her father's phone and email account open, and Sutherland reviewed the contents regularly, hoping to receive another message from Baskin's anonymous source. After so many days since Baskin's death, Sutherland was surprised and excited to hear Baskin's ringtone.

He dashed across the hotel room and grabbed the iPhone. "Sam Baskin's phone," he announced.

No response. But there was noise in the background, Spanish-speaking people in lively exchanges. Was this Baskin's secret source?

"Mr. Baskin isn't here. No está," Sutherland said.

Still no response—only the murmur of Spanish banter and the clatter of dishes.

"I'm Sam Baskin's friend. Su amigo," Sutherland said. "Tengo malas noticias. Señor Baskin está muerto."

During the silence that followed, Sutherland knew that this was the pivotal moment. If this was the informant and Sutherland couldn't gain his or her confidence, Baskin's story wouldn't be complete. But if this was just a random caller or someone who intended to suppress the story, Sutherland had to tread carefully. He struggled for the Spanish words. "Quiero terminar el trabajo del señor Baskin. Su historia. I want to see his story published."

"You can speak English," the caller said with a slight accent. "What happened to señor Baskin?"

"He was killed by an assassin. Many people don't want his story to come out."

"That's understandable. And who are you?"

"My name is Doug Sutherland. I was a good friend of Sam's. He told me he'd heard from another source of information, but I have to be careful of what I say and who I'm speaking to. Who are you?"

"My name's not important at this stage. How can I trust you, señor?"

"I can prove we were friends. I'll send photos of us together, and you can search his name and see his photo online," Sutherland said, retrieving his own phone and opening it to his photos. "Text or email?" he asked as he flicked through his albums.

"I'm on a pay phone, but there are internet stations in the back of this café. Send your proof to this address, and if I'm convinced, I'll call you back on the same number."

The man gave an email address, and Sutherland sent pictures of him and Baskin on a boat, at a bar, and at a wedding, and then he added a real-time selfie to establish his own identity.

Ten minutes later, when the man called back, he seemed less suspicious but still cautious. "Sorry for the delay," he said. "But one more question. I sent señor Baskin a package. What was in it?"

The question was a great opening. It convinced Sutherland that he was speaking to the authentic source and would prove his own claim to be in Baskin's confidence.

"You sent him a book written in Spanish, along with chronicles of medical experiments," Sutherland said. "He had the book translated, and I have a good idea of its subject. A Dr. Ortega."

After another unresponsive moment, the man said, "What good is my information if señor Baskin is dead? Are you a reporter?"

"Before he died, Sam Baskin contacted two reporters for our largest newspapers. They agreed to publish it. I'll give them Sam's material and add yours to it."

"Your government will try and stop us. My government will as well."

"They won't know until the story is out," Sutherland said, relying on the newspapers' reputation for investigative journalism in the face of government attempts to silence them. "What was the plan for giving your material to Sam Baskin?"

"We were going to meet in Cuba. But unexpectedly, I was sent to Miami for a conference at the Continental Hotel. We were all watched very closely, but I escaped down the freight elevator and out to a loading dock early this morning. They will be searching for me."

"They?" Sutherland asked.

"The Cuban security police who accompanied us here. Probably your security forces too," the man said. "That's why I called. I needed to ask señor Baskin for help."

"I'm a few hours away by car. Where are you now? I'll come and get you."

Sutherland listened carefully to the man's instructions on where and when to meet.

"I have your photo," the caller said. "If you aren't being followed, I'll contact you. This matter is very dangerous, señor. Nos matarán!"

After the man hung up, Sutherland was left mulling over the translation of his last words. "They will kill us."

CHAPTER 18

Sutherland drove Baskin's seven-year-old Buick out of Key West over the Cow Key Channel Bridge and thought about the drive ahead. He'd read that before he reached Miami, there would be forty-two bridges to cross and about 160 miles to traverse. On an expressway, it would be a fast trip, but the only route was the Overseas Highway Route 1, a road that was often only two lanes and that passed through the reduced-speed communities of Sugarloaf, Big Pine, Marathon, Islamorada, and Key Largo.

On an open stretch on Boca Chica Key skirting the US Naval Air Station, Sutherland called David Hurly of the *New York Times*, one of the two journalists Baskin had communicated with about his Lawrence investigation. After Sutherland read Baskin's last journal, he had emailed Hurly on Baskin's behalf without divulging that he had Baskin's research.

"I was sorry about Sam," Hurly said after he learned who was calling. "A great journalist and fine gentleman. What's your connection? Some information?"

"Not just information. I have all of Sam's research on Lawrence Labs. It's dynamite."

For a few moments, there was silence. Then Hurly said, "Who else knows about this? Sam told me he'd been warned off the story by a government agent."

"His editor called him off too. But no one knows I have his files. And there's more material coming from another source. If you promise to publish it, you're welcome to all of it. Sam also offered it to the *Washington Post*."

"But after Sam was killed, we thought the story was dead too. What now? You going to bring us the material?"

"No. You're going to want to interview Sam's other source about the evidence he's providing. For reasons that will become obvious, he can't travel by commercial air. You, or someone you trust, will have to come here for him and his material."

"We can do that," Hurly said.

"Meanwhile, you'll need to form a top-secret team from both your papers to go through everything. You'll want Spanish translators, doctors, and a scientist or two. There's a lot to sort through, and it's not all here yet. Some material is in Chicago, and there's more coming from the source I'm on my way to meet. You're going to need a private plane or a boat to transfer this new source safely out of reach of our government."

"I don't understand," Hurly said.

"Because I'm not giving you the whole story yet. What's to say your paper decides not to publish under government pressure? Don't tell me it couldn't happen."

"It's not out of the question," Hurly said.

"I'd post it all on the internet right away, but it wouldn't have the credibility of your newspapers. But if necessary, I will. I'm not letting anything stop Sam's story from seeing the light of day. That's what he would've wanted. Are we clear?"

"Perfectly," Hurly said. "And this is all about that pharma company? Lawrence?"

"For a start. I'll call you tomorrow. One more thing," Sutherland said. "Regarding the source, you're going to need some good lawyers. Governments will want to shut him up."

"Governments? Was that plural?"

Sutherland drove through Key Largo, passed by Homestead, and left the Overseas Highway, getting onto I-95, heading north to Miami. Well into the city proper, he exited I-95 and headed west on Flagler to the Little Havana Medical Center, where he was to meet Baskin's anonymous source. He parked on a nearby street, intentionally avoiding the parking garage in case he needed a fast getaway. He tucked Baskin's gun in his waistband under his loose tropical shirt and entered the emergency room, a large bright space filled with evidence of the damage a Miami neighborhood could cause in the course of a day. A dozen or so Spanish-speaking men, women, and children sat in wait of attention. Sutherland found a chair in a corner, far from the check-in desk and anyone with a hint of curiosity. It was ten minutes to eight o'clock, the agreed time he was to meet his yet unnamed source.

Trying not to be obvious, Sutherland checked out each of the male faces among him, looking for anyone daring a glance in his direction. Nothing. A half hour passed, and although several more people had entered, no one approached him or gave him a second look. Sutherland began to think that Baskin's source had been caught and his material lost. But he couldn't risk missing his contact if he'd been delayed for some reason.

At a quarter to nine, a heavy man in an ill-fitting suit entered and scanned the room, obviously looking for someone. Then he walked to the check-in desk and had a conversation in Spanish with the admitting nurse. The interchange became heated, and when it ended, the man turned red-faced and walked to the exit. "No está," he barked at a man waiting there. "El café?"

The second man shook his head. "Se fue."

"Bastardo," the burly man said. "Ve a la estación para ver. Yo voy a la iglesia."

Both men rushed out into the night, leaving Sutherland to figure out what to do next. The men were splitting up, one to check a church, the other a station of some sort. It seemed likely that the object of the search was the man Sutherland was to meet, meaning he hadn't been caught.

Sutherland waited another fifteen minutes before deciding that his contact must be hiding somewhere. He phoned the number that the man had called from earlier, and a woman answered, "Raúl's Café. Habla Victoria." That didn't help. Who was he going to ask for? Feeling stymied and frustrated, he walked out of the emergency room wondering where to go. He decided to return to the car and wait, hoping that his contact would call Baskin's phone again.

He was on the side street nearing the car when a man jumped out from behind a parked van a few steps behind him. Sutherland grabbed the handle of Baskin's gun and spun around. Before he could pull the gun, the short man standing there held up his hands.

"Señor Sutherland?"

"That's right. And you?"

"Silvio Delgado," he said. His hair was black with silver flecks, his skin was bronze, and his dark eyes were deep-seated behind black-framed glasses. His sport shirt and pants might have been designer rip-offs.

"And what?" Sutherland asked guardedly.

"You are the friend of señor Baskin, right?"

"That's right. Sam Baskin," Sutherland said. "And so?" Sutherland was being careful, not certain this wasn't a trap.

"I have information for the story," Delgado said.

"What happened? We were supposed to meet," Sutherland said.

"They were waiting outside the hospital."

"OK. My car's this way," Sutherland said, waving for Delgado to follow. "Where is the information?"

"En mi maleta. Sorry, a small suitcase."

Sutherland looked over his shoulder to realize Delgado wasn't carrying anything. "Where's your case?"

"La iglesia. Nuestra Madre de Merced. Under the altar."

Just where Delgado's pursuer was heading. "Why'd you leave it there?"

"I was hiding, and a security man entered. I hid it under the altar and sneaked out the side door."

"Did the man see you do that?" Sutherland asked.

"I don't think so."

"Then it still could be there. Let's go."

After hurrying back to Baskin's parked car, Sutherland opened the rear door and asked Delgado to lie down on the back seat to avoid being spotted. It took only a few minutes to drive to the church where Delgado had hidden his suitcase. Sutherland parked around the corner on a dark street and left Delgado in the rear. The Roman Catholic church was open for confessions, and when Sutherland entered, a few parishioners were waiting in the pews for their turn. He sat in the back and surveyed the interior for the man who'd come to the hospital, but he was nowhere to be seen. The altar was a hundred feet in front at the head of the aisle, with no one near it. Acting as devoutly as he knew how, Sutherland walked to the altar, genuflected and crossed himself cursorily, and waited a moment to sense whether anyone took notice. It was then he saw what he'd missed when he first came in. The overweight man from the emergency room was sitting in one of the choir benches, and he was looking directly at him.

Delgado had said, "They will kill us," and Sutherland figured that the man glaring at him was one of the *they*. Sutherland laid his hand on the handle of the gun, and after an intake of breath, he circled the altar, snatched the suitcase from under the altar, and strode back down the aisle toward the front door.

He was nearly to the door when he heard shoes shuffling on wood and stamping down the choir-section steps. Picking up his pace, he passed through the door and set off at an awkward run, hindered by the weight of the case. The car was forty yards ahead, and when Sutherland looked over his shoulder, he glimpsed his pursuer lumbering at a labored pace. Sutherland reached the car, threw in the case, and sped off without turning on his headlights.

Sutherland turned the corner, turned on his headlights, and drove through Little Havana's streets with Delgado out of sight until they were well out of the Cuban neighborhood. Once on the turnpike, they continued south past Homestead and through Key Largo, then stopped in Tavernier after Sutherland spotted a Vacancy sign at the Rusty Pelican Motel. The ten-unit motel must have been one of the last of its kind on the long ribbon of Keys. Most of the others had been razed and replaced by more upscale accommodations over the last few decades. Sutherland paid cash in advance for a room with twin beds and, after they were settled, ordered a pizza to be delivered.

Animated by the food and his new freedom, Delgado wanted to talk, and Sutherland was happy to listen while he recorded their conversation on his cell phone. Delgado began with a brief autobiography, beginning with his upbringing in the home of a Canadian diplomat in Havana. "My mother was the housekeeper, and I was friends with the attaché's son. That's how I learned English. After I earned my medical degree from the Universidad de la Habana, I was given a position in el Centro de Ingeniería, Genética, y Biotecnología. Over the years, I worked on many research studies involving viral and bacterial diseases, searching for defenses or cures."

"Where did that take place?"

"Our clinics were in Venezuela, the Dominican Republic, and Angola during our involvement in the war there. I was a working doctor and researcher, far from the politics or administrative functions of el Centro. When my projects showed sufficient promise, they were taken out of my hands, and I rarely knew what happened to them. We assumed that there would be further testing, and if the drug or therapeutic was found effective, it would be sold to countries Cuba had friendly relations with. It never occurred to me that the US would be part of that."

Delgado explained that he was later transferred to a section of the CIGB that was doing early research on gene manipulation. They tested on fleas, mice, and monkeys, subjecting them to the actual disease. But he learned more recently that testing on drugs with potential was shifted to an area where humans were used as involuntary test subjects, following the methods of Dr. Ortega.

"You sent Sam Baskin a book about Ortega. Wasn't he called Dr. Death?" Sutherland said.

"Dr. Muerte. And with good reason, though no one ever dared say it," Delgado said. "The author of that book, Benjamín Salvat, disappeared soon after it was printed."

"You knew the author?" Sutherland asked.

"My mother did. They were friends, and Salvat knew that my mother was related to Dr. Ortega. He gave her the copy I sent to Baskin. She had kept it hidden from me. I found it when I cleaned out her room after she died."

"Why'd she hide it?"

"I found out that Luís Ortega is my mother's half brother, an estranged and hostile relationship that must have gone back to my womanizing grandfather. She knew that I worked in the same organization as Ortega, and she must have worried that we'd meet and I'd turn out like him. Anyway, I was new in the CIGB when he was conducting his experiments, and I never did run in to him."

"That explains the book and how you learned about Ortega, but what about the journals you sent Baskin?"

"A few months ago, el Centro was preparing to move our labs to a new facility, and I was assigned to head a team to go through the archives and catalog or destroy them. That's when I uncovered the clinic's journals and charts that documented Dr. Ortega's tests, a program of using Castro's prisoners as unwilling and unsuspecting subjects of these studies. Hundreds, maybe thousands, died. I was horrified. But Ortega was appointed by Castro himself and apparently had his blessing to proceed in whatever way possible to advance Cuba's medical research."

"And it still goes on," Sutherland said.

"Mainly in our satellite clinics. The development of variant viruses, bacteria, vaccines, and antibiotics is done in the center's main labs in Cuba. It's too sophisticated these days for the remote clinics. CIGB is even using CRISPR techniques to alter genes. But all these modern techniques haven't reduced the number of fatalities in the test clinics."

"Let me understand this," Sutherland said. "This has been going on for years, and what? Didn't anyone protest?"

"Señor Sutherland," Delgado said gravely, his eyes darkening. "I had heard about it but only had this proof for a short time. As for others? Do you understand what it's like to live under a dictator—being watched by your neighbors and work colleagues? To fear that if you say or do the wrong thing you may be put in jail or killed and your family will starve or worse. You just don't know …"

"I'm sorry," Sutherland said. "I didn't mean to imply …"

"But now I can do something. My wife died years ago, and as I said, my mother just passed away. I no longer have any family to protect."

"My condolences."

"Thank you. But it's late, and I'm getting tired, so let me finish my story tomorrow."

"One last thing tonight," Sutherland said. "What do you know about el Centro's connection with Lawrence Laboratories?"

"Ah," Delgado said and grinned. "Until recently, nothing. But after conferring with señor Baskin, I unraveled a mystery about that association that will astound everyone. You'll be one of the first to know. But you have to arrange for my safety first."

After Delgado slid into one of the motel room's twin beds and began snoring, Sutherland went outside, circled around the Rusty Pelican Motel's end unit, and sat on a lounge chair by the small swimming pool. The building served as a noise buffer to the Overseas Highway, and the only sounds were the ocean waves lapping the dock and the wind rattling the palm fronds. The air was heavy with the fragrance of flowers—maybe honeysuckle or jasmine, he didn't know. As Sutherland lay there, it was nearly calming enough to forget what he'd been through and had yet to do.

Connecting with Delgado was an encouraging development, but as a defector with sensitive information, Delgado would be the subject of an extensive search. There was nowhere in the United States he could be safe if the government really wanted to find him. There had to be another solution.

❧

Having fallen asleep in the motel pool's lounge chair, Sutherland was awakened when his burner phone rang. It was Kelly, and it was nearly midnight.

"You'll be happy to hear that I'm arriving in Key West tomorrow around five o'clock on American," she said without preamble. "I've arranged to stay at a friend's vacation house that she isn't using. We should be safe there."

"You're finally leaving? Smart girl."

"How could I stay any longer? One thing after another. When we learned that Lawrence was essentially owned by Paolo, the son of a bitch who ordered all the hits, it became clear that Doc had to know and be complicit. Then, in my meeting with Jim Ridgeway's replacement, I was threatened with treason. Finally, Jim's wife called me. She was going through his things and found a tape proving that Jim was involved in arranging Sam's murder. She played a little of it for me, and it sounds like Matt threatened Jim and Hugh Trent into paying two hundred thousand for the hit on Sam. I told her to get a good lawyer and turn over a copy, keeping the original just in case."

"Good advice. I'll pick you up at the airport, and you can meet our new source. A microbiologist from el Centro."

"Great, a Cuban," she said with a groan. "I hope you know we aren't allowing Cubans free entry anymore since the wet-foot, dry-foot policy was revoked. He should have chosen another country to defect to."

"Didn't have a choice. He was attending a conference in Miami," Sutherland said and then paused to consider what Kelly had just said. Another country. What if?

179

"Doug? You still there?" Kelly asked.

"I have an idea," he said, still refining his thoughts. "You went to law school with a Canadian guy who became a diplomat, didn't you?"

"Yes. Didier LeComb," she said. "He's in the Canadian state department now. Ottawa. Why?"

"We're going to need him," Sutherland said. "And when you come tomorrow, don't forget to bring your passport."

Sutherland and Delgado left the motel early the next morning, and on the drive from Tavernier to Key West, Sutherland asked, "How did you learn of Sam Baskin's interest in el Centro and its connection to Lawrence Laboratories? How did you even hear about Lawrence?"

"I first heard of it when a half dozen visitors were escorted through my lab that was conducting genetic research. Everyone was speaking English, and even though the guests were dressed in civilian clothes, the guide addressed one man as General and a woman as Colonel. At one point, the escort said, 'We want to assure Lawrence Laboratories and Washington that we're taking every precaution,' and then he was out of earshot. I'd never heard of Lawrence Laboratories before then, but I assumed it was an American company because of the mention of Washington. When I thought about the incident later, I couldn't come up with an innocuous explanation for the United States having a military interest in Cuba's work in mutated genes."

"Then how did you find Sam Baskin?"

"I used to eat my lunch in a public park near our labs, and someone had left a copy of the *Chicago Tribune* on the bench where I was sitting. I always like to read in English, so I opened it and read Sam Baskin's story about Lawrence Laboratories. The Lawrence name jumped out at me from when I'd heard it mentioned by the guide in the lab, and Baskin wrote about a defective drug that was developed in an entity he labeled el Centro. He wrote that in the next installment he was going to reveal undeniable evidence of a cover-up and the unethical practices used in Lawrence Labs' el Centro.

"Learning that someone with influence was determined to expose el Centro's operations was my inspiration. I realized that Baskin only had part of the picture, and I decided to reach out and give him the pieces he was missing. That's when I met an American doctor in a cultural exchange held in Havana."

"You gave that doctor that package to take back to the States and send to Baskin, right?" Sutherland said. "A cigar box with the book and medical charts in it."

"I could hardly use our mail," Delgado said.

CHAPTER 19

With Paolo Aguilar's wealth, he could afford a yacht of any size and cost. But he never liked being on the water, and he didn't understand why so many people wasted their time living on a rocking boat when they had a perfectly stable and comfortable option on dry land. It had never occurred to him to buy one, and he probably would never have set foot on a boat again if hadn't been for the very bad luck of one of his casino patrons. If Jeremy Watson had stuck to craps, blackjack, or the slots, it likely wouldn't have happened at all. But in one of the casino's private, unlimited-stakes poker games, Jeremy had a rotten string of bad cards and poor judgment, and he put up the title to *Buena Suerte*, a 150-foot yacht, as security. His fortune didn't change, and when he tried to get out of settling the debt, he was visited by Matt Kirkland, who persuaded Jeremy to sign over the title.

Buena Suerte turned out to be a worthwhile acquisition for Magnífico Enterprises. Many of the conglomerate's companies used it for internal and client entertainment, but it began to play a special, personal role for Aguilar as the setting for his periodic carnal indulgences, events that occurred whenever his libido and licentious id beckoned.

Aguilar and Renata were in his penthouse reviewing a few business issues when Margarita knocked on the door and entered. "Tío, you have a message from Washington," she said, passing him a note.

Aguilar snatched the note and quickly scanned it as Margarita scurried from the room.

"What's it say?" Renata asked.

"Nothing important. One of the visiting Cuban delegation in town disappeared," he said, handing her the note.

She read it and said, "Not important? The man is from el Centro."

"A researcher, a scientist. They'll find him, and that's that. Anyway, what would he know that people would listen to?"

"Just the same, it's not good timing. How can you be so unconcerned? Getting careless in your old age, Papi. Like with Matt or sending those bunglers to Key West with a fucking dart gun. Why not just let them shoot the bastard and be done with it? We lost two men because of it."

"Enough! Basta!" he bellowed. "We're not through with him. If you were on top of things, you'd know what he's up to."

"He moved out of his hotel, but the sheriff or local police want him to stay while they finish their investigation of the death of our men. He's in Key West, and we'll find him."

❦

A few hours after Sutherland and Delgado arrived at the motel in Key West, David Hurly of the *New York Times* and Francis DeMarco of the *Washington Post* conferenced together on a call to Sutherland.

Hurly said, "When we spoke last night, you were on the way to meet another of Sam's sources. How'd it go?"

"He's with me now, and he's got a hell of a story to tell," Sutherland said. "Have you talked about what I said last night?"

"A team with Spanish translators and scientists," Hurly said. "We'll get started on that today. Lawyers, OK, but what kind? And regarding the plane or boat, where are we going?"

"If all goes well, Ottawa."

"As in Canada?" DeMarco asked. "You joking?"

"Sam's other source is a Cuban defector with information highly damaging to both the US and Cuba," Sutherland said. "If he's caught in the US, he'll be sent back to Cuba and killed."

"Wait," DeMarco said. "I thought this was a story about the drug company—Lawrence. What's Cuba and our government got to do with it?"

"That, my friends, is what you're going to win a Pulitzer over," Sutherland said. "But first, we've got to see this man safely in Canada."

"Why would Canada take him? This could cause a major diplomatic clusterfuck," DeMarco said.

"First, when Canadian leaders learn about this story, they will be as incensed as you will be and act to protect this man," Sutherland said.

"Second, neither the US nor Cuba knows about his connection to me, Baskin, Lawrence, or your newspapers. Finally, no one in Cuba or the US needs to know he's in Canada. Your story doesn't depend upon his identity or open testimony. It only requires the material he brings, coupled with what Baskin amassed."

"Christ, Doug, this is getting hairier and hairier," Hurly said.

"I'll repeat what I said last night so Francis can hear it firsthand," Sutherland said. "If you don't want the story, I'm going to start posting emails and files on YouTube or some other site."

"All right, all right," Hurly exclaimed. "We're in. What's the next step? Who's going to open Canada's door?"

"That's going to be up to your lawyers, an attorney named Kelly Matthews, and her friend in Canada's state department," Sutherland said. "You can start with Kelly. She's Lawrence Laboratories' corporate counsel and knows the whole story. But you have to call her on this number. It's a burner, just like the one I'm using."

"Jesus," DeMarco said.

Sunset Key is a twenty-seven-acre residential island located about five hundred yards from Key West's waterfront. It was once a fuel depot for the navy until it was developed into a privately owned luxury community. Homes cost millions of dollars, and nightly rentals can reach thousands. Residents and visitors reach the island on a small ferry that runs regular trips back and forth to the dock by the Margaritaville Hotel.

If Sunset Key spells wealth and luxury, Wisteria Island represents squalor and shabbiness. It lies a few hundred yards to the east, is owned by the federal government, and has never been developed. It is supposedly uninhabited, though a walk through the scrubby brush would quickly disprove that notion. It is home to all manner of drifters, fugitives, and homeless people living in makeshift camps without electricity, drinkable water, or bathroom facilities.

Buena Suerte dropped anchor between these two keys in lieu of finding a slip with enough privacy in one of the busy harbors. It had taken the yacht fourteen hours to travel along the keys between Miami to Key West and its anchorage there. Another hundred-plus-foot yacht was anchored off Sunset Key, and further to the east and south of Wisteria Island, a field of several dozen smaller sailboats and motor cruisers tugged at their anchor lines in the light breeze. Owners and passengers living on these boats motored back and forth to Key West in dinghies to buy supplies or seek entertainment. Those residing on *Buena Suerte* traveled on one of the two comfortable launches that were stored in the yacht's aft hold. As soon as the yacht dropped anchor, the captain and two of the crew motored to the main dock to make arrangements for the next several days. Aguilar and Renata remained in Miami occupied with the management of the former's empire via an array of computers and telephone lines. The two were expected to arrive by helicopter some days later.

Matt Kirkland had served as a guard several times over the years of his indentured service to Aguilar and was familiar with the yacht layout and all the usual arrangements. During these dissolute events, most of the crew spent the night onshore. The captain, an armed security guard, and three servants confined to their cabins would remain. After bringing the young guest on board, Renata would also stay and partake in the entertainment. The only difference this time was that the yacht was anchored in Key West waters instead of one of a number of other locations chosen for their privacy.

Matt's biggest challenge would be getting from shore to the anchorage with his dangerous cargo.

Sutherland left Delgado in the motel and picked Kelly up at Key West's airport in Baskin's Buick. After they shared a warm kiss and a hug, Kelly threw her suitcase and ski jacket in the back seat, took off her sweater, removed her boots and socks, and slid into a pair of flip-flops. "Whew, that's better," she said. "By the way, whose car is this?"

"Sam's, but it's in his daughter's married name and shouldn't show up on anyone's radar," he said. "So have you officially quit Lawrence?"

"No. After my meeting with Colonel Lansing, I said I needed a few days off. Doc and Lansing are probably relieved."

"Now the crucial piece," he said. "How did your discussions go with your friend in Canada?"

"Didier said it could start a ferocious pissing contest among the US,

Canada, and Cuba, but after I told him the whole story and added the latest bit about X-ops, I think we're moving forward."

"We better be," Sutherland said. "The newspapers are making plans to move Sam's secret source, the man you're about to meet. His name's Silvio Delgado, and if he can't get to safety, he's not going to cooperate. Meanwhile, what's the address of your friend's house? I want to get Delgado out of that crappy motel."

Kelly said they needed to buy groceries, so Sutherland parked in the Publix shopping-mall lot, and Kelly went in to stock up on the basics. If Delgado had been there, he would have been right at home inside the supermarket. A good percentage of the cashiers, clerks, and food handlers were either from Cuba or descendants of the island's immigrants.

While waiting for Kelly to return, Sutherland's burner phone buzzed.

"That you, Doug? Rafael Aguilar calling."

"It's me. What's the story? Matt Kirkland still planning his attack?"

"Definitely. And now the old man's yacht is in Key West. He plans to arrive by helicopter. His yacht is anchored east of Sunset Key. You can see it from Mallory Square."

"What are his odds?"

"Better than fifty-fifty. Most of the crew and staff are sent ashore while these things go on. There will be an armed guard, the captain, and my sister Renata on board, along with his latest young victim. Matt won't take any prisoners, so it's either him or my father. If Matt's the last one standing, he'll have to get off the yacht by whatever means he arrived. If he's ever going to be vulnerable, it's then."

"And if your father wins?"

"All it takes is one shot, so it's possible. I can't tell you what would happen next," Rafael said. "But if you're planning to be there, the website yachtbuenasuerte.com has all the specs and deck layouts for the yacht."

"Will Margarita, your spy, be on board?"

"I'm going to advise her to go to shore if she can," Rafael said. "Speaking of her, she repeated that Renata and my father have spoken about going after your girl if they can't find you. Renata researched where she lives, works, exercises—you name it."

"Fortunately, she's nowhere near there right now," Sutherland said as he watched Kelly exit Publix carrying two grocery bags.

❧

After picking up Delgado at the motel, Sutherland drove to Kelly's friend's place in a neighborhood called Bahama Village. The home was originally a conch house, a small single-story structure built for the Cuban immigrants who rolled cigars for the Gato Company in the early twentieth century. It had been expanded in the early 1990s, when another bedroom, bathroom, and a small dipping pool were added. Sutherland dropped Kelly and Delgado off with the groceries and parked Baskin's car on a street two blocks away. When he returned to the house, Kelly was in the kitchen putting items into the refrigerator, and Delgado was in the living room.

"Silvio," Sutherland said, "let's have a look at what you brought. We may find something that pushes Ottawa's verdict over the goal line. Lawyers and diplomats aren't known for making quick decisions."

Delgado opened his carry-on suitcase on the coffee table and retrieved a large leather portfolio. "Some of these records precede my time at el Centro—journals and charts for prisoners Ortega used as laboratory rats. They were prisoners, so who cared?"

"You have the actual journals, not copies?" Kelly asked.

"The original paper journals. Later the journals were copied on microfiche, and nowadays the data is digitized. But current records still document that some clinics are following the same practices Ortega devised."

"No controls, placebos, or blind tests," Kelly said.

"That takes too much time," Delgado said. "But let me be clear: I was not involved with any of these human trials. I only experimented on fleas and mice. It was only after I was asked to clean out and organize el Centro's archives in preparation for a relocation that I found out about these atrocities. After my first discovery, I did more digging and eventually stole the material you have here."

"These mutations that el Centro's playing fast and loose with," Kelly said. "Are they virulent? Deadly?"

"That's the problem," Delgado said. "And the scary part. You may never know until it's too late. It could be one small change, a random switch in some DNA or RNA that could cause a global catastrophe. Like in that chaos theory."

"That chaos thing sounds familiar," Sutherland said. "What is it again?"

"The notion that a flap of a butterfly's wings in Brazil could bring about a tornado in Texas," Delgado said. "Who knows what furies gene manipulation could release?"

Kelly groaned in exasperation and said, "Pandora's box. Escape of the Furies. And there's an impatient general who's eager to take control and use those Furies. He's in that secret organization X-ops I told you about."

Sutherland sat with Kelly at the dining-room table reading through Delgado's material when his phone buzzed. It was Hurly. He didn't waste any time.

"We've got a tentative yes," Hurly said. "But there are some conditions."

"As long as we can get our man to safety," Sutherland said as he raised an affirmative thumb to Kelly and Delgado.

"At least wait till you hear them," Hurly said. "The terms include a Canadian newspaper sharing the byline, Canadian intelligence experts in attendance to vet the material and make certain it meets their standards of veracity, and veto power on certain disclosures."

"Just what I was afraid of," Sutherland said. "Now it won't be Uncle Sam that suppresses the story—it'll be Canada?"

"I don't think so," Hurly said. "We want the story to be bulletproof. If they want to double-check some of the technical, political, or historical material, that's all good. They may be better at it than we are. We plan to send a private plane to Marathon's airport to take the defector to Ottawa. Tomorrow night at six o'clock. Can you deliver him?"

"There will be two people. Kelly Matthews is joining him. She knows this stuff better than anyone else alive."

After they disconnected, Kelly gave Sutherland her steely-eyed stare. "Kelly Matthews is joining him? Did I miss the part where I was asked? Why not you?"

"The sheriff department and medical examiner aren't through with their investigation. They may want to see me again. And I did tell you to bring your passport, didn't I? Where did you think you were going? Cuba?"

CHAPTER 20

Agent Donald Radoff lay on his queen bed in his Chicago Marriott hotel room cradling his phone between his cheek and shoulder. He was on hold, waiting for yet another hotel clerk in Key West to answer his inquiry about whether a man named Douglas Sutherland was staying there. Operations had informed Radoff that Sutherland would be remaining in the Keys until the county authorities finished their review of the deaths on Baskin's boat. But now X-ops was in disarray after the entire organization had been hacked and everything was exposed. So for the moment, that left it up to Radoff and his mouthy partner to locate Sutherland if they were to satisfy Paolo Aguilar's lust for revenge and determine what he and the Matthews woman knew about el Centro and X-ops. It also meant that if he couldn't locate Sutherland remotely, he would have to take another trip to Key West. And the fact that he, an agent with over thirty years under his belt, was left to make these calls and chase the man down himself infuriated him.

There was a knock on the door, and Radoff rolled off the bed to let Alex Hernandez in.

"Find him yet, Gramps?" Hernandez asked as he walked over to the minibar and looked inside. After retrieving a can of Budweiser, he popped the top, took a swig, and expelled a loud belch.

Radoff knew that Hernandez's coarse behavior was meant to piss him off, just like the ribbing over missing the kill shot on Baskin's town house steps and insisting that he was over-the-hill at fifty-seven years old. So were the jibes about wearing a suit and tie, pronouncing it a sign of living in the past. The truth was Hernandez had succeeded in baiting him, and it had taken Radoff a great deal of willpower not to show his irritation and to hide any signs of his simmering internal burn. But there was a limit to his tolerance, and Hernandez was approaching that line with each new taunt.

"He's totally disappeared," Radoff said. "His girlfriend too. But because of all the shit flying around X-ops, Lansing has given us the green light for both of them when they're found."

"Finally," Hernandez said. "Lansing's letting us handle it instead of Paolo's fuckups. About time."

"But first we have to learn how they hacked X-ops and where they're hiding Baskin's files," Radoff said.

"And after that, I'll be the trigger. Two clean shots. I don't think you've got the *cojones* anymore."

Radoff allowed the dig to sink in for a moment before resolving himself to what had seemed inevitable ever since he had been hooked up with Hernandez. This story wasn't going to end with just two shots.

Sutherland and Kelly wandered along the Key West Bight's harbor walk, passing the hundreds of cabin cruisers and sailing yachts rocking in their slips. When they reached the Schooner Wharf Bar, they found two stools and ordered draft beers. He hadn't shaved since leaving Chicago, and between the stubble, the baseball cap, sunglasses, shorts, T-shirt, and flip-flops, he doubted anyone would pick him out of a crowd of locals. Topping off his disguise was his permanent sailor's tan, which stood in stark contrast to the pasty legs and sunburned faces of northern visitors. Kelly's features were well concealed by her wide floppy-brimmed hat and her oversize sunglasses. Delgado was content to remain in the house, where he had unlimited access to the internet for the first time in his life.

The restaurant's motif was tropical rustic, and the building was open on two sides, one facing the crowded marina, the other an alley-sized street. That afternoon, a singer sat onstage with a guitar, crooning covers in a deep languid voice.

"What's so special about the island you were staring at?" Kelly asked. "Is that Sunset Key?"

"I was looking at the yacht that was moored to the east of it."

"I saw it. Nice. Planning on buying it, are you?"

"It's Paolo Aguilar's," he said before sipping his beer and bracing for what Kelly would say next. He had debated whether to tell her. "But he's not on it yet. He arrives by helicopter."

"Damn it, Doug," she said, turning on her stool to get in his face. "I thought there was something weird going on when you wanted to risk coming downtown. Now you tell me that the very person looking for you will be here on his fancy boat. What are you not telling me?"

"Matt Kirkland is supposed to come too."

"Great! A convention of people who tried to kill you," she said.

"He's here to kill Aguilar, not me. During one of Paolo's evenings of debauchery."

"Matt's going to shoot him while he's beating off watching porn?" Kelly said mockingly.

"If it happens, one or the other will be dead, anyway."

"Wait a minute," Kelly said. "I'll need something stronger than beer if you're planning what I think you are. That's why you're sending me to Ottawa, isn't it? Get me out of the way."

"Admit it. You'll be more useful to the reporters than I would be. You've been through Ridgeway's files and emails."

"Yeah, I know. And then you've got that convenient 'medical examiner hasn't ruled yet' excuse. Admit it—you're planning something, aren't you?" Her lips were pinched into a determined line, her eyes as hard as emeralds. You didn't win arguments with Kelly—you hoped for a draw. She called it tenacity, and he called it stubbornness, but then the same could be said of him.

"Don't jump to conclusions," he said. "My plan is to let this play out. Until then, I'm not doing a thing."

"You're just saying that so I'll stop worrying. Let me tell you something, mister," she said as she brandished her index finger in his face. "If you do this and get killed, I'll never forgive you."

Although her comment was darkly amusing, he didn't dare smile, because her eyes had suddenly gone misty, and she pulled out a handkerchief and sniffled into it. A few hushed moments later, she gathered herself, took a deep breath, and in a controlled tone said, "You think you're a lone wolf, that it's your life to risk, but you're wrong. Other people are affected— people who care about you and will be hurt."

Sutherland had never found an adequate response for what he termed the "no man is an island" argument she'd just pulled on him. Maybe there wasn't a good answer, because every time she'd employed it before, he'd merely feigned his agreement. But this time, he might have to apply a little more finesse if he wanted to avoid a real donnybrook.

"Look—I promise I won't do anything rash. We don't even know if this comes together at all. But if it does transpire, Rafael calculates that Matt could succeed. If he does, I can live with that."

"What does that mean? You can live with what?"

"With Paolo dead, I won't be on the Aguilar family hit list anymore. Neither will you. I'll settle for that."

"And if Matt doesn't succeed?"

"We're back where we are right now. We either hide in a bunker until the old bastard dies, or we find a way to kill him. I include you in the *we* because he'll come after you to get at me."

"That's what I thought," she sighed.

"It's ironic, in a way. Our fate may lie in the hands of the man who killed Sam and put me and you in Aguilar's crosshairs in the first place. If you believe Rafael, Matt has an even chance. A toss-up."

"I'd never bet my life on those odds," she said, shaking her head firmly.

The wrong side of those same odds had already put Sutherland in the situation he faced with Aguilar. He'd been lucky so far. He wondered how fortune would treat him when he tested that luck the next time.

Back at the house in Bahama Village, Sutherland and Kelly spent the rest of the day comparing Delgado's records to Baskin's to confirm there were no discrepancies. Afterward, Sutherland copied everything digital onto his laptop and flash drives to be hidden in a safe place. He also kept duplicate files and journals in hard-copy form, all to ensure that the truth wouldn't be lost if the newspapers didn't publish the full story.

Before setting off for Marathon to meet the airplane, Sutherland opened a bottle of wine and proposed a toast. "Here's to Sam's story and Dr. Silvio Delgado's future," he said, raising his glass. "Now that we've arranged your safety, Silvio, can you tell us the big surprise?"

"Did you look at the book I sent señor Baskin?" Delgado asked.

"And the page you mentioned to him. It's a grainy black-and-white photo of a couple dozen bearded men in prison garb, lined up in front of a large tent with men in lab coats inside. You're not in it, are you?" Sutherland asked.

"No. I was a new doctor when that was taken. Dr. Ortega was inside, but the critical person is the patient that was leaving. I'll explain it when the time comes. But now I have a question for you. Señor Baskin told me that he was there when Dr. Castillo was rescued from a raft."

"It's true," Sutherland said. "I was there too. Did he give you the details?"

"Just that the other man on the raft died," Delgado said.

"There isn't much more to tell," Sutherland said. "That's the whole story."

"I wonder," Delgado said.

Ten minutes into the trip from Key West to the Marathon airport, Sutherland asked Kelly to turn on the car radio. "Let's get the news," he said. "I'm a little out of touch."

"Nothing but politics," Kelly said. "It's an election year, in case it slipped your mind."

"But there's also that new flu from China they're talking about. *Corona* something—like the beer."

"Yeah. It was on CNN this morning," Kelly said. "The president's saying it isn't a problem, but some doctors believe we should be preparing, whatever that means. They said it's spreading fast in Italy."

"They think it might be from bats, Silvio? Does that seem possible?" Sutherland asked. "Or is it more likely something created in a lab? Like the methods they're using at el Centro?"

"I'm not sure," Delgado said. "In the past, new viral strains came from chickens, birds, and pigs, so why not bats? Then again, with today's technology, you can almost engineer whatever you want."

"Great," Sutherland said with a groan. "Another bunch of egotistic geniuses messing with nature. We're doomed."

The trip from Key West to the Marathon airport took Sutherland an hour in light traffic. While they waited for the private plane to land, Kelly said, "I've never been to Ottawa before. Probably won't see much once we get to work. What are you going to do while we're there?"

"With Sharon laid up, I agreed to work out the details on the sale of the condo and the boat," Sutherland said. "I also may have to see the sheriff again. Don't know what the problem is—clear case of self-defense."

"Self-defense?" Delgado asked from the car's back seat.

"Just a couple dead shitheads," Sutherland said. "Nothing to do with you. Another matter."

"You lead a complicated life, señor," Delgado said.

"That's not the half of it," Kelly said, frowning.

After Sutherland dropped Kelly and Delgado at Marathon's aviation terminal, he drove to Stock Island and the marina where Baskin's boat was docked. Charlie Little was hosing down the deck of his boat a few slips away, and he dropped the hose and sauntered down the dock to Sam's slip. "I heard it was quite a mess the other night," he said. "A deputy told me about it."

"Has anyone else been nosing around?"

"Not since the sheriff and crew left. Quiet."

"Good." Sutherland pulled out his phone from his pocket and showed Charlie a closed-circuit TV image of a visitor taken in Sutherland's office lobby several days earlier. "Is this one of the guys that broke into the boat?"

Charlie studied it for a moment and nodded. "He's the guy in the suit. Is he one of the men you killed?"

"Not him. They were just two lowlifes from Miami," Sutherland said. "I stopped by now to see what I need to fix that broken lock and clean up some things. There may be a boat broker coming around in the next couple days. Sam's daughters approved it."

"Poor Sam," Charlie said, shaking his head. "Did those guys the other night have anything to do with Sam's death?"

"Yeah. They were after me because I killed one of Sam's hit men."

"Killed the hit man? You some kind of cop or something? That's three guys you knocked off."

"Four, if you count the one my girlfriend finished. The problem is they keep coming!" Sutherland shouted as he opened the door and went into the cruiser's salon.

When Sutherland called to confirm the meeting with the sheriff and medical examiner, he was told that the ME's panel had completed the investigation of the deaths on Baskin's boat and no additional testimony was necessary.

Free to make his plans, Sutherland printed out the specifications for *Buena Suerte* from the website Rafael had told him about and spread them on a patio table near the dipping pool. *Buena Suerte* was 150 feet long with two fifteen-foot launches that could be hauled into the stern's lower deck when the yacht was underway. Sutherland studied each deck layout from bow to stern, looking for the best route to reach Aguilar's forward suite which lay directly below the wheelhouse. After fifteen minutes, he had decided on an approach that no one would expect and then measured off the critical distances he had to equip himself for.

In Sutherland's mind, killing Paolo Aguilar was logically, if not legally, an act of self-defense. But as Rafael had said, Sutherland was about to take a leap across the moral chasm from serial survivor to single-minded assassin. He would leave it to chance to decide which of Baskin's killers survived Matt's attack. But he couldn't live with himself if he allowed either one of them to walk away.

He was planning the equipment he needed to buy, when he fell asleep in the lounge chair.

When he opened his eyes, he stared straight up into a cloudless sky speckled with frigate birds and turkey vultures soaring overhead. From the gumbo-limbo tree next to the house, a mockingbird chirped and trilled its random warble. The tropical birds living here were so different from Chicago's winged fauna it was like comparing horses to giraffes. Sutherland's favorites were the pelicans—when they skimmed low over the water or plunged headfirst into the ocean pursuing a snack. In flight, a flock reminded him of war movies in which a fleet of flying fortresses advanced on their targets over Germany.

He realized that these musings were his way of temporarily forgetting the challenges he faced. He rolled off the patio lounge chair and padded in bare feet to the kitchen to make coffee. While the coffee maker gurgled, he finished his mental list of purchases to make before Rafael called with the news of Matt's planned attack.

Sitting at the desk in the Looe Key motel, Matt Kirkland finished his delicate task and leaned forward to double-check each detail of his assembly. The primary circuit went from the battery through the digital clock and arming switch to each of the blasting caps plugged into the stacks of C-4 bricks. A second wire connected a separate arming switch for the vibration sensor. Once the vibration sensor was activated, the bomb would detonate if it was jostled. He knew that arming it would be an indirect act of suicide—his last resort if he found himself cornered.

His sensitive work done, Matt wrapped the heavy package with duct tape and wedged it into a large metal toolbox with holes punched for the leads to the countdown clock and arming switches that he'd taped securely to the top of the box. Now all he had to do was wait until he received word from Rafael, and he would head to Key West for his surprise appointment with Aguilar.

From her small cabin on Aguilar's yacht, Margarita pulled her cell phone from its hiding place and placed a call to Rafael in Boulder. He answered her call immediately, as he usually did. Margarita chose the timing of her calls carefully, fearful that she would be discovered with the phone that Rafael had managed to sneak to her via one of the mansion's gardeners. She wasn't allowed to venture out of the penthouse or mansion alone or have any contact with anyone outside the household.

"Hola, querida," Rafael said after seeing her number pop up on his iPhone. "¿Cómo estás?"

"Como siempre," she said. "Triste y cansada."

"I'm sad too, little one. What is new with you? Have you been to shore?"

"Renata wants me to stay on the boat."

"When is his next arrangement?"

"February ninth," Margarita said. "I don't want to think about it."

"You have to get off the boat. It's going to be dangerous. Matt Kirkland is coming, and there will be shooting. Go on the launch with the other crew."

"Your father won't let me."

"Say you're sick and need a doctor. Go to the emergency room. If you can't do that, hide. There's lots of places on the boat."

"What will happen to me if Matt kills your father? Will I be sent back to Guatemala?"

"You're a grown woman and can do anything you want."

"Without papers?" she said. "No birth certificate, driver's license, or passport?"

"If you like, you can live with my family until we straighten that out."

"I hope that can happen, Tío."

"I do too, querida," he said before disconnecting.

At that moment, Renata opened Margarita's cabin door and flinched when she saw her on the phone. "What's this?" she bellowed. "A cell phone? Who are you talking to?" She charged into the room and snatched the phone from Margarita's hand, shouting into it, "Who is this? Who's on the phone?" She tapped to call the most recently dialed number, but no one answered, and there was no greeting. Furious, she turned and seized Margarita by the hair. "Who was it, bitch? Tell me, or I'll tear your hair out."

Margarita let out a cry, and Renata slapped her hard across the face.

"You tell me who that was, or I'll slice off your tits and use them for shark bait." Her eyes blazed as she pushed Margarita against the bulkhead and slammed her fist into her stomach. "Tell me!"

Margarita doubled over onto the deck, sobbing and gasping for air. Renata kicked her in the ribs and screamed, "Puta, tell me, or I'll make you wish you were dead."

Between gasps, Margarita whimpered, "Uncle Rafael."

Renata knelt down, clutched a handful of hair, and yanked Margarita's head up. "What did you and Uncle Rafael talk about?"

"He was warning me," she sniveled, rubbing her tearing eyes. "He said get off the boat when the rest of the crew leaves."

"Warning you?" Renata said. "Why? What is he up to?"

"Not Uncle Rafael. Matt. He's coming to kill us."

"How does he know?"

"He didn't say. Just that he was coming and it wouldn't be safe."

"Jesus," Renata hissed as she stood and walked to the door carrying the cell phone. "We're not through with this. Stay in this cabin."

Moments later, Renata rushed into Aguilar's office off the yacht's master suite. He was at his desk facing his computer screen, savoring a cigar, and when he faced her, he knew she was agitated. "What's the problem? Nothing about the girl, I hope," he said.

"We have a problem, Papi. Margarita's been speaking to your son on a secret phone."

"Where did she get the phone?"

"What difference does it make? Point is, Rafael just told her that she should get off the boat before the girl gets here because Matt is coming for us."

Aguilar puffed on his cigar and frowned. "How would that fucking traitor know that?"

"How would he know we were even on the boat?" she said. "In Key West? Or that you had plans for that night?"

"It's not hard to figure it out, is it? She has a secret phone. She talks to Rafael, he talks to Matt."

"What are we going to do?" she asked. "Leave Key West?"

"We're here for that hijo de la chingada Sutherland. Our friends will tell us when and where as soon as he's located."

"And the girl? Cancel?"

"No, my dear. Let's welcome Matt. A surprise party." He smiled, drew on his cigar, and blew a smoke ring.

"He'll come armed to the teeth."

"Make it easy for him. Put on two more guards, but hidden, so he can walk right in. We'll set a trap for him on the stairs."

CHAPTER 21

It was early in the evening, and Matt was waiting in his Looe Key motel room when he finally received word from Rafael. The text said that Aguilar planned his next night of debauchery in two days. Matt decided to travel to Key West the next morning, giving him a day and a half to complete his own preparations. In the meantime, Matt was already experiencing the edginess and impatience he frequently felt with the approach of a chancy operation. The restlessness was like a nagging hunger or craving, and over the years, he had found only one way to satisfy it.

Matt strolled a few hundred yards down the highway from his motel on Looe Key to the Boondocks Grille and sat at the bar, checking out the other patrons for likely candidates. Soon, he struck up a conversation with a woman who said her name was Clara Baker. She looked to be about thirty-five and had bleached-blonde hair, a tiny but passable figure, big eyes, and a cunning smile. Clara told him she was a hairstylist from Georgia visiting the Keys for the first time. To save money, she'd been sleeping in her van and using public and hotel bathrooms.

"That's no way to live," Matt said, fantasizing her petite body pounding up and down on his stiff dick. "And here I'm staying all alone in an air-conditioned room with a soft queen bed and a hot shower. Why don't you join me?"

Matt's sidewise glance followed Clara greedily eyeballing the wad of bills he'd produced to pay the check. It didn't surprise him that she agreed to his invitation; he knew the type. He left a big tip on the bar, and the two of them drove back to his motel in her van.

The next morning, it was still dark when Matt left his motel room carrying Clara's naked body wrapped in a sheet. On the drive to Key West, he stopped her van on one of the bridges, and seeing no approaching cars, he dumped her over the rail into the channel. As her shrouded body was swept away with the outbound tide, he felt no remorse. It wasn't that she was a grifter intending to roll him; if it hadn't been her, it would have been someone else. Sometimes you've got an itch that's got to be scratched. He had never needed another reason.

Over the past several days, Sutherland had completed everything he'd promised Sharon Pietrazak he would do. She had returned to Chicago with her husband and was still recovering from the concussion. The real estate broker's agreement for Baskin's condo and the boat broker's contract were finalized and emailed to Chicago for her and her sister's signatures.

Since he'd purchased all the items he would need and was adequately familiar with the yacht's layout, there was nothing for Sutherland to do but wait for Rafael's call. He hadn't spoken to Kelly since dropping her and Delgado at the Marathon airport, so he called her in Ottawa.

"How's it going?" he asked.

"We've taken over a small suburban building, and all three newspapers and the Canadian analysts are working here. There are twenty-four-hour armed security guards and closed-circuit television cameras everywhere. With the volume of material to sift through, translate, validate, and analyze, nobody's getting much sleep. We have the material Sam received from Lawrence's whistleblower, what I copied from Ridgeway's files, the files Fadi hacked from X-ops, and the new information Silvio provided. It's going to be a hell of a story."

"When will it be through?"

"Shooting for Monday or Tuesday. You coming to Ottawa?"

"There may be something just as important happening here. We still don't know when or if he'll show."

"I'm just hoping that Aguilar is the one killed and we won't be targets anymore. Tell me you'll back off if it gets too risky. Promise you won't make me a widow, damn you!"

"I wouldn't dare. You said you'd never forgive me," he said.

Sutherland's phone pinged, rousing him from a repetitive dream that had been lasting for what seemed a long time. In it, he was sitting at a table tossing silver coins in the air, each one spinning and landing perfectly balanced on its edge. The table was littered with on-edge coins, and as soon as one landed, he would toss another with the same result.

Blinking himself awake, Sutherland swung his legs to the floor and turned on the lamp. On his phone, he saw he had a text from Rafael, and it was succinct: "Paolo arrived yesterday, and the rendezvous is on for tomorrow night. It's the moment of truth. If you decide to act, *buena suerte.*"

The moment of truth—a test of courage in the face of an impending challenge. Sutherland had learned from fateful experience that courage and foolhardiness were opposite sides of the same coin. That truth wasn't lost on him when he considered what lay ahead.

Matt stood at the water's edge in Mallory Square staring out at the long silhouette of *Buena Suerte* anchored five hundred yards away. Aguilar was supposedly on board now, and his latest young victim was expected tomorrow tonight. It was nearly sundown, and the square was overflowing with tourists enjoying the sight of jugglers, acrobats, ropewalkers, animal acts, fire eaters, and sword-swallowers. While the audience watched the acts, they would occasionally sneak glimpses westward lest they miss the sunset. But Matt hardly noticed the activities around him. His eyes were on Aguilar's yacht, hoping to get a glimpse of his former tormentor smoking one of his cigars on his suite's balcony overlooking the bow. But Aguilar hadn't shown his face, so Matt would have to take Rafael's word that his father had arrived. In any event, Matt planned to be on board tomorrow night and wait for him, if that's what it took.

He had considered a number of alternatives for crossing from the island to Aguilar's yacht and finally decided on using a Jet Ski again. Early that evening, he'd been walking along the waterfront by a water-sport rental outlet and noticed that the machines were left on their docks at night with the keys removed to prevent theft. He approached a young worker cleaning up and preparing to close. The boy was lean and deeply suntanned, and when he saw Matt looming over him from the dock, he stared up with stoned eyes. "Sup, bro?" he slurred.

The name Davy was printed on his grimy T-shirt under the company logo.

"Davy. Anyone ever take these out at night?" Matt asked.

"Daylight only. Why you wanna know?"

"I want to see a friend who lives on a boat moored out there. How much would it take for you to forget to lock up the key to one of these?" Matt asked. "Couple hundred? You tell me."

Davy chortled. "Must want to see that friend pretty bad. But I could get fired."

"Only if you got found out. How much you make in a day, Davy? In a week, say?" Matt said.

Davy chewed on the inside of his cheek and looked up, thinking. "I get good tips. Three hundred, maybe."

"I'll give you five hundred if you give me the key to one of those machines. I'll take it out tomorrow night and bring it back a little later." Matt pulled a hundred-dollar bill from his roll and handed it to him. "This is a down payment. We got a deal?"

"Fuck yeah," Davy said. "Take your pick."

The next night, Matt straddled his borrowed Jet Ski and focused his attention on *Buena Suerte*'s cabin lights hundreds of yards across the water. He'd found a sheltered spot on the lee side of Key West's seawall while he made his final preparations. A half hour earlier, he had watched Renata lead a young girl by the hand to the yacht's launch before it sped off into the wind and waves. After checking his watch, Matt pulled his windbreaker over his Kevlar vest, zipped it to the neck, and tightened the breast strap on his heavy backpack. Then he revved the engine and pointed the machine toward the yacht and what he envisioned would be Aguilar's death. He figured by the time he arrived at the yacht, everyone would be settled, and the events of the evening would have commenced, providing Matt the element of surprise.

Matt knew from his own experience that the guard usually stationed himself on the open stern deck, making him an easy target. He felt his luck was holding because the wind would muffle the sound of his silenced gunfire. He doubted that the guard's shots, if he had a chance to fire, would be heard by Aguilar or Renata in the master suite, up wind and over a hundred feet away.

The trip from the seawall to the yacht was rough, and Matt was getting soaked, but his pistol was in a dry baggie in his jacket pocket, and the bomb lay at the bottom of the waterproof backpack. Approaching from downwind at the stern, he eased close to the platform, grabbed a handhold, and turned off the ignition. With line he'd brought with him, he tied the Jet Ski to an empty cleat. Then he pulled out his pistol, screwed on the suppressor, and eased onto the platform, where he had a clear view of the open deck and the door to the main salon. But the guard he was expecting to see wasn't there.

After climbing to the deck, he peeked into the dimly lit salon. The flat-screen television was dark, and no one was in the lounge chairs. The guard might be in his quarters or the galley, but Matt's ingrained radar sensed a trap. He shrugged out of his backpack, set the countdown timer to fifteen minutes, and armed the bomb. Thinking he might joggle the bomb while combating his welcome party, he didn't activate the vibration sensor. Unless it was the only way to finish off Aguilar, blowing himself up was not in Matt's plan.

Matt assumed that he'd been double-crossed, and he expected to be ambushed after being allowed to enter the salon. If so, where would an assailant be hiding? He knew there was a stairway on his port side rising from the lower-level hold, and the liquor bar to the right could also provide cover. Gun in hand, he pulled open the lounge's sliding glass door, took one step inside, and then quickly shuffled to the left, where he peered down the staircase at a very surprised crouching man. Matt shot him once in the forehead and pivoted to face the bar, where another guard was aiming his gun. Matt fell to one knee and fired, sending the guard crashing into the bulkhead while frantically trying to stem the blood spurting from his throat.

As Matt stood up, another man appeared from a forward door and fired twice, hitting Matt squarely in the midsection. Matt clutched his belly, fell to his knees, and pulled off three shots before the shooter crumbled. Matt scrambled across the lounge and hid behind the bar, waiting for another assault wave. He probed under his Kevlar vest and flinched when he touched the wet wounds. The bullets had penetrated the vest, and he guessed he'd been hit with cop-killer bullets. He looked at his watch. Only a few minutes had passed since he set the clock, but he had plenty more to do.

When he'd worked on the yacht on Aguilar's rendezvous nights like this, there was only one guard. But this time, there was no telling how many more were waiting. And Renata, no stranger to killing, would also be with her father in his suite. He knew that he could motor back to shore and leave the bomb behind to do its worst. But he had come this far, and the appeal of witnessing Aguilar and Renata die consumed him.

With his belly a cauldron of pain, he stepped over the dead guard and staggered to the foot of the private spiral staircase that led from the lounge to the master suite on the deck above. He heard a noise behind him and spun around to see the captain in his white uniform raising a shotgun. Matt shot him before he could fire, painting a bright red blotch on his formerly spotless shirt.

Bent over and holding his stomach, Matt began to climb the staircase while he strained to see around the curving path above. Three-quarters of the way up, he felt a sharp sting in his neck and slapped at it, hoping he'd knocked off the dart in time. In a burst of pain and willpower, he lurched up the last treads, intent on shooting his attacker. But his legs gave out, and he stumbled onto the carpet, losing his grip on the gun. The last thing he remembered was Renata looming over him with a menacing leer on her face.

CHAPTER 22

It was dark when Sutherland left the house and drove Baskin's car to a side street a few blocks from the waterfront hotels. He had just turned off the engine when his phone buzzed. It was Rafael, and from the pitch of his voice, he was excited.

"I'm glad I got you," Rafael said. "I don't know your plans, but there's something you should know."

"About your father's rendezvous?"

"Exactly. I expected to hear from Margarita today, and I'm worried. She hasn't called and I'm afraid I know why. During my last conversation with her, I told her she should find a reason to get off the boat tonight because Matt Kirkland was coming. At the end of the call, just as I was disconnecting, I thought I heard Renata's voice. If my sister saw Margarita on a phone, she would have grilled her and forced her to tell her who it was. I know my sister, and she would beat it out of her and enjoy it."

"And learn about Matt's plans?" Sutherland asked.

"Probably. I tried to warn him and got no answer. He's probably on his way. Since he doesn't know they're expecting him, my guess is that he plans to climb onto the rear deck, take out the guard, and get to my old man," Rafael said. "If my father is expecting him, he'll put on more guards, and Matt won't have much of a chance. You won't have the opportunity to get at him when he's scrambling off the stern into whatever vessel he came on. That's where he'd be vulnerable."

"If Matt does run into a buzz saw, wouldn't everyone let their guard down afterward?"

"You have a point," Rafael said. "But you'd still have to get on board and face the same guards Matt did."

Not if I avoid boarding from the stern, Sutherland thought, visualizing his planned approach.

"Any way you look at, it's a gamble, and I thought you should know how the playing field has changed. You'd face Matt, if he survives the ambush, or more likely my father and his guards. I'm glad I don't have to decide."

Sutherland had no trouble borrowing the kayak. None of the hotel guests were around the dock after dark. Sutherland had simply walked through the lobby like any guest, strolled to the rack of kayaks at the water's edge, and cut the cable lock with the cutters he'd purchased at the same time he paid cash for two grappling hooks. He put on his gloves, slid the kayak into the water, climbed in, and set off. Paddling furiously through the windblown surf, he wondered whether Matt could survive the ambush that Aguilar had waiting for him. If he didn't, and Aguilar's men won, the tactic Sutherland had decided on to enter Aguilar's suite directly and circumvent the guards was the only way he could succeed.

He had gone over every step of his assault a dozen times, mentally executing every move, and had estimated every distance. He wore a sailor's harness over his windbreaker, carried two grappling hooks in his backpack, and had Baskin's gun in its holster at his side. Approaching the yacht broadside and upwind, he could see that the launch was secured to the closed starboard gangway door. There was also a Jet Ski trailing behind the stern, and he assumed that had been Matt's method of reaching the ship.

The anchor line was a thick hawser, and Sutherland tied the kayak's painter around it and steeled himself for what was to follow. After he shackled the grappling hooks to a D ring on his harness, he climbed the line hand over hand until he reached the hawsehole. There he thrust the spring-loaded hook through the hole and set it, allowing him to hang without holding on. Then he tossed the other hook up and over the bow coaming that, being six feet higher, would have been impossible to reach by stretching. He tested the hook's grip and shinnied up and onto the foredeck, where he lay for a few moments, waiting for the pain in his weeks-old flesh wound to subside.

As he inspected the balcony and the sweeping windshield of the wheelhouse above it, he focused his hearing for signs of danger, but he heard only the droning wind and rhythmic waves clapping the hull. After drawing Baskin's semiautomatic from the holster, he chambered a round and began climbing the external ladder leading to the suite's balcony. At the top of the steps, he got his first view of Aguilar's sleazy lair.

A movie playing on the large flat screen on the far bulkhead cast enough light to swathe the entire space in a soft glow. In the film, a group of naked prepubescent boys and girls were frolicking around a backyard pool. It was possibly a prelude to some child pornography, because in the room itself, a live naked woman, fit out like a dominatrix, stood at the foot of the king-size bed taking a video of the activity there. She wore leather belts and chains and a red phallus strapped to her groin. A naked old man lay in the bed with his back against the headboard. He was petting a young blonde girl, who seemed spaced out and compliant. She couldn't have been more than ten or eleven and was wearing skimpy black lingerie. Sutherland couldn't help thinking of his own daughter at that age, and he had to repress an urge to burst in, firing. He had to keep his head.

Judging from the X-rated scene proceeding inside, Sutherland assumed that Matt had already been killed by the guards in the ambush Rafael had predicted. Sutherland wouldn't have to worry about Matt, but he still had to get in and out of the suite while being prepared for the appearance of any guards. After a deep breath, he opened the sliding door, stepped in, and pointed the gun at the woman. "Take the girl away from that pig," he ordered.

"Aye, you!" Renata screamed, snarling. "¡Bastardo, hijo de la chingada!" She hurled the video camera at him, and he had to duck or be struck in the face. Then, with the phallus still dangling between her legs, she charged at Sutherland with her fingers spread like talons. He sidestepped her and slammed the gun butt into her temple. She fell to her knees and slumped over on the carpet.

Gunshots coming from the stern of the yacht awakened Margarita, and she tried to open her eyes. She strained, but only the right eye would open all the way—the other was swollen shut. She touched her face and winced as her fingers explored the puffed lips and the large bump under her good eye. She sensed that she lay on her back but wasn't in her bed. It had to be the floor of her cabin, and she began to piece together how she'd ended up there. Taking a deep breath, she gasped when an eruption of pain shot up from her ribs, a reminder of the multiple kicks she'd withstood. Renata hadn't been content that Margarita had told her everything. She had continued beating her until she had lost consciousness.

Rolling over to her stomach produced more discoveries of the damage Renata had inflicted. Every small movement caused another twinge, throb, or ache. When her head began to clear, she gingerly struggled to her hands and knees, gritted her teeth, and stood. Then she heard another several gunshots.

The shooting could mean only that Matt had come aboard and a gun battle was underway. He wouldn't have a chance now that Renata knew his plans. He'd surely be killed, and she knew that she alone was to blame. It might be too late for him, but she knew she had to act, or it would end badly for her as well. The Aguilars were going to kill her, hand her over to ICE, or send her back to Guatemala, and she guessed it would be the former. She had nothing to lose.

Every step sent an excruciating message, one that told her to stop. But despite the pain, she left her cabin, tiptoed aft down the port passage, and entered the common lounge, where she found the first body. He was lying on his face, with a spreading pool of blood on the carpet. His pistol lay by his side, and she picked it up. Scanning the lounge, she noticed blood spatter on the bulkhead behind the bar, and she spotted a pair of legs sticking out on the floor. On the other side of the lounge, the head and shoulders of another dead guard rested over the top tread of the staircase from the hold below. Since Matt had seemingly made it this far, he would have gone up the spiral staircase that went directly to Aguilar's suites and avoided the aft main stairway. That's where she was headed, and if Matt hadn't killed the Aguilars already, she intended to.

Margarita left the lounge and limped forward along the corridor to the spiral stairs, where she found the captain sprawled on his back, obviously dead. With the pistol in hand, she climbed the staircase and was disheartened to find Matt passed out on his stomach at the top, his ankles and wrists bound with cable ties. He still had his backpack on, and blood was collecting beside him from under his windbreaker. He had obviously been hit by one of the guards.

She recognized immediately what had happened. It was a common tactic when Aguilar wanted to capture someone for the purpose of killing them slowly later. Margarita had heard Renata and Aguilar discuss using tranquilizer darts or drugs a few times, and she couldn't help hearing the results. The screams of the victims carried all the way from the basement of Aguilar's Palm Beach mansion to Margarita's small bedroom in the attic.

The twin doors to the master suites were closed. The Aguilars would be beginning their revolting games by now, and she didn't need to guess what would be going on in Aguilar's bed. She had experienced it firsthand when she first arrived in the United States fifteen years earlier.

Aguilar would be planning to deal with Matt when they were through playing with their latest victim. That could take hours, but she couldn't risk a change in their normal pattern. She limped into Renata's office, found a pair of scissors, grabbed two water bottles from her refrigerator, and went back to Matt. After cutting the cable ties, she emptied both water bottles over his head and face. His eyes opened halfway, and he coughed. She shook him hard.

"Huh?" he muttered.

She slapped him. "Señor Matt. Wake up. We have to kill them."

He blinked a few times and shook his head, seeming to try to rouse himself. "The bomb," he said. He struggled to sit up, peeled off his backpack, and looked inside. "Not much time, but I have to watch them die first."

"That's a bomb?" Margarita cried. "There are innocent servants in the crew quarters. They're told to stay there."

"Take the launch," he grunted. "Gimme that gun. I'll take care of Paolo and Renata."

Margarita hesitated a moment, handed him the gun, then rushed limping to the stairway.

Matt reached into the backpack, felt around for the switch, and activated the bomb's vibration sensor. Then, with his knapsack over his shoulder, stooping and holding his stomach, he staggered to the double doors, ready to burst in.

Renata lay on the floor bleeding from the temple where Sutherland had smashed her with the gun butt. With his back against the bed's headboard, Aguilar held the girl against his wasted, naked body like a shield.

"Let her go, pig!" Sutherland called.

"My friends will cut your balls off. You fuck with the wrong guy," Aguilar growled.

Just then, the doors crashed open, and a voice from outside Sutherland's vision rasped, "Nice work, partner."

Sutherland spun to see Matt standing in the bedroom suite's doorway with a backpack draped over one shoulder and a gun hanging loosely at his side. He was unsteady, his eyelids droopy, and he was evidently wounded in the stomach.

"So we meet again," Matt slurred.

"You don't look so good," Sutherland said, keeping the gun pointed at Aguilar.

Matt, grayish and heavy lidded, took a wobbly step and leaned against the doorjamb. "Some kind of dart," he said. "Fell asleep."

"Renata, you fucking puta," Aguilar shouted as he held on to the girl and edged out of the bed. "Didn't you tie him? Wake up, bruja!"

Renata pushed herself up from the carpet to one knee and squinted at Sutherland with unfocused eyes. She touched her temple and inspected the blood left on her fingertips. Then her eyes turned steely, and with bared teeth and flared nostrils, she lunged at him in an insane fury.

Sutherland fired once, and she fell dead at his feet with a hole in her bare left breast.

"One fucker gone," Matt muttered as if it was all he could do to stay awake. "One to go."

Aguilar scrambled out of the bed holding the lethargic girl by one arm. Stumbling, he grabbed her by the hair and dragged her toward a desk ten feet away. Sutherland saw the silver-plated gun just as Aguilar seized it and spun toward him. Sutherland fired twice before Aguilar could aim, and both rounds hit him in his withered chest. As he crumbled to the floor, the girl emitted a pitiful whine and scuttled into the bathroom.

"That's two," Matt said.

Sutherland pointed the gun at Matt. "How about three? Sam Baskin was a very good friend."

"It won't matter. I'll show you why." Matt listlessly tossed his gun on the carpet, dug into the backpack hanging at his side, and slowly pulled out a toolbox by the handle. "I fall, and it goes boom."

"Bullshit. You already fell, from the look of things."

"Before I activated it. Now it blows when it's jostled or …" He pointed a trembling finger at the digital clock and said, "In seven minutes."

The words had barely come out of his mouth when Margarita hobbled in holding her side and cringing in pain. Her one functioning eye immediately fixed on Aguilar's dead body, then shifted to Renata's. "Gracias a Dios," she said, crossing herself. "Los monstruos están muertos. Que vayan al infierno!"

"You must be Margarita," Sutherland said, shocked by the sight of her injuries. "The girl's in the bathroom. Grab her, and let's get out of here."

"I don't think so," Matt said, straining to stand without the support of the doorjamb. "Margarita must've told them I was coming."

"Are you crazy?" Sutherland said.

"You have a choice," he said as he strained to hold up the toolbox. "Shoot me, this hits the floor, and *kaboom*. Or wait for the countdown."

"You *are* crazy."

"Make it a head shot so I'm dead before it blows," he mumbled as he staggered to the desk chair and eased himself down. He cradled his stomach while his free forearm rested on the chair arm, the bomb hanging by the handle in his upturned palm.

Sutherland frantically weighed whether to shoot, wondering if a drop from that height would detonate the bomb. Matt's eyes gradually closed as if he was about to fall asleep or die, thereby settling Sutherland's question.

Margarita desperately looked to Sutherland for guidance. Thinking quickly, he pointed the gun at Matt as if shooting, then gestured to her with a grabbing motion. She nodded and inched closer to Matt, ready to take hold of the bomb. Sutherland flashed his fingers in a count of *one*, *two, three* and fired. The round hit Matt in the eye, and he sank backward just as Margarita supported the bomb with two hands and gingerly eased it to the floor.

"Let's get the girl—hurry. In there," Sutherland yelled, pointing at the bathroom.

Margarita opened the door, and they found the girl huddled against the bulkhead with a drowsy stare. Margarita lifted her to her feet, and Sutherland seized her around the waist and carried her out under one arm.

When they sidestepped Aguilar's body, Sutherland noticed Aguilar's gun and cell phone lying on the floor. "Grab that. We may need it," he shouted as he pointed at the gun.

Margarita, rattled and hurried, scooped up and pocketed the phone without slowing her pained shuffle.

When Sutherland entered by the yacht's bow, he hadn't planned on leaving with Margarita or the girl. He couldn't take them down the anchor line, so he was counting on the yacht's launch. They hurried down the main stairway to the second deck and the starboard gangplank. The door was open wide, and the launch was gone.

"We'll have to swim," Sutherland shouted.

"I can't," Margarita cried.

"The Jet Ski," he said, remembering seeing it when he arrived. When they reached the stern deck, he mounted the Jet Ski, and Margarita followed with the girl. After he untied the painter and started the engine, the machine drifted off to stern before he gunned it and headed for safety. If Matt had been telling the truth, it wouldn't be long before the bomb exploded.

They were fifty yards away when it went off—a brilliant light, a deafening blast, and a shock wave that felt like a giant hand slapping them. He turned to see the flames shoot up, along with hundreds of pieces of the yacht. Adios, *Buena Suerte*.

When Sutherland, Margarita, and the girl cruised past Mallory Square on the Jet Ski, there was already a crowd gawking at the burning wreck. Sutherland dropped Baskin's gun overboard but kept his gloves on to avoid leaving prints on the ski. Margarita spotted an open slip by the Hyatt hotel, and after Sutherland docked, he put his windbreaker on the girl, and the three of them walked down the pier, through the lobby, and out to the street.

They hadn't spoken at all on the trip to shore or the drive to the house. The girl was still apparently on some sedative, and Margarita seemed numbed by it all. Inside, after the girl stretched out on the couch, Margarita finally said, "So much killing."

"They all deserved it," Sutherland said, examining her face. "Did Renata do that to you?"

"After she found my phone. She made me tell …"

"It looks bad. Maybe we should go to the emergency room."

"I don't have any papers. No ID."

"Then let me see what I can find in the medicine cabinet. Not much we can do about your ribs without an x-ray," he said.

The young girl was still wearing the skimpy lingerie under Sutherland's windbreaker, and Margarita's clothes were covered with blood and vomit. Sutherland rummaged through their host's closets and dressers and found clean underwear, shorts, and T-shirts, everything many sizes too large for either of them. While Margarita was helping the drowsy girl get dressed, she learned her name: Maureen.

"She'll come around by tomorrow," Sutherland said. "Rafael told me that Paolo or Renata pays off the parents for these disgusting arrangements with the girls. That right?"

"True. I never understood how a mother could do that. They must have guessed what was going to happen."

"The only thing to do is to get her to a family-services organization that takes care of abused juveniles. Tomorrow I'll drop her off with an anonymous note explaining why she shouldn't be taken back to her mother. That's the best I can do without incriminating myself."

"What about me?" Margarita asked. "Rafael said I could stay with his family."

"Let's call him," Sutherland said, pulling out his phone and punching in Rafael's private number.

"The fact that you're alive and calling," Rafael said, "means you wisely decided against it, or it was a success of some kind. Which was it?"

"Paolo, Renata, Matt, and the guards are dead," Sutherland said. "The *Buena Suerte* is destroyed."

For a moment, there was total silence. Then Rafael said, "Did I hear that right? The three of them? The yacht?"

"The captain too."

"I gotta hear this," Rafael said. "How about Margarita? She wasn't on the boat, was she?"

"She was. She's beat up but OK. She tells me she's got nowhere to go and no papers. Any suggestions?"

"She can live with my family as long as she likes. My firm has a private plane and a pilot. We'll fly down and bring her back. I can arrange it right away."

"Let me know when. I'm staying in Key West a few more days arranging the sale of Sam Baskin's assets."

"If you're staying there, keep a very low profile. Just because my old man's dead doesn't mean his cronies have given up the hunt."

"Why would they care if he's dead?"

"I have the impression they don't live by the same parameters. Or, for that matter, have given up on their mission. Ask Margarita. She said my father had a name for his dark friends: *los clandestinos.*"

"A name that doesn't give me a very warm feeling."

CHAPTER 23

The next day when Sutherland woke up, Margarita had already made coffee and was frying bacon. Maureen was still sleeping soundly. Sutherland got on to his laptop and typed a note explaining that her parents had sold her to a pedophile. After he printed it, he said to Margarita, "When she wakes up, you should explain what her mother or father has done and that she has other options besides going back to them. After you talk to her, I'll drop her off at one of the family-services offices."

"You are a good man, señor," she said. "You saved her from horrible people."

"They aren't the only bad ones in my life at the moment. Do you know the name Dr. Castillo? Or James Ridgeway? Maybe Paolo and Renata spoke about them?"

"Many times. The company called Lawrence Laboratories. I can remember other names too. Even the phone numbers, because I usually had to connect the call."

"You're my hero, Margarita. Could you write them down?"

"Better than that," she said as she held up an iPhone. "You wanted his phone—remember? Hundreds of names in here. Even a senator or two. We were about to be blown up, and you wanted his phone—I thought you were loco."

"His phone?" he said, astounded. "Paolo's? Unbelievable! It was his gun. I thought we might need it if any of the guards were waiting."

After Maureen woke up and had breakfast, Sutherland dropped her outside the Wesley House Family Services building. When he returned to the house, the television station was showing video of the burning *Buena Suerte* lighting up the night sky, followed by a daylight scene of the floating debris. The commentary shed little light on the cause or fatalities, only that the yacht was owned by a conglomerate named Magnífico Enterprises.

A few minutes later, Sutherland's phone rang.

"Tell me you had nothing to do with that," Kelly said.

"It was Matt Kirkland," he said.

"And how do you know that?"

"Who else could have done it? I told you he was going to kill them. He evidently chose to blow up the yacht and everybody on it," he said. "What do I know about bombs?"

"You know damn well answering a question with a question doesn't work with me."

"Then you tell me how I could have bombed that yacht," he said. "Just think about it."

"I'm not convinced," she said. "I'm thankful that you're all right and the bastard trying to kill you is dead, but we're not done with this discussion, mister."

"Fine, but for the moment, let's talk about Ottawa. I've got more red meat for you," he said. "I have Paolo's phone. Give me an address, and I'll overnight it to you. The reporters can research the names he regularly called and make it part of their article. I'm particularly interested in what they find about one of the names listed in the Rs," he said.

"Intriguing. You're not going to tell me how you came by his phone?"

"I take the fifth. And you should too," he said. "But I would like to know about the super surprise Silvio promised."

"You can read about it next week. It wouldn't be a surprise if I told you."

The next morning, Sutherland drove Margarita to the Key West International Airport's General Aviation office, the operations center for private airplanes. Rafael Aguilar had just landed, and his company plane was being fueled while his pilot filed his flight plan back to Colorado.

While they sat in the waiting room, Sutherland recounted the events leading to the deaths of Rafael's father and sister and Matt Kirkland.

"Amazing," Rafael said, shaking his head at what he'd just heard. "You've survived one close call after another, but if I'd known Matt had a bomb, I would never have helped you. The gods must be on your side, my friend."

"True enough," Sutherland said. "The thing is, if those gods had been with me a few weeks ago, I wouldn't have had to survive. I wouldn't have been with Sam at the time he was killed, I wouldn't have shot your son, and I wouldn't have been on that yacht in the first place."

"That's the problem—those gods can be fickle. That's why I'm not a gambler."

After Rafael's plane took off, Sutherland met the dealer buying Baskin's car. Sharon's husband had told him to get rid of it, even if they got less than it was worth. So in exchange for a cashier's check, Sutherland handed over the car and the title Sharon had signed before she left Key West. Then he caught a flight back to Chicago.

That evening, after Sutherland arrived at his Chicago condo, he called Kelly in Ottawa. She was still working with the reporters and analysts finalizing the articles due to be published the following week.

"We're getting there," she said, sounding tired. "No one can believe this stuff. Did you know Lawrence sent fifty million or so every year to Cuba's overseas accounts? Not a bad arrangement. Cuba couldn't sell the new drugs they developed because of the embargo, but Lawrence could. But it was when the analysts started to delve into the research on viral mutations and what was going on with X-ops that matters got heated here."

"They trying to censor that? Dammit, I knew it," Sutherland said.

"Hold on. There's been some intense discussions with Canadian intelligence and the diplomats. We think they're overly sensitive because the facts are there in black and white and hard to refute. And although we've had to back off some of our assertions, the story still paints a shameful picture of el Centro, Lawrence Laboratories, and America's role in this. It will still be a sensational story."

"So will they allow the unethical mutation experiments, the X-ops connections?"

"They're still working on it," Kelly said. "Speaking of X-ops, the person R on Paolo's phone list was a man named Donald Radoff."

"Agent Donald Radoff. That's what I thought," he said. "Was he acting in an approved FBI capacity?"

"We don't know how connected the X-ops group was with the official FBI. May never know," she said. "By the way, did you have any trouble leaving Key West?"

"Why would I? They gave me the OK. Self-defense."

"I was thinking of Paolo's death," she said.

"All they've reported is that there was an explosion. No details. Anyway, I'm back, and no one's said a word to me. You think they will?"

"The man who has allegedly been trying to kill you for weeks has been killed, and you were in the same town at the time. Yes, I think you'll be questioned. I'm surprised it hasn't happened already."

Kelly left Ottawa when she was satisfied the story was ready to be published. The newspaper team's plan was to disclose an abbreviated version to the news networks the evening before the first installment hit the newsstands. When she arrived at O'Hare International Airport, she called Sutherland and told him she was going directly to her Lawrence Laboratories office in the hope that she could be present when the networks aired the story.

"You want to be with Doc when it's first broadcast?" Sutherland asked.

"At the same time that I resign. I want to see his face."

"What if he flips out?"

"I'll be all right. Then I hope to catch Lansing as well. They both should be there because there's an emergency board meeting at five o'clock."

"You want to throw it in their faces. To gloat."

"Why not?" she said. "After the way I was treated."

"All I can say is *be careful*. You never know how someone's going to react when they see their life flushed down the crapper."

Sutherland hadn't been in his office for a week, and the stack of mail on his desk made him wish he hadn't come in at all that afternoon. On the top of a pile of phone messages was the name Agent Radoff.

"What's this?" Sutherland asked Eileen, his assistant.

"He left a message on your voice mail to call him."

"Let's pretend we never got this message," he said, winking. "Must've been a voice mail glitch."

"OK," she said as she passed him another memo. "This other voice mail was from Rafael Aguilar. He said that Margarita remembered another contact. He said it won't be on Paolo's phone list because someone named Renata always called her. Her name is Catherine Lansing."

Lansing. The woman taking over for Ridgeway. And Kelly was about to see Doc and her this very evening to throw the story in their faces. Kelly might have changed her mind had she known about Lansing's familiarity with Paolo Aguilar.

Sutherland tried Kelly's phone, but she didn't answer. It was nearing the time that the television news would be airing the story's headlines, the time when she planned to drop into Lawrence Laboratories' offices. All he could hope for was that neither one of them went berserk.

It had been over a week since Kelly left Lawrence Laboratories' headquarters offices after her meeting with Catherine Lansing. She'd explained she needed some personal time, and after she'd been pushed aside in dealing with the BioVexis matter, no one had thought it odd. Before she boarded the plane in Ottawa, she'd learned that Lansing and Castillo would be in the office for a short board meeting that afternoon, and she calculated that it would conclude around the time the national evening news would be airing. Her briefcase contained the final copy for the front-page article in the next day's *New York Times*. It was to be a present for Castillo.

Kelly took a taxi from the airport to Lawrence's offices, cleaned out her personal items, and checked to see whether the board meeting had adjourned. Noting that the boardroom was empty, she marched into Castillo's office, sat herself down assertively in front of him, and said, "Do you read the *New York Times*, Doc? Or *Washington Post*?"

He glowered at her brazenness as he removed the cigar he'd been chewing on. He set the cigar in the crystal ashtray on his desk. "I'm surprised to see you. What is it now? Another conspiracy theory?"

"We're well past theories," she said. "Paolo Aguilar's death is only the beginning of things going south."

"I thought Catherine Lansing made it clear that you're to stay out of this."

"Perfectly clear. I'm pleased to say I will no longer be part of a company that's going to be out of business in a few days"

"You're delusional," Castillo said, his face darkening. "I don't have to listen to this. Take your crazy ideas and leave before I call security and have you thrown out."

Kelly looked at her watch. Just five thirty. "I suggest you turn on your TV. CNN, Fox, whatever," she said. "I think you'll find the news interesting tonight."

"Just get out!" he shouted.

"You're in the news. Don't you want to know?"

Scowling, he snatched the remote and turned on the flat screen on the wall. The introductory music and graphics were just winding down, and the announcer began his presentation. "The *Washington Post* has just released a bombshell of a story this evening. Chicago-based pharmaceutical company Lawrence Laboratories for years has served as a secret intermediary between a Cuban medical research center, the American military, and a clandestine organization involved in international dirty tricks. The research methods of this Cuban center consisted of experiments on unwilling and unknowing humans who often died as a result. Not since the experiments in the Nazi death camps have such horrendous and immoral practices been carried out."

Castillo stared wide-eyed at the screen, his mouth agape.

The announcer continued, "More recently, Lawrence made headlines for the deaths caused by the faulty drug BioVexis, but what was not known was that the company was also circumventing FDA protocols and supplying unapproved medications to the military, in some cases causing the deaths of servicepeople. The most alarming activity of the associated Cuban research center is that it was experimenting with mutated viruses."

Castillo sat stiffly with his hands gripping the chair arms, staring with bulging eyes. "You!" he bellowed. "This is all you!"

"No, Doc, it's all you," Kelly said, standing. Then she dropped a paper-clipped sheath of paper on his desk. "There's the full text of tomorrow's front-page article. But don't worry—you have time to disappear. The series doesn't get into details about your identity until the last installment."

"What do you mean?" he said, seething to the point of spitting.

"You know exactly what I mean," she said. "You've hidden for years. Posing as the medical genius, when all your discoveries were stolen or provided by el Centro. But that isn't the worst of it, is it?"

"Get out!" he shouted as he grabbed the heavy ashtray and prepared to throw it. Kelly quickly backpedaled to the door and shielded herself with her briefcase. But the ashtray slipped from his hand and clattered on his desk, and the cigar landed on the carpet at Kelly's feet.

When she turned to leave, Castillo was glowering at her menacingly, standing with his fists resting on his desk like a rabid bulldog.

Kelly walked out of Castillo's suite, strode down the corridor to Ridgeway's former office, and found Lansing on the phone with her back to the door. As Kelly watched, Lansing's torso suddenly stiffened as if she'd been hit with an electric shock. "What? On the news? Now?" she cried. "The *Washington Post*, for Christ's sake? How can they? Can't we stop them?"

Lansing listened for a moment, then said, "And we're not shutting it down? We're the government!" Her interlocutor spoke for a moment before Lansing said, "How did they get that stuff? They even know what went on in el Centro? And the third-world shipments? Jesus, we're fucked."

"Yes, you are," Kelly said, stepping into the office. "You, this company, and your buddies in Virginia. Fucked."

Lansing spun around and stared at her a moment before putting the receiver down. She took a deep breath and shook her head. "You stupid bitch. Think you'll get away with this? You'll be prosecuted for sedition."

"Try pinning that one on an assassinated reporter, a murdered whistleblower, and a Cuban defector, if you can find him."

"You were involved," Lansing said. "All your questions. Don't deny it."

"Questions that no one would answer honestly. Evasions, denials, and lies. I can't even count the number of crimes involved."

"You violated the secrecy act," Lansing said.

"Uh-uh, Colonel. My position in this company never fell under that act—nor did I ever sign anything of that nature. Furthermore, nothing I ever laid my hands on was designated confidential, secret, or anything of the sort."

"You have no idea how much—"

"Save it. If I were you, I'd crawl in a deep hole before the shit really hits the fan. This is only the beginning."

Before Lansing could respond, a gunshot went off down the corridor.

"What's that?" Lansing blurted, jumping to her feet.

Kelly flinched. "Whoa. That didn't take long. I think the figurehead of this corrupt enterprise just offed himself."

It was six o'clock, and Eileen and Sutherland's skeleton staff had left for the evening, leaving him alone in his office to catch up on some paperwork. He tried to reach Kelly again, but the call went into voice mail once more. When he disconnected, he looked up to see Agent Radoff standing in the doorway leering.

"How did you get in here?" Sutherland demanded. "The office is closed."

"You didn't return my call," Radoff replied as he walked in and boldly seated himself across the desk from Sutherland. Then, in an act obviously calculated to intimidate, he unbuttoned his suit coat, revealing the butt of his pistol in his shoulder holster. It was as if he was announcing he meant business and had the upper hand. "We know you were involved in that explosion. You're in a heap of shit, my friend."

"You haven't got a shred of evidence of that, so don't pimp me."

"I don't need evidence. I can take you in right now."

"If it's another fishing expedition to find out what I know, you can save the questions. You'll know everything soon enough. And before we get too far with this little chat, you should know that in my business, I sometimes have occasion to record conversations with concealed mics. There's also closed-circuit TV in the lobby and a hidden camera in here. We keep the recordings off-site."

Sutherland had witnessed Radoff's glare before, but this time, the agent's raptor eyes bore into Sutherland with an intensity that made him seem rabid. Undaunted by the agent's fierce reaction, Sutherland met his gaze with an indifference that said, *You don't scare me.*

Gradually, Radoff's angry ferocity morphed into an insincere smile. "No matter," he said, shrugging. "And Kelly Matthews? We need to speak to her as well. She's another person off the grid."

Sutherland looked at his watch. "Fact is, she's probably in Lawrence's offices right now speaking with Doc Castillo and Catherine Lansing. She's going to ruin their day."

"Not by resigning, she isn't."

"Odd that you would know about her awkward situation there. I wonder why a federal agent would be privy to that. But you're not your typical agent, are you?"

Radoff narrowed his eyes and jutted his jaw pugnaciously. "You think you know something, but you don't."

"I'll tell you what I know," Sutherland said. "With the recent death of the two men most responsible, Sam Baskin's murder is avenged. I also know that Sam's story is getting published this week."

"You're bluffing," Radoff said.

"It will be all over the news tonight and carried in the papers for the next few days. From Lawrence Lab's illegal relationship with the Cuban labs to your organization's international meddling."

"We'll close down those papers first," Radoff said, snarling.

"Do your people, X-ops or whoever they are, control the Canadian press? Even if our government succeeded in silencing the American newspapers, the US media would be all over the *Toronto Star*'s disclosures. Besides, our government is going to be so disgraced and dishonored by these revelations they'll be hanging people left and right and claiming it was just a few bad apples, a rogue operation. You among them," Sutherland said and smirked.

"What do you mean? Me?"

"The federal agent who tried to silence Sam Baskin with threats—maybe even with a rifle. The guy who spoke on a regular basis with Paolo Aguilar knowing that he ordered Baskin's murder. And the man who searched Sam's boat and condo for incriminating evidence against Lawrence and el Centro. From the video of your last visit here, a property manager and a boat owner in Sam Baskin's marina identified you."

"You're way out of your league here, buddy. You have no idea."

"And phone records. The reporters have Paolo's cell phone and tracked all his calls. You and Paolo, and he with Castillo, Lansing, and others up your chain of command. They won't be happy when they read about it."

"You're going to regret this."

"Not one bit," Sutherland said as his office phone rang. The ID indicated it was Kelly, and he grabbed the receiver. "How'd it go?"

"Not like I expected. Doc shot himself. I'm still here with the sheriff's deputies."

"Jesus! He did?"

"Yep. Couple minutes after I gave him the news."

"Dead?"

"Very," she said. "And messy. I'm going to need a few stiff drinks tonight."

"Come to my place when you're through. We'll drive down to the University Club," Sutherland said. "Gotta go. Agent Radoff paid me another visit. I'll give him the news."

"Who's dead?" Radoff demanded after Sutherland hung up.

"Doc Castillo just killed himself."

"Castillo?" Radoff said, stunned. "I don't understand."

"You will. Watch the news tonight. Read the papers tomorrow."

"You're saying—you weren't bluffing?" he asked, incredulous.

"Not at all."

Radoff sprung from his chair, his face flushed, nostrils flared. "If that story got out, I'll fucking break your neck, you cocksucker!"

"Duly noted," Sutherland said. "On your way out, feel free to smile at the lobby camera."

Agent Radoff spun around and stomped out of the office. Sutherland checked the switch under his desk to verify that he'd recorded their conversation. He had a bad feeling that Radoff really meant what he'd said.

CHAPTER 24

A fter giving the sheriff's deputies her statement, Kelly couldn't get out of Lawrence's headquarters building and the smell of death fast enough. It was nearly nine o'clock when she arrived at Sutherland's building, and as soon as she walked into the apartment, Sutherland handed her a glass of scotch. She downed a mouthful and sighed. "Not a pleasant sight. Blew off the back of his head."

"Horrible," was all Sutherland could say as he imagined the scene.

She finished off the rest of the drink. "While I was calling 911, I watched as Colonel Lansing read through the text of tomorrow's story that I'd left with Doc. When she finished, she flung the sheaf of paper on the floor and stared at me with an expression so apoplectic I thought she was going to tear my eyes out. I'm probably six inches taller and thirty pounds heavier, but I wouldn't have wanted to fight her right then. I was giving the emergency operator directions at the same time I was retreating toward the corner bar and a few crystal liquor carafes that I figured could do some damage if it came to that. But instead of attacking me, she glared and in a measured growl said, 'Girl, you and your boyfriend are sooo dead,' before turning and hustling out of the office. She must have left the building, because I didn't see her again."

"Agent Radoff was more explicit. He said he was going to break my neck," Sutherland said. "You want another drink, or should we get going? We have reservations at the University Club, and my car should be ready downstairs."

"Then let's go. I'll get another drink there."

They took the elevator to the ground floor, and Sutherland used his key fob to open the door to the valet garage, expecting to see his car in the first space. The garage was arranged with cars lined up on both sides facing the long middle aisle that stretched from the overhead entrance door to several cars parked at the far end. "Damn," he said. "The valet said he'd leave it here by the door. He's probably digging out someone's car on the other level. Shouldn't be long."

While they waited, the overhead door opened, and a car drove in and parked in the designated drop-off area at one side of the aisle. A woman got out and walked out the door carrying a grocery bag she'd retrieved from the back seat.

Getting impatient, Sutherland pulled out his phone and tapped in the valet's number. They heard the ringtone sound close by.

"It's over that way," Kelly said, walking down the line of parked cars farther into the garage. On the fourth ring, she slipped between a BMW and a Mini Cooper and stopped short. "Jesus!" she cried and turned around, gasping.

Sutherland ran to her side and nearly tripped over a uniformed man lying on the concrete.

"That's right. He's dead." The booming male voice came from behind them and echoed around the garage. They both whirled around to see a man appear from the driver's seat of a doorman's parked Chrysler. It was Radoff, and he had a gun. "So good to see both of you at once. Save me time."

They were a hundred feet into the garage, and he was sixty feet away with his back to the overhead door, blocking that means of escape. There was a back way out that led to the lobby, but a good shot could probably take out at least one of them before they made it there.

"I take it you've seen the news, Agent Radoff," Sutherland said as he tried to unobtrusively turn on his phone's recorder.

"If you're dialing 911, there isn't time," Radoff said, taking a step toward them. "Quite a commotion you two have stirred up. Too bad your celebration will be short."

"This your idea, or are you following orders?" Sutherland said as he took Kelly's arm and retreated a few steps. "Trying to make up for your failure at stopping the story?"

"What's the difference?" he said.

"You know you're on video?" Sutherland said, pointing to a closed-circuit camera.

"Won't matter," he said, taking another step.

Just then, the overhead door opened again, and a Jeep drove in and stopped just before bumping into Radoff, who was blocking the lane. The Jeep driver leaned on his horn insistently until an agitated Radoff spun and fired, putting a hole in the Jeep's windshield. The Jeep sprang forward and hit Radoff a grazing blow as he tried to get out of its way. He was knocked to the concrete, and Sutherland pulled Kelly by the arm and took off running farther into the garage. The three cars parked at the end faced directly up the lane, and Sutherland knew the keys were usually left inside. Sutherland pointed to a Chevy, and he and Kelly scrambled in. He started it and cried, "Get down!"

Radoff was on his feet limping unsteadily toward them, waving his gun. Behind him, the Jeep driver was yelling into his phone. Sutherland put the car in gear and gunned the engine, squealing rubber as the Chevy leapt forward. As Radoff raised his gun, Sutherland slumped down and braced himself. Two rounds pierced the windshield before he and Kelly felt the jarring thump and saw Radoff's body sailing over the hood and bashing onto the glass. The next jolt came when the Chevy crashed into the front of the Jeep, came to an abrupt stop, and inflated the airbags.

Chicago's weather forecast was for a frosting of snow overnight and frigid weather the following day. It would also be the second day of the newspapers' series that began with Lawrence Laboratories' association with el Centro. The *New York Times*, the *Washington Post*, and the *Toronto Star* were coordinating the publication of each of the installments, and every television news program was buzzing with the revelations and waiting for the next bombshell. The US attorney general was seen ranting on every channel after seeking an injunction to stop any publication and threatening to put every editor in jail. But the newspapers had no plans to be silenced, insisting that none of the material published in their articles had been identified as classified, confidential, or top secret. The story might be embarrassing to those involved, but it wouldn't be detrimental to the security of the country.

Kelly and Sutherland watched the evening news in his living room as they sipped chardonnay and nibbled on brie and crackers. She glanced at his face and couldn't stifle a guffaw.

"What?" he said.

"Oh, nothing. Just that you look like a racoon." The Chevrolet's airbags had performed as intended, inflating on impact and preventing both him from hitting the wheel and Kelly from going through the windshield. But they were both slumped down and without seat belts. He was left with a broken nose and black eyes, and Kelly suffered a swollen jaw and fat lip.

"Don't laugh," he said. "You look like a casualty of botched collagen injections. At least we ended up better than Agent Radoff. He may not make it. His partner certainly didn't. One of the officers last night told me they think Radoff shot his partner—agent named Hernandez or something. There was already an APB out for Radoff."

"The local papers and channels haven't said a word about his attack on us. Makes you wonder how much the FBI knew about his activities," she said.

"Or the rest of X-ops' machinations, for that matter," he said. "A secret organization messing in the politics of America's allies and enemies—I thought the reporters would be on that like wild dogs on a meat truck. Is that in the next installment?"

"Nope. I had the impression that Canadian intelligence wanted to save evidence on that operation as an ace to play in discussions with the US state department. But Didier did tell me that Canada sent the American ambassador a sampling of X-ops' emails, files, and records that Fadi hacked. Guess what: X-ops' office and monitoring center went dark within hours."

"What about el Centro's testing new vaccines on engineered viruses and the potential for biowarfare? Nothing?"

"Canadian intelligence said it was too speculative, and besides, they didn't want to scare the crap out of half the population. But for my money, like with X-ops, they wanted it for diplomatic leverage."

"Will the next installment bring Dr. Ortega into the story? Or did that get squelched along with the bioweaponry conjecture?"

"Not at all. That book about Dr. Death confirms the rumors that circulate in Cuban expatriate communities. And Silvio Delgado's latest clinical charts from Venezuela and Nicaragua prove that the practice of experimentation on prisoners and unknowing humans continues today. Ortega was the architect of the very program that had a role in Lawrence's production of BioVexis. And since Ortega disappeared from Cuba about the time Doc Castillo arrived, one has to make the connection. Now it's a matter of the newspapers getting Doc's DNA results back soon enough for the last installment."

"With all the secrecy, how did the reporters get his DNA?"

"Last evening, after Doc shot himself and we ran to his office, I saw the cigar that Doc had been chewing minutes before. It had landed near the door."

"Let me guess. You picked it up and kept it. You destroyed evidence, counselor," he said and grinned.

"I was convinced what Silvio Delgado believed about Doc being Ortega was true. The cigar was the evidence we needed. If there's a DNA match with Silvio, it will confirm that the man that passed himself off as Doc Castillo is really Silvio's mother's half brother, Dr. Luís Delgado Ortega. Dr. Death."

"Well done, detective," Sutherland said. "That's interesting, because in one of Sam's journals, he mentions seeing Dr. Ortega's name among the material Doc had in the suitcase when we found him. So the thinking is Ortega pushed the real Doc Castillo off the raft and took his identity?"

"The reporters wanted to believe that, and it would have made a good story, but Silvio had to disabuse them," she said.

"How? This have to do with the prisoners in the photo?"

"It was the convict leaving the tent. His prisoner number on his shirt was barely readable, but Silvio matched some dates in the records they were clearing out, and he identified the man by that number. He brought that chart with him. The man's name was Dr. Jorge Enrique Castillo, one of Castro's political enemies. He died during a trial of a vaccine they were testing—meaning the vaccine didn't work."

"So Ortega took the identity of Castillo, a man he'd killed in a Cuban clinic," Sutherland said. "Did anybody dig up anything on who the dead man on the raft could have been?"

"So far, nothing. Silvio looked into it, but no luck," she said. "Could have been anyone."

Sutherland looked out his living-room window and saw nothing but a swirling veil of white as wind gusts shook the windowpanes. He sighed and said to Kelly, "Why are we here? You're unemployed, and I have zero projects in my backlog. We should be in the sunshine celebrating."

"Unemployed and no projects? What are we celebrating?" Kelly said.

"In the last month, we got Sam's story published, and we rid the world of a pile of toxic genome waste."

"I'll give you that," she said and raised her wineglass in salute.

"But now that it's over, I've been wondering. If I hadn't been the target of Aguilar's attacks, would I have pushed to see Sam's story get out? I mean, I didn't know anything about Lawrence or Aguilar or el Centro—I could have simply mourned a good friend and got on with life. It was my being a target that really provided the impetus."

"You're forgetting that I was right in the middle of Lawrence's corruption and had a lot to do with the story."

"I'm not forgetting that. But I'm not sure we would have been so tenacious if our lives weren't in danger."

"Bottom line—we'll never know. So let's just enjoy the moment." Then Kelly paused and put on her no-nonsense face. "But speaking of danger, I know you were on that yacht. Despite your promise, you couldn't miss that opportunity. So? When do you plan to tell me what happened?"

Why fight it? he thought. *She already knows.*

He shrugged and said, "OK, I'll give you the whole bloody story. But let me get you a drink first. You may need it. I know I will if I have to relive it."

Fifteen minutes and two glasses of scotch later, Sutherland finished his narrative of the events on the yacht and waited for Kelly to say something. She was sucking on an ice cube from her drink, rolling it around in her mouth, while she stared blankly at her empty glass. Then she slowly shook her head and exhaled a long sigh.

"Well?" Sutherland said. "You wanted to hear it. Can we put it to bed now?"

"Doug. What you did ..." she said, her voice cracking, her eyes moistening. "What you went through, the risks you took, the danger you faced and overcame ... and the results ... is all so terrifying—so incredibly amazing—I'm at a loss for words."

"Evidently not," he said, attempting to lighten the mood. "You just said a mouthful."

"Planning and precision," Kelly said. "*Bang*, the woman; *bang*, the old pervert; then taking out Matt without detonating the bomb. I don't know how you kept your cool through all that."

"That's the interesting part—the other times I shot someone, like the time in Sam's suite or on his boat, they were reflexive acts taken in self-defense. This time it was calculated. Once I planned it and faced them, I intended to kill, and I didn't think twice beforehand or feel a twinge of remorse afterward. You could even say it was cold-blooded. And the thing that scares me is that it exhilarated me. I was flying high."

"It doesn't make you a murderer, if that's what you're worried about," she said. "Maybe the law would see it that way, but it was the only way to extricate yourself from the situation you fell into. And I know that feeling—it's how I felt when I coldcocked that Patrón creep in your apartment. So here's an ethics question for you: Since we both got high killing another human being, what does that make us?"

"There's where you're wrong. I wouldn't call any of them human," he said.

Kelly and Sutherland were preparing to retire for the night with the late television news playing in the background in his bedroom. The newscaster finished coverage of the Lawrence Laboratories story by stating, "And as an apparent result of these astounding disclosures by the *New York Times*, Dr. Jorge Castillo, president and founder of the disgraced company, committed suicide in his office last evening."

Sutherland's cell phone buzzed, and he answered. It was Hurly of the *New York Times*.

"Sorry to bother you this late," Hurly said, "but we're going to press on the final installment and wanted to let you know. There was no DNA match. Not even close. It would've been a great finish to the story, but we still have a winner, thanks to the two of you. Tell Kelly, will you? And thanks again for everything. There wouldn't be a story without you two."

"What was that about?" Kelly asked as soon as he disconnected.

"No DNA match. Castillo is not Ortega."

"Wow. The papers must be disappointed. And Silvio too. He was certain he was right."

"DNA doesn't lie," Sutherland said. "But based on the date Ortega disappeared, and his link to the real Castillo who died as his patient, there's still a possibility that Dr. Ortega was on that raft. He could have been the one pushed off."

"Then who the hell was the guy you rescued before he was Doc Castillo?" Kelly said.

"Could have been anyone—some jamoke who learned of Ortega's plan while on the raft and decided he'd kill Ortega and do it himself. Hell, we already figured out that the pretend Castillo's great creations came from el Centro. So into the ocean Dr. Death goes. Adios, *pendejo*."

"Can't feel sorry for him," Kelly said. "From what we know of him, he was a sadistic and merciless monster, on a par with Mengele, who deserved whatever came next."

"Let's say he sank to the bottom and was picked apart by crabs and maggots and other disgusting creatures," Sutherland said. "I'd hate to think that any self-respecting shark would have the stomach."

EPILOGUE

May 2020

Throughout the week before Memorial Day, the first of summer's doldrums blanketed Key West, the only relief from the suffocating heat coming from the occasional and fleeting rain squall. Unlike the normality of the tropical weather patterns, almost everything else about the small island town had been eerily altered since mid-March. Duval Street was as quiet as a ghost town. Storefronts were shuttered, boarded, or dark, with For Lease signs posted on every third door. In contrast to Sutherland's previous trips, there were no cruise ships looming over the harbor's docks, no hordes of tourists in shorts and T-shirts carrying shopping bags and open glasses of beer, wine, and margaritas. For months now, COVID-19 was in total control. Key West, like most of the country, was in lockdown.

Sutherland and Kelly had spent the morning away from their rental condo being driven around the traffic-free Key West streets in a large van by Suzanne, a local real estate broker. Taking precautions against the mystifying virus, they had sat in the very rear seats wearing masks, with the van's windows open for ventilation. As they crisscrossed different neighborhoods, Suzanne explained the critical considerations when buying property on an exposed island in a hurricane zone where the highest point was seventeen feet above a rising sea level. Important factors included flood and wind insurance, pool service, gardeners, parking, termite control, and finally whether one preferred a single-family house or a condominium. COVID-19 restrictions prohibited entrance into any of the properties, but the tour was still informative, if a bit tiring.

In the afternoon, overlooking the Atlantic Ocean on the balcony of the condominium they were renting, Sutherland turned to Kelly and groaned, "Information overload. Too many options."

"No hurry," she said and sipped on her chardonnay. "Nobody's breaking down our doors to buy either of our Chicago places."

The plan was to sell one of their Chicago condominiums, whichever sold first. They were also waiting to see to what extent a supposedly remorseful Uncle Sam would compensate Sutherland for Lawrence's default. Even though Sutherland's financial survival didn't hinge on that settlement, he was ambivalent about what to do next. Maybe it was time to retire and move on. The Keys were far from the cold he detested and a mecca for fishing, tennis, golf, or scuba diving.

After lunch in the condo, Sutherland took a nap on the balcony's hammock and woke to his cell phone buzzing. It was David Hurly, and he was on FaceTime. He must have been calling from his home because there was a cat sleeping on a bookshelf behind him.

"Wait—let me get Kelly into the picture," Sutherland said, signaling to her where she lay sunning in a lounge chair. She quickly put on her bikini bra, and Sutherland squeezed next to her on the lounge holding the phone so Hurly could view them both.

Kelly waved and said, "Hi, Dave. A little warmer here than our time in Ottawa."

"From all the skin you're showing, that's obvious," he said, chuckling. "Warmer in New York too, not that you can go anywhere. We're in COVID-19 lockdown like the rest of the world. Everything closed, deaths keep climbing, emergency rooms overrun, and our government is still in denial. By the way, is that a palm tree I see behind you?"

"We're in Key West for a month or so," Kelly said as she swung the phone around to bring the beach and ocean into the picture. "What's the latest on the fallout from our story? I hope the pandemic hasn't stopped those investigations like everything else."

"Matter of fact there's a whole lot going on," Hurly said. "They're talking about a full congressional investigation of X-ops for one thing. Another is the latest on Castillo's DNA, the main reason I called. You'll remember that the phony Doc Castillo's DNA proved he wasn't related to Silvio Delgado so couldn't be the infamous Luís Ortega, who we know was Silvio's mother's half brother. We've taken it further since then, and believe it or not, between threatening and begging, we got the FBI to use their CODIS DNA database and the National DNA Index System on Castillo's DNA. They matched the phony Castillo with a convicted felon in Texas, a Cuban immigrant named Ricardo Cruz. He was out on parole and agreed to a phone interview."

"He knew who the fraud was?" Sutherland asked.

"Oh yeah. He said it had to be his brother Hugo. They both worked in el Centro de Ingeniería, Genética, y Biotecnología as maintenance workers. It seems the brothers were fabricating an escape raft and Dr. Ortega overheard them whispering about it. He threatened to turn them in unless he could go along. But the raft would barely hold two. So he told them to choose which of them went with him."

"Did they know Dr. Ortega intended to assume Doc Castillo's identity?" Sutherland asked.

"Not according to Ricardo. His brother must have learned of the plan on the raft. They both knew what kind of monster Dr. Ortega was, and either one of them swore to kill him before arriving in the United States. But Ricardo would never have been able to assume Castillo's identity and start a company like Lawrence. He's as dumb as the proverbial stump. He told us Hugo was the smart one, having spent a few years at the Universidad de la Habana, where he learned Russian and English."

"Then Hugo Cruz hears about Ortega's plan and decides to run with it himself. That's ballsy," Sutherland said.

"Brilliant, if you ask me," Kelly added.

"He needed Dr. James Ridgeway's help," Hurly said. "Ridgeway was recruited from a defense department lab by Paolo Aguilar when he made arrangements with el Centro."

"This Ricardo must have been pissed off when he heard what Hugo did," Kelly said.

"I don't think he's smart enough to understand," Hurly said. "He escaped from Cuba a few years later and began a bungling criminal career here. He was just happy to learn that his brother killed Dr. Ortega."

Sutherland's thoughts were whirling as he tried to unravel the implications of what he'd just heard. Finally, he said, "If the dumb brother had been the one on the raft … maybe he'd have killed Ortega as planned, but because he didn't have the brains, Lawrence Laboratories wouldn't have existed. There'd be no BioVexis causing hospitalizations and deaths and no cover-up or conspiracy for Sam Baskin to write about. In other words, Sam would still be alive."

"Probably," Hurly said, frowning.

"Because the wrong … fucking brother … got to go," Sutherland said, exasperated.

"How did the brothers decide who went?" Kelly asked. "Did Hugo, the smart one, trick his brother?"

"You won't believe this," Hurly said. "They tossed a coin. Hugo won."

Sutherland and Kelly sat in silence staring at each other for several moments. Hurly finally broke the spell. "I told you you wouldn't believe it," he said.

"Like that theory Silvio talked about," Kelly said. "A butterfly flaps its wings, and we get tornados—except this was a frigging coin."

"Crazy when you think about it," Hurly said.

"I'll tell you something else that's crazy," Sutherland said. "Something I never told either of you. That night, when I was in Sam's hotel suite, Sam talked me into staying and having another drink with him by flipping a coin. He tossed a quarter—leave or stay—and stay won."

"And that's why you were there when the gunmen arrived and nearly killed you?" Kelly asked, flabbergasted. "The Cuban brothers' fates, then yours—there has to be a moral in there somewhere."

"At least a painful observation," Sutherland said sullenly. "If luck really is a lady, she's an awfully fickle one. Just as soon screw you over as smile on you."

"That's why I never gamble," Hurly said. "Betting on a big story is worry enough."

"Speaking of stories, David, what's the latest on el Centro? They close it down yet?" Sutherland asked.

Hurly's reflexive grimace was followed by a stubborn shake of his head. "I really can't get into that," he said tersely. "Sorry."

"Come on David," Kelly retorted, stung by his response. "You know us. We can keep a secret. After all, we handed you the goddam story."

Hurly took a deep breath and sighed. "OK. This is super sensitive, and you didn't hear it from me or anyone else for that matter. It has to do with all that encoded correspondence we found in el Centro's digital files Silvio Delgado brought to us. Maybe you remember it, Kelly."

"I do," Kelly said. "Silvio couldn't help us with its significance or content, and the Canadian intelligence people wouldn't comment. So you couldn't use any of it in your articles."

"And if the NSA or CIA are able to decipher it, they aren't talking either," Hurly said.

"So why is it important if you don't know the substance?" Kelly asked.

"Because we finally identified who el Centro was communicating with," Hurly said. "Hundreds and hundreds of encrypted messages back and forth over a period of years."

"So? Are you waiting for a drumroll? Tell us, David," Sutherland said.

"It was the Wuhan Institute of Virology."

After a moment's stunned silence, Kelly said, "What do you think el Centro and the virology lab in China that produced the COVID-19 virus could have been discussing in all those messages? Could we be looking at a locally grown version of that mutation—compliments of el Centro? That's a frightening possibility."

"Worse than that," Hurly said, shaking his head. "We've just learned that a virulent strain of the mutated viruses was unaccounted for in a recent relocation of one of el Centro's labs. It seems Cuba is worried enough that it has secretly sought help from the World Health Organization and are also speaking to our Centers for Disease Control and Prevention. They're desperately trying to find and destroy it before it escapes and spreads. I hate to say this, but we really need a smile from that fickle lady."